THE VANISHING POINT

Recent Titles by M. R. D. Meek

POSTSCRIPT TO MURDER
THIS BLESSED PLOT
TOUCH AND GO
A HOUSE TO DIE FOR *
IF YOU GO DOWN TO THE WOODS *

* *available from Severn House*

THE VANISHING POINT

M.R.D. Meek

This first world edition published in Great Britain 2002 by
SEVERN HOUSE PUBLISHERS LTD of
9–15 High Street, Sutton, Surrey SM1 1DF.
This first world edition published in the USA 2003 by
SEVERN HOUSE PUBLISHERS INC of
595 Madison Avenue, New York, N.Y. 10022.

British Library Cataloguing in Publication Data

Meek, M. R. D.
   The vanishing point
   1.   Kemp, Lennox (Fictitious character)
   2.   Lawyers - Fiction
   3.   Detective and mystery stories
   I.   Title
   823.9'14 [F]

   ISBN 0-7278-5840-8

Except where actual historical events and characters are being
described for the storyline of this novel, all situations in this
publication are fictitious and any resemblance to living persons
is purely coincidental.

Typeset by Palimpsest Book Production Ltd.,
Polmont, Stirlingshire, Scotland.
Printed and bound in Great Britain by
MPG Books Ltd., Bodmin, Cornwall.

One

'What's the matter, Glumface?' Joan addressed her boss pleasantly and without disrespect.

'Sorry.' Franklyn Davey was always saying he was sorry. He deplored the habit but was unable to remedy it. 'Your nature is unnecessarily apologetic,' his girlfriend, Dinah, had told him; 'that's why it always sounds sincere.' Dinah was studying psychology.

Joan was still standing in front of his desk, looking down at the top of his head. 'There isn't any gloom in the morning mail,' she said, 'even if it is a Monday. And your clients for the day are all pussy cats . . .'

Franklyn stopped himself from apologizing again. 'It's got nothing to do with the office. Just that Dinah had some bad news this morning.'

Now it was Joan's turn to feel sorry. It was unlike Franklyn to look unhappy. He had the sunniest temperament of any man she'd ever worked for, never subject to moods the way many of them had been – trailing domestic woes round their offices in spreadsheets of personal anguish, possibly on the premise that troubles shared were troubles dissolved like Disprin in a glass of water.

'Not from her family?' she asked now, for she liked Dinah and hoped that she and Franklyn would soon get married and give her a wedding to look forward to . . .

'No, it's not any of her family. Its an old college friend . . . Dinah has just been told that she was in that awful thing in New York . . . This girl – her name was Annabel – is dead . . .' Franklyn wondered why he'd used that silly word 'thing' for something so terrible; because, he supposed, the actuality transcended words. Even at the time he'd thought of

1

Wittgenstein's 'Whereof one cannot speak, thereon one must remain silent.' Of course nobody did remain silent: talking heads on the media filled up empty space; conversations sometimes stopped, but they ran on in the mind – as now.

Joan had sat down as if her legs had given way. The same image was in both their heads, that image pinned there for all who had eyes to see; and, despite all the daft and dangerous events since, it was the image that stuck.

'Were they close friends?' Joan asked, 'this girl and Dinah?'

Franklyn shook his head. 'Not for some time. I gather they were best mates at college but had drifted apart since. Annabel Angus was very ambitious and got a job with a Scottish television company, where she became something of a high flier. She and Dinah exchanged Christmas cards and the odd e-mail, but I don't think they'd actually met for some time – not since I've known Dinah, anyway. But you know how it is with the friends you make at college: you don't forget them . . .'

Like the girls in the first office you ever worked in, Joan was thinking; they're somehow special even though you might not see them again for years. At the time, you were new to the job, you felt so nervous and there were all those others who knew so much more than you did; but in the end they turned out to be ever so helpful and even sometimes became your best friends . . .

'How did Dinah get the news?' she asked; 'I mean it's been more than a month.'

'She was on Annabel's e-mail list – it was as simple as that. The firm she worked for went through it and let people know what had happened. There'd been a conference that day with possible American sponsors who were interested in one of the Scottish serials Annabel's firm had produced, and she had been sent along to represent them. The meeting was being held that morning in an office on the eighty-first floor of the World Trade Center . . .' His voice trailed off, and they both found themselves looking instinctively out of the window at the low grey clouds hanging over Newtown.

Joan refused to allow the other image back into her mind. She got up briskly. 'I'll get you a coffee,' she said, 'while you tackle the mail. Then you'll be ready for Mrs Sinclair-Brown, who's first in line for you this morning.'

'Thanks.' Franklyn shook himself and got down to the day's work. After all, what he was feeling was only a remote sadness on behalf of Dinah, and some degrees removed from the real thing; but at breakfast Dinah had been upset as much by that as by the news. 'If only I'd kept in touch,' she'd wailed, 'but we went different ways, and I suppose we changed – Annabel more than me. She'd become harder, really quite abrasive in fact; you know how the Scots can get when they set out to be somebody?' Franklyn had been reminded that someone had said there was nothing so impressive as a Scotsman on the make, but he'd decided this wasn't the time for smart comment. Dinah had been shaking and he'd put his arm round her shoulders.

'Annabel was so full of life . . .' She'd been speaking more to herself than to him. 'I can't believe she's dead . . . Oh, how I wish I'd seen her before . . .'

Franklyn had never known Dinah to cry, but there were tears in her eyes now as she warded off his encircling arm. 'I'm better on my own,' she'd said. 'You didn't know Annabel and you can't really grieve for someone you've never met. I'll be all right. I don't have classes this morning, so I needn't even wash my face . . .' She had given him a wan smile as he left.

'Talk to me about Annabel,' he said that evening after supper. 'It might help.'

'Like people do at a wake?'

'Something like that; it's a way of remembering.'

'I think this morning I cried out of regret,' said Dinah slowly, 'because I'd let Annabel down by not making the effort to meet her again. Last year she'd suggested we have a holiday together like we'd done in the past, but I put her off, said I couldn't fit it in – which wasn't the whole truth. Actually, I didn't want to go on holiday with her, because the last one hadn't been a success . . . Anyway, you and I . . .' She paused.

'Were becoming significant others?'

'Well, yes . . . I told her I had other plans . . . I did feel a bit guilty, and now it's worse . . .'

'Where did you go on that last holiday with Annabel?'

3

Franklyn asked, hoping to steer her out of the remorse that he felt unwarranted.

'It would be nearly three years ago, and we went no further than her native Scotland. I was still with Leversons.' Dinah herself had had a fairly high-powered job in the City before having taken a leap back into the groves of academe by enrolling for post-graduate study. 'Annabel had got this wonderful job at ClydeSight Scottish television and was over the moon about it. Perhaps that's why I didn't enjoy my time with her; maybe I was just the teeniest bit jealous – her career was going places, and she was making the most of it while I was stuck with Leversons without much future . . .'

'Only because you didn't see yourself as City material,' Franklyn assured her. 'You were obviously not happy, while your friend Annabel had achieved the start she wanted. Not exactly the recipe for a great holiday together . . .'

'Looking back, I think you're right. At the time all I remember is that Annabel grated on me, going on the whole time about making a name for herself; she was already doing interviews and had been told she had talent . . . And of course that's just what happened; Annabel Angus was fast becoming a household name – in Scotland, anyway.

'When did you last hear from her?'

Dinah grimaced. 'Isn't that the trouble with e-mail?' she said. 'Especially the kind between Annabel and me: just girlish gossip to start with and a real interest in each other; then it was all about her exciting work and the foreign places she was off to . . . It was like holiday postcards, really, and I trashed them much the same way. It's not like getting letters – letters you might keep, if they were amusing and interesting.' Dinah suddenly caught what she was saying. 'I'm not really criticizing Annabel; it was the way she was. Her centre was herself and others simply revolved round it, without lives of their own. I know I told her when we got engaged – that's months ago now – but when she mailed me again she never mentioned it. She was excited about a new production she'd been put in charge of. Oh, now I remember: she did mention another trip to New York – she'd been there before and made a lot of friends, she said . . . When did I get that last e-mail?

It must have been at the end of the summer. I know I was a bit relieved, because if she was going to New York she couldn't be too bothered about me turning down that earlier idea of us going on holiday again . . .' Dinah took on a brooding look.

'You'd been good friends at college. What sort of a girl was she?' Franklyn was by now genuinely interested.

'We kind of clicked from the first time we met. We were both aliens – that's how we thought of ourselves. I was from the depths of old Ireland and she from some outlandish Scottish island, so all the other lot from London and the home counties thought us a bit weird. We played it to the full – dressed like country bumpkins and talked like hillbillies. We had a lot of giggly fun – especially when we were the only two in that year to get Firsts . . . Annabel, she sure was smart . . .'

'What happened that last holiday you had with her in Scotland?'

'We hadn't seen each other for a while and I suppose I'd forgotten just how self-centred she was, or maybe she had simply become that way through success. That good degree she'd got obviously mattered up there in Glasgow, and she got a plum job straight from college while the rest of us were dithering about not sure what we wanted to do. Well, the time we spent together I soon learned that the new Annabel was a bit hard to take. We did the tourist spots up the West of Scotland because I'd never been north of the Border before, and then the last week we went to her island.'

'What's it called?'

'Bute,' said Dinah.

'But that's only in the Firth of Clyde. You made it sound like Ultima Thule.'

'It was the way Annabel spoke of it, as if it was way over the edge – fitted in with her sense of drama. She'd always had that . . . She said she couldn't stand the place: the people were all pursed lips and "wee frees". Which wasn't true, but the idea of it she wanted to hand over to you . . . Actually, I don't believe her family had ever really lived there. She herself was brought up in a Glasgow suburb and it was only when her mother was widowed and bought a croft on Bute that Annabel began going back. She'd made a documentary about

5

the island, which seems to have been successful; it was in the new mode – searingly truthful about rural poverty – although I don't think it went down well with the natives . . .' Dinah stopped. She was remembering how Annabel had scorned her mother's neighbours, the farmers' wives who chattered endlessly over tea and scones, as much as she scorned the tourists spilling out of their buses on the quay at Rothesay in search of toilets and shelter from the sometimes incessant rain . . . It was then that she had found her friend's tone – her whole attitude – too acerbic, too dismissive of what was in fact a not unattractive way of life. It was all very well for Annabel to think of herself at the sharp, cutting edge of the new style in the media – anything to get away from 'couthy old Scotland', as she'd called it – but Dinah found it wearisome to live with.

'I liked her mother,' she found herself saying now, 'and I fell in love with the island itself – so like Ireland, the scenery and the people. Well, nothing like as relaxed as we were, but maybe they'd had it harder.'

Franklyn made no comment. He considered Dinah's father the most relaxed individual he'd ever met, a doctor down there in the lush south-west of Ireland who'd have been content to do his rounds in a pony and trap, had his wife allowed it. Speed was not for him, he would say, nor excessive diligence – just enough to get by on . . .

Later that night, before she slept, Dinah thought that once again Frank had been right – when it came to serious stuff he often was, though fallible in minor matters – to encourage her to talk about her friend who was now dead; but she had held a lot back. It had suddenly seemed disloyal to talk of Annabel's faults; had she been still alive Dinah would have enjoyed a good gossip about her, the way she and Annabel had used to tear their mutual friends to pieces over long night sessions of girlish gab. Now, though, it seemed wrong, like telling tales, to speak of those things she had come to deprecate in her friend. Better simply to remember the liveliness of the brown eyes, the sparkle in them, the whole vibrant personality of Annabel; talking about her had indeed pinned her into memory.

There were practical things she could do, too. 'I'll write to Annabel's mother,' she told Franklyn at breakfast. 'I have the address because that's where we stayed. It'll not be an easy thing to write, but as I've met her . . .'

'I gather you've already acknowledged this.' Franklyn held out the letter from ClydeSight plc. 'A highly regarded and popular colleague, they say . . .'

'The brightest and best – yes, that would be Annabel. I thanked them for letting me know. Isn't it strange: if I'd not been on her e-mail list, they'd never have written, and I wouldn't have known . . . ? It would have been in the Scottish papers, I suppose. After all, there were other firms up there who had people over in New York. But I might never have heard . . .'

'No Christmas card might have set you wondering.'

Dinah shrugged. 'The way we were drifting apart I'd probably just have thought she'd given up on me. How long would it have been before I realized I wasn't going to hear from her ever again?'

Franklyn nodded. 'I always found it hard to keep up with old friends from university days. There's that terrible gap when you all scatter and you're so busy getting on with your career and making new friends that the others are history. Anyway, men don't keep up friendships the way women do. You always seem to have had a network, even if some, like Annabel, were out on the fringe. You'd have heard about her death sooner or later.'

Dinah shivered. 'That kind of death,' she said; 'I don't want to think about it . . . Oh, her poor mother . . . Such a kindly soul she was to me that holiday . . . I hope the news was broken to her gently . . . But I shall write to her tonight if I can find the words.'

'I'll pick you up at college and we'll go somewhere to eat – save you bothering with an evening meal. I happen to have an easy afternoon and can leave the office early.'

Dinah knew this was probably not true, but she accepted, as she always did, that Franklyn wanted her to believe she was his first priority and that, if necessary, office work could be subordinated to that end.

Two

W hether or not Franklyn spoke the truth about his office work, the senior partner of his firm was certainly not having an easy afternoon. Lennox Kemp did not like his client, Mervyn Prentiss, and although there is no Law Society ruling that solicitors must actually like all their clients, a certain degree of mutual respect does get an interview running the way it should.

He had been told that Prentiss was a man to avoid – it was better to step to one side than to get in his path; this from several Newtown citizens who, for one reason or another, had not done so . . . The fact that Prentiss had recently become Chairman of the Council – by an inexorable rotation system – meant that his name tended to crop up more than ever, and always with a tag of active dislike or the restraint that means the same thing.

'I know he's in the same line as me,' Alan Brinscombe had said to Kemp when the name was mentioned, 'and property developers ain't the flavour of the month around Newtown, but Mervyn Prentiss – well, he's just about the nastiest man I've ever come across in the business; and I've met a few . . . The building trade's no bed of roses, whether you're at the bottom or up there where he is, but some of the tales I could tell about him . . . Now I know we all had to scramble around for contracts at the start – me more than most as I was doing it the hard way – but there were limits, weren't there?'

Kemp agreed. He had known the Brinscombe brothers from his own early days in Newtown, when the Development Corporation had been seen by property men as a milch cow to be sucked dry as plans for new homes, new roads, new schools and shops, superstores and business blocks fell off the drawing board and became concrete reality. The Brinscombes had done well enough out of it but had kept their hands clean, more or less, in a business where mud and money alike stuck to the fingers. Others, it seemed, had not been so moderate. Alan was now retired and could talk about it.

'It's not like Mervyn had to fight his way. His old man had the business going for him; all he did was step into it out of that posh school he went to. Me, I started out under them railway arches in Hackney, gettin' the brass out of dumped gas cookers . . .' Alan Brinscombe threw back his head, and laughed. With a house in Spain and a newly built mansion up by Emberton Woods, he could afford to. 'Anyway,' he continued, with a sly look at Kemp, 'it can't be matrimonial. He's never been married. Lots of women, I hear, but he's been too mean to share any of his worldly goods with them. What I mean is, he's always used Roberts's as his solicitors, and that goes for the Prentiss Company, so what's he coming to you for?'

'You know I can't comment,' said Kemp, primly. 'It was you brought his name into our conversation; how did you know he was coming to see me? That kind of thing is supposed to be confidential.'

'Brenda's niece works in his office; she saw the appointment in his diary,' said Alan, smugly.

Kemp sighed. 'Talk about old wives' gossip . . . Surely Newtown's got better things to discuss over the teacups . . . Well, perhaps not . . .' He was thinking that perhaps local petty issues were preferable to the wider topic in everyone's mind, casting its shadow across these golden days of splendid Indian summer . . .

After introducing himself and settling his chubby frame into Kemp's client chair, Mervyn Prentiss had immediately hit the wrong note by saying he was all for bombing the shit out of them; he didn't say who, but made the remark as if it was mere comment on the weather.

Kemp looked at him from opaque grey eyes that gave nothing away, and made no reply.

'We've gone soft in this country,' Prentiss went on. 'Reckon it's only the Yanks now who know how to kick ass . . .' Despite what sounded like a studied attempt to sound American, or at least mid-Atlantic, his accent was that of a public school, possibly a minor one. He hitched his trousers higher on his knees and gave Kemp the benefit of his views on the present situation, which were somewhat to the right of President Bush.

In order to stop this flight of the ego, Kemp looked pointedly at the clock on his office wall. The movement got instant attention.

'Yeah, I know, I know. Time's money in my business too, eh, Mr Kemp? Let's get down to it . . . I want you to find my wife.'

'I was not aware you were married.'

'Nor is anyone else. And don't you go blabbing the fact among the hoi polloi of Newtown . . .'

It was as close to an insult as anything Kemp had heard in years. It could be dealt with either by a haughty exposition on the merits of lawyer–client confidentiality, making Prentiss feel the sharp edge of his legal jargon; or it could be ignored. Kemp decided on the latter. He examined the lines on his notepad for a few seconds, then asked in a voice which, he hoped, dropped the temperature of the room by some degrees:

'If I could have some details, Mr Prentiss.'

Mervyn was more concise on facts than he was when airing his opinions, and in a few minutes Kemp had noted all that his client thought necessary for him to know. Listening to the Prentiss story, he had found that the only thing they seemed to have in common was their age – both near fifty.

'Why have you never looked for your wife, Linda, before now?' he asked. 'You say you haven't seen or heard of her in some twenty years.'

'There was no need.' Throughout the interview Prentiss had spoken of his wife as he might have done a set of golf clubs he'd left on a train. 'When she told me she was leaving, I wasn't sorry, but we parted amicably enough. If she'd wanted to get in touch, she knew where to find me. As she never did, I took it for granted she'd found someone else with money and stuck to him.'

Linda Prentiss: the name seemed ordinary enough, but her background was more complicated. Before she'd married Mervyn Prentiss she had been Sieglinde Neumann, the daughter of the housekeeper Colonel Prentiss had brought home with him from Germany, where he had been stationed at the end of the War.

'Housekeeper was what they called her – both my parents – but it was common knowledge it was his bed she kept. My mother simply didn't care whose bed he was in, as long as it wasn't hers. She'd had enough of sex by the time she'd produced me and my brother. I gather the only stipulation Frau Neumann made when she came from Germany to England was that she could bring her daughter Sieglinde with her.'

'And you married Sieglinde?'

'Well, she cheated me – her and her mother: accused me of seducing her and getting her pregnant.'

'And had you? And was she?'

Prentiss made a fist of his right hand, stuck out a forefinger and aimed it at the side of his head. 'Shot-gun wedding . . . There'd been no seduction; she was up for it, was Linde – and there was no baby. Frau Neumann said there'd been a miscarriage. That was a lot of bullshit . . . By the way, the name's Linde, like Lindy, not Linda. Linda's so common, don't you think?'

'How long were you together before she left?'

'I can't honestly remember. We got wed in the swinging sixties, and she left about five or six years later. I was up to my eyes in the company, trying to revive a business that was more or less moribund, so I'd more things to worry about than anything that was going on in Linde's head. I'd given her a house, plenty of money for clothes, a decent lifestyle; there was no reason for her to be discontented, but discontented she was.'

'No children?'

'I made bloody sure of that. I wasn't going to be caught out twice.'

'Did she give any reason for leaving? Another man?'

'Just said she was fed up living with me. Well, that made two of us. I wouldn't have minded if she'd got a chap, but I never

11

saw any sign of one. We came to an arrangement about money. I let her have a few thousand; it was all I could spare at the time and she said it'd be enough till she got herself a job. I always expected she'd be back for more, but she never came.'

'What kind of work could she do?'

'She'd never worked. She was a few years younger than me, so she was still at school when it happened.' Mervyn Prentiss shifted uneasily in his seat and had the grace, for the first time, to look somewhat sheepish. Kemp wondered just how much younger the housekeeper's daughter had been . . . The Colonel and his wife must have been more afraid of scandal than of acquiring a new daughter-in-law – probably considered a quick divorce in a few years' time.

'You could have divorced her for desertion,' he observed. 'Why didn't you?'

'Never got around to it, old son. If she'd come back, I suppose we'd have talked about it. I'd certainly not have had any objection if she'd wanted it. As for myself – well, I'd no intention of getting married again. All my energies were going into building up the business at that time.'

Alan Brinscombe had said Mervyn Prentiss had the name of a womanizer. For all his faults, he was a good-looking man, and when a little younger might well have been attractive to women; to have an absent wife was a sure way to stifle any wedding bells they might have deluded themselves into hearing . . .

'But now you want her found?'

Melvyn nodded. He leaned forward. 'Now this is for your ears alone: things have changed for me lately. I am thinking of getting married.' He leaned even further forward, putting his elbows on Kemp's desk and lowering his voice, as if he feared being heard in the corridor outside. 'In fact, Alicia Simon has accepted me. And you must know who she is . . . Lord Allen's daughter.'

Kemp had to suppress a grin. An old ballad had sprung to mind: 'Oh, I'm the chief of Ulva's Isle, And this Lord Ullin's daughter . . .' With another client he might have shared the allusion, but Mervyn Prentiss would have been too concentrated on his own trouble, too intent on the seriousness of his mission, to have appreciated it. Now he spread his hands palms upwards on the desk and spoke earnestly.

'It is important, Mr Kemp, that this matter be dealt with top secret . . .'

'I don't quite see what you mean by that,' Kemp said, not seeing it as a matter of national security. 'But of course none of what you have told me will be divulged outside this room.' Prentiss's dilemma was plain: he might be head of the local bigwigs of Newtown, but Lord Allen was London, and the biggest wig of all, a judge in the High Court. Kemp wondered where Mervyn had met the daughter, Alicia; she would not be exactly young . . . His thought was interrupted by his client.

'That's why I want you to handle this personally.' Prentiss lay back in his chair as if in expansive mood. 'I don't want any of your underlings on it. It's too damn delicate.'

Kemp demurred. 'Well,' he said, after a moment's pause, 'I'm not sure that I can take it on. There are many other agencies who look for missing persons; it's not really a solicitor's job.'

'I don't want any other agencies, as you call them. They're too large, there's too many people in them, and they blab. I want you, Mr Kemp.'

Nice to be wanted, but not in this context. Kemp shook his head. 'I'm sorry, but it's just not my kind of business.' He was aware that he was being too abrupt, letting his dislike of the man colour his judgement. 'Have you been to the police? or have you employed anyone in the past to look for your wife?'

'D'you take me for an idiot? Of course I've had enquiries made – discreetly, I may say. Ever since I knew I wanted to marry Alicia I've done everything I could. I've advertised widely; yes, I've even been to the police – they don't want to know and a fat lot of good they'd be anyway – but I've kept to the name Sieglinde Neumann, and said she'd come over here with a German family in the fifties, and I was simply concerned for her welfare since her mother had died. I knew Linde herself would come forward if she thought there was money in it . . .'

'Then you could have a quick divorce, rather than risk

committing bigamy.' Kemp had to admit Prentiss was no fool. He'd gone about things the right way, but . . .

'Why me?' he asked his client bluntly.

Prentiss laid a well-manicured forefinger against the side of his somewhat fleshy nose in a gesture that Kemp thought had gone out with the death of vaudeville. 'Discretion, old boy, discretion. Didn't you once work for a detective agency down in Walthamstow?'

'What's that got to do with it?' asked Kemp, though he well knew what was coming.

'At a time when you weren't all that popular with your fellows at the Law Society, eh?'

Kemp sighed. It wouldn't have needed much homework on Mervyn's part to discover that some twenty odd years ago Kemp had been struck off by that eminent body for embezzlement of trust funds. There had been a choice for Kemp: either pay his wife's gambling debts or she'd get acid in her face. At the time – and he had never regretted it – taking a loan from those trust moneys had seemed the right thing to do. It was unfortunate that he had been found out before he'd had time to repay the fund, with the consequence that he was out of his profession for six years until full reparation had been made, and he'd climbed back in again. Most people knew about his lapse – which he himself now regarded as history – and the circumstances that had caused it; Muriel had become his ex-wife and was now dead and it was, in fact, a long time since he had thought about the days he'd spent outside the legal profession. Had anyone asked him directly, he would have said that he had rather enjoyed them . . . They had brought him into contact with the underside of society, where the law was not printed in black and white. The experience had done him no harm, and the fact that he had solved some murder cases as a result of it had impressed members of the Law Society so much that when he had eventually applied for reinstatement, it had been granted. There were times, however, when he had wondered if he was not more suited to detective work. Already he was beginning to be hooked by this tale of the mislaid wife, but he was determined not to show it. It was interesting that Mervyn Prentiss should bring up the old story of his exclusion from practising law: the man must be desperate to obtain his services.

'Are you trying to blackmail me, Mr Prentiss?' After he'd asked the question, he grinned, to show that neither it nor the man's attempt to embarrass him need be taken seriously. 'My life's an open book, both inside the profession and outside. Which brings me back again to the point I was making: why come to me?'

'Who better,' said Prentiss, 'than a lawyer who can also detect? That way I get complete confidentiality plus the know-how of a private eye.'

'You've been reading too much detective fiction,' said Kemp. 'I don't do that sort of work any more.'

'And of course there'll be a fat fee.'

Mervyn Prentiss mentioned a sum – a very large sum. Kemp had to laugh. 'First blackmail, then bribery. You can't be serious.'

'Oh, but I am – very serious. I want this information about my wife. I need to know whether she's dead or alive, and I'm willing to pay highly for your services. That's the way I work, Mr Kemp.'

'You'll pay my bill of costs when I present it, Mr Prentiss. That's the way I work.' As he said it, Kemp knew he was lost. Not for the first time in his life, curiosity had overtaken prudence. 'Now I shall require to take some further notes on Sieglinde Neumann, as you have called her. Did you never think of the obvious: that she might have returned to Germany?'

'Of course that might have happened. That's another reason for coming to you. I've been asking around. That agency you worked for – McCready's, wasn't it? They've expanded a bit, I hear. Got themselves into Europe. Business enquiries, checking up on credit ratings within the Common Market – you know the kind of thing. Of course I wouldn't think of going to them myself – discretion and all that – but you could use them and the matter be treated in confidence. See what I mean?'

Kemp saw what he meant. What a clever boy, Mervyn Prentiss. He had to give credit for the man's perseverance.

15

He nodded. 'All right, I'll see what I can do; and if I do use McCready's, I shall ensure the same confidentiality as exists between you and me. Have you a photograph of your wife, and any papers or letters of hers?'

On the way home that night Kemp found himself thinking of that very large sum of money he had been offered, and had so primly turned down. One of the consequences of his crime all those years ago was that he would never rise into the highest-earning bracket of his profession; there would always be the slur . . . It had never concerned him before; indeed, he was approaching his middle years with some measure of contentment, pleased to be the head of Gillorns, a reputable enough practice and modestly prosperous. Of course, every firm could do with more money. He'd like to take over the empty premises next door to the office to provide a better reception area, perhaps take on another conveyancer now that the property market had taken off . . . Stop it, he had to tell himself firmly; you're being influenced by what the likes of Mervyn Prentiss offered with such ease. Don't be. But he'd been influenced, enough to take on the job.

Three

'Now there's a coincidence,' exclaimed Lennox Kemp, interrupting Franklyn's story. 'But do go on . . .'

They were seated in the back room of their local pub, the Cabbage White. When Newtown Development Corporation had first arisen it had taken some existing hostelries under its wing and given them the name of butterflies, hoping to evoke a country or garden image – green oases in the surrounding brick and concrete housing. They had found that green space cost money, however, so gradually the pubs had been squeezed into the usual urban shape, with only the odd minute beer garden to the rear. By now only its name reminded anyone who cared to ask that the Cabbage White had once had pretensions to being a country inn.

However, it suited the senior staff of Gillorns well enough, and it had become their custom to walk round there on Friday evenings when the office door had been firmly closed at six o'clock. The small room at the side of the bar was little used and Lawson the landlord made sure they weren't disturbed. He owed Kemp a few favours anyway, and it did no harm to the standing of the pub with the local police force that Gillorns should be seen frequenting it on a regular basis.

For Kemp it was an opportunity to keep up with those aspects of his firm that tended to escape his notice as each department got on with its own business during the week, leaving not enough time within the office for interchanges of views. Recently there had been an overlap of clients that had gone unnoticed, and Kemp was determined such a thing should not happen again.

The custom had now become quite a social occasion and, once the business side was over, the members of staff relaxed

17

and enjoyed one another's company. Kemp had found the weekly meetings often ironed out minor arguments and prevented the kind of abrasive personality clashes almost inevitable in a highly motivated work force such as his.

Sally Stacey had been asking Franklyn Davey about Dinah's friend, who had been lost in the disaster of 11th September. 'I know Dinah told me they hadn't seen each other for some time, but even so . . .' She shivered. 'Has she heard from the girl's mother? I know she was going to write.'

'You said something about a coincidence when I mentioned where Mrs Angus lived.' Franklyn had turned to Kemp. 'What was that about?'

Kemp shook his head. 'Tell you later,' he said. 'Did Dinah get a reply to her letter?'

Franklyn nodded. 'Only made things worse . . . much worse. The old lady had died. Seems she had a dicky heart, and when the news of her daughter's death reached her, it was just too much . . .'

'Christ!' Mike Cantley muttered. 'Two tragedies. Unbearable . . .'

There was a silence that nobody wanted to break. Two people collected glasses and went over to the bar. Kemp took the opportunity to have a word with young Davey. 'Bring Dinah to dinner on Sunday. She can have a talk about it with Mary.'

'Thanks, we'd both like that. This has had quite an effect on Dinah. First time in her life she's been aware of death so close – that's what she keeps saying. Up till now she's been lucky: still got parents, never lost someone she was fond of . . . And she does feel remorse that she had been so out of touch with Annabel. She knows it was her fault, but it's too late now to do anything about it. And she genuinely liked Mrs Angus, even though she'd only known her during a short holiday on Bute.'

'I was on Bute once,' said Kemp, 'a long time ago. That's why I said it was a coincidence, hearing the name of the place.' He didn't add that Bute had cropped up again recently when he'd contacted McCready's Detective Agency in the matter of Mervyn Prentiss. He had been told that the old man, McCready

18

himself, had retired with his Scottish wife to that very island. But the Prentiss case must be kept under wraps.

Franklyn explained that it was a lawyer's letter to Dinah that had brought the sad news of the death of Annabel's mother. 'The executors are a legal firm in Rothesay; they found Dinah's unopened letter in the mail box. Apparently Mrs Angus died in the cottage, but her body wasn't found for some time. There's no other family,' he ended, bleakly.

Cantley, who dealt with wills and probate, sympathized with the Scottish solicitor. 'Don't they call them writers to the signet, up there? I hate this sort of case,' he went on: 'old folks dying, a will names local lawyers but there's quite literally no one to deal with practical matters such as going through the mail, making the bed, washing up the cups. There's only neighbours, and they don't want to get involved lest they're accused of meddling. This friend of Dinah's – this awful trail of circumstances makes a sad situation even worse . . .' He stopped, having no words left.

'Events triggering other events,' Sally Stacey murmured, 'so far away from each other. And all we can do is get on with our everyday lives . . .'

Somebody muttered that all work, particularly their work – the quick-quick-slow dance of legal processes – seemed now trivial and unreal, as if out there was the only true reality. Kemp was asked for his opinion.

'I have none,' he said, although he realized it had been a serious question. 'Everyone reacts in their own way, as they must do with events in their own lives. It's personal, I think, not something you take from the media, not other people's words; but everyday happenings go on even against the background of tragedy, even – heaven help us! – against the background of the daft things governments have to do. People will still come to us with their matrimonial quarrels and their business troubles and their need to make provision for death. I notice your department's busy, Mike.'

Michael Cantley made a wry mouth. 'People who've never thought to make a will before . . .'

'I guess we just carry on,' said Perry Belchamber, their expert on family law. He had a soft voice for women who

19

wept, but only if tears meant truth; he had no time for the lying kind, especially where children were involved.

'So, we just carry on.' Kemp repeated the familiar phrase that night when he was home with his wife, Mary. 'Some do it with reluctance, some with alacrity. It serves one great purpose, though: it stops one from overmuch thinking. Life must go on . . .'

'And that's another one,' said Mary, getting up from the dining table at a sound from upstairs; 'cliché, I mean. The trouble is that they're all true. There's the reason, now, for the "life going on" bit. Elspeth wants her supper.'

The little noise that had started as no more than a low gurgle was fast growing into a high wail as the baby of six months found herself awake and hungry.

At home in their flat, Dinah and Franklyn had no such distraction to take them away from sombre discussion.

'I feel so useless,' said Dinah. 'Two people have gone right out of my life and at the time I was giving neither of them a passing thought.'

'You weren't to know,' said Franklyn mechanically. He too felt useless. His dear, high-spirited Dinah whom, up till now, he'd never seen downcast, seemed to have changed into someone he hardly recognized. And he could do nothing . . .

'There's our holiday to look forward to,' he said, still feeling inadequate. She turned her huge blue eyes at him, but with no spark in them.

'I'm being so stupid,' she said. 'I can't even think about our holiday.'

They were to spend a week in Ireland with her parents. Franklyn had taken no time off that summer because she had been studying for exams, and in fact it had helped at the office too, for Lennox Kemp, becoming a father for the first time, had found himself in need of more assistance at work than he had cared to admit.

'I'm being so bloody ungrateful,' Dinah went on, 'and you're being your usual forebearing self.'

'Hey, don't overdo it.' Frank kissed the nape of her neck as she put her head down on the table. 'I've got an idea . . .'

He had given the matter a great deal of thought, far into the night as he lay awake with Dinah inconsolable beside him. He wondered if psychologists would agree with his plan of action . . . That was the word: 'action'. Now he picked up the letter from Dinah's desk – the one from the Rothesay solicitors.

'This firm, Robert McFie & Son, sounds like a one-man show; he's signed Dougal McFie and his is the only name on the letterhead, but he's written a good letter in the circumstances. This bit about "you might like to have something of the late Mrs Angus's" – that's a kind thought.'

'Yes, isn't it? There's an echo of Victorian custom about it – didn't they used to have mourning brooches and the like? I can't bear the word "mourning" – gives me the creeps . . . Besides, in my case it would be spurious. I can't mourn for Annabel – not properly I mean. I don't know enough . . . When I think of her, all I see is the way she was, the way we were. How long did I really know her? Three or four years in college and a couple of summers since. Yet we were so close – almost like sisters. If she'd died then, I'd have been devastated. Now . . . I had let her go, almost forgotten her. But I have this terrible hollow feeling, this kind of ache in my chest. Is it grief? Is this mourning?'

'Of a sort.' Franklyn didn't know whether this was true or not, but it reminded him of something he'd been thinking of during the long nights: that Dinah was having difficulty in coming to terms with what had happened because it was so wildly out of her control. She liked to know things, she liked to search for answers, she wanted to get at the core of any matter; it was the reason for her having taken that degree course in psychology instead of the MBA that would have advanced her career.

Now, though, she was stumped, not only because of her helplessness in the face of a distant tragedy but because her own personal sorrow had to be distant too. 'I never even replied to her last two e-mails,' she said, miserably. 'All I can remember is that she was going to get her big chance . . . Now I wish I knew more about her – what she was doing in that television company, how was she coping with being a sort of celebrity. Instead I had that little niggle of envy, and binned the only link I had left with her – those bloody e-mails.'

'Come on, darling, enough of this soul-searching; it's not doing you any good. I've been thinking about our holiday, and you can turn this idea down flat if you don't like it.'

'Well, what is it?'

'If you don't feel like going to Ireland, I'm sure your parents won't mind. Would it help if we made a trip up to Scotland instead? Got in touch with ClydeSight TV, and talked to some of Annabel's colleagues . . .' He stopped, conscious that Dinah had whirled round and was staring up at him. He couldn't read the expression in her eyes, so he stumbled on. 'We could visit this island, call on this lawyer chappie and do what he says: choose a memento of Annabel's mother . . .'

Dinah didn't know whether to laugh or cry. How right Franklyn often was, how ridiculously right!

First, through, she had to voice her doubts. Because her self-esteem was presently at its lowest ebb, she had wondered if she was somehow making too much of what had happened, as if the immeasurable effects of 11th September were tempting her into a false display of grief . . .

'Won't it seem like morbid curiosity, wanting to talk to people who knew her up there?'

Franklyn shook his head. 'I'm sure they would understand. After all, you knew her for many years, and for a while she was your closest friend. To want to talk about her would be the natural thing.'

'I do think it will help,' Dinah said, slowly, picking her way through the words. 'It's the lack of knowledge of her that's upset me, not lack of feeling. I know that nothing can bring her back, but I would dearly like to have a proper memory of her, and I might be able to get that by talking to the people she worked with. And going back to Bute – that would be lovely . . .' She was quiet for a moment. 'You're a genius, Frank – and you say you don't know a thing about psychology!'

22

Four

It was some days before Franklyn Davey broached the subject of his holiday with Lennox Kemp.

'Thought you'd never ask. You played the honest martyr all the summer without a word of complaint until I could have strangled you. Of course you must take whatever time off you need. Things are a bit slack anyway in these uneasy days. Will you be off to Ireland then?'

Franklyn explained the situation.

Kemp commiserated with him. 'Studying psychology doesn't make one less vulnerable. That friendship Dinah had with Annabel came at a precious time in her life, though she would hardly recognize it as such. The emotional impact only strikes now because of Annabel's death; otherwise they'd have gone on drifting apart, and eventually her friend would have become just one of Dinah's memories of college days. I think you're right, though. She wants to fill in that gap, and talking about Annabel in the company where she last worked could help Dinah come to terms with her death.' He sighed. 'So many people are treasuring so many trivial last things because there is no other proper way to express what is felt . . .'

Franklyn nodded. 'The Victorians used to compose last letters when they were dying, change their wills, summon the family to their bedsides . . . There was time, then . . .' He didn't say any more, but they both knew what he meant and could almost see those who had fumbled at the numbers on their mobile phones as the unforgiving skies flew past the plane windows . . .

'You said you were on Bute once,' said Franklyn, to change the subject.

'It was a case I had when I was with that detective agency in

Walthamstow. In fact, it was the wife of the boss himself who sent me up there, Grace McCready, a Scots body as hard-fisted as any; but they paid me well, and she and George were a great help to me on my road back to the law. She got him to retire to Rothesay in the end; it would be the golf, I suppose. If you and your Dinah get to Bute, I'd be glad if you'd call on them – George must be bored to tears by now and will be glad of a breath of air from the South. I'll give you their address.'

'We'll do that,' said Franklyn. 'We've this lawyer to see in Rothesay, the one looking after the estate of the old lady.'

'Bute will not be at its best in November,' Kemp warned. 'They have harsh winters. I was there in February and there was a bite in the wind for days on end. But the summer – ah, the summer in Bute: if the weather's good, it's magic . . .'

It was most certainly not summer in Bute, nor in Glasgow. The streets were swept daily by surges of rain brought in from the south-west by winds that deliberately rose at the corners of buildings to take the feet from passers-by. Dinah clutched Franklyn's arm. 'Did you see that woman over there?' she said, 'the one with the umbrella and the short mac that makes her look like a pawn? I'll swear she was up in the air a minute ago and would have taken off if her man hadn't held her down. What a country! Let's get into the shopping centre before I'm blown away.'

'You have to admit it's a great city.'

Dinah allowed that it was indeed. 'But only because of the special effects,' she added as the wind tore at the guttering on a nearby building, sending a gush of dirty water over the heads of those below. She and Franklyn ducked and fled under an archway that opened out into warmth and a glitter of glass, the ever-open arms of shops, and cafés, and restaurants – not simply shelter from the storm but temptation on all sides.

'Very Scottish,' said Franklyn, remembering what Kemp had told him: 'It's a land of extremes, hard-edged like treacle toffee, but with a good chewing it goes soft.'

Dinah wasn't impressed when he told her. 'Its only weather,' she said. 'No need to go all philosophical about it.'

Sitting in the tea room – a much nicer word than café, he

24

thought – he looked at her with love. The tip of her nose was pink, and from under her furry cap the strands of pale hair dripped their share of Glasgow wetness on to the table top. She was back, his own matter-of-fact, clever Dinah – or almost back. They had been three days in Glasgow, three days of wind and rain, but it had been worth it.

Dinah had written a tentative letter to the television company, ClydeSight, and it had been warmly received. They understood her need and would very much appreciate a visit from her. All who had worked with Annabel Angus were anxious to meet her, and to talk about their lost colleague. They were only sorry that a memorial service had already taken place for Annabel and other Scots who had perished in the New York tragedy, but they were sure that if Dinah could bring herself to visit Glasgow they would make her welcome, and see that she met everyone who had known her friend . . .

There had been half a dozen people on the production of the series that Annabel had gone to the States to promote, and Dinah talked at length with them all.

This evening they were to have a second meeting with one of them, Sandy Duncan, who had worked more closely than the others with Annabel. It was he who had suggested that he would like to see Dinah again, and they had invited him to dinner at their hotel.

'Was he more than a friend, do you think?' Franklyn asked her. 'Or have you come up with any other possibles in that sense?'

'Difficult to tell. Remember, I talked to them in their offices and mainly about the project that took her to the States. They were all very friendly, of course, but in that atmosphere you couldn't ask much about her private life. Perhaps that's why Sandy Duncan wants to talk to me again. He does have a personal link – apparently it was touch-and-go which of them would be sent to New York.'

'That's quite a thought to live with,' Frank observed. 'Makes you feel the ground under your feet's a bit shaky. And that goes also for the person who made the decision who to send.'

'And I can tell you who that was.' Mr Sandy Duncan didn't

look as if the ground beneath his feet was anything but firm. He had the self-confident look of one who has appeared in front of the public and liked it. He was carefully and correctly dressed for dining at their rather expensive hotel, and spoke with a cultivated accent that slipped easily into soft Glaswegian when occasion demanded. 'Adelaide Bristow herself; it was she who chose Annabel.'

'I've heard of Adelaide Bristow,' exclaimed Dinah, 'but I've no idea what she's famous for. Is she in the new Scots parliament?'

'She'd like to have been, but age was agin her. She's getting on for seventy, though you'd never know to look at her. She owns ClydeSight – among a lot of other things – and is in effect our boss.'

'I thought she was in politics too,' said Franklyn, 'because she only seems to have become well known since you people went your own way.'

'How nicely you put it,' said Sandy, helping himself to more sauce for his grilled salmon steak. 'I wish they'd leave our guid Scots fish alone instead of giving it an Aussie barbecue. A wee bit of a poach is all it needs, and it'll flake apart like silk. It'll be an English chef in the kitchens here. You could make a purse out of this piece of old leather . . . Sorry. Yes, you're right. It was politics brought our beloved Mrs Bristow into the public eye once again. You see, she came of a family that was aye for the home rule when most folks thought the idea was too crazy. It's said that as a wee lassie she sat on the Stone of Scone when it was pinched from Westminster back in the thirties. Wendy Wood was supposed to be some kind of relative of hers. I see I've lost you.'

Sandy proceeded to lead them through a short but full history of the movement for Scottish political independence from its early days of nationalistic fervour – seen by many as just a funny wee sect out on the lunatic fringe – to its present position as a grown-up parliament subject to the same kind of financial squabbles as its big sister in the South.

By then they had reached coffee and brandy and Sandy's audience felt time passing but they had not been bored. He was a brilliant reconteur and the subject gave full rein to his gift for ironic comment coolly delivered – save for the odd hot shot of Glasgow vernacular. Dinah was thinking, if this man had been beaten to the post by Annabel, then her late friend must have been all she had set out to be: a television lioness in the making . . .

'And that's why Adelaide Bristow treats the Scottish parliament as if it's her ain hoose, and she the keeper of its conscience.' Sandy stopped, and wetted his lips with a good swirl of cognac.

'One of the tabloids has called her the Mary Whitehouse of the North,' remarked Franklyn, who tended to read everything within reach.

'Aye, she's a right Calvinist at heart, especially when she gets the smell of corruption in high places, and as there's a lot of it about, she gets into the papers fairly often. No bad thing for us at ClydeSight; it gets us noticed. As a matter of fact, we're doing a profile of her in the New Year; there was already to have been an interview . . .' His voice tailed off. He picked up his glass, and gazed gloomily into the bottom of it.

As Frank signalled a waiter to bring them another round, Dinah watched Sandy's face. 'Was it something Annabel was concerned in?' she asked. Sandy nodded but didn't speak until they had their refills.

'It was what she was working on before she went to the States . . . Well, we were both in on it, part of the team. But the American trip was different, just a hangover from our last project, there'd been a nibble from over there they might buy it. Either myself or Annabel could have done the representation and up to the last minute I thought it would be me . . .'

'Was Annabel Mrs Bristow's choice?' Franklyn asked.

'She'd taken a liking to her. Adelaide sometimes did that with young people if they had a bit of go in them, and Annabel had that, as you've probably realized . . .'

Dinah agreed. 'It came into any correspondence I had with her, and I'd always known she was ambitious. Of course, when I actually saw her last was before she went to your company. Wasn't she with a smaller outfit in Glasgow?'

'We poached her. Sorry, I mean she was head-hunted. Someone saw her and her potential. Anyway, once she arrived, she was clearly going to be unstoppable. The fact that Adelaide fancied her . . .' He stopped.

'You don't like Mrs Bristow?' Dinah was being direct.

'Och, I like her fine; it's just some of her decisions I can't take. Yes, it was noticed in the firm that Annabel had caught the attention – or maybe the affection – of our boss. It had happened before – Adelaide has been known to encourage favourites; she's a lonely woman herself.'

'Is there a Mr Bristow?' asked Franklyn, who liked facts.

'He must have faded years ago, but he left her enough money to fuel her need to be in the public eye, and the good causes she takes up to that end.'

Dinah was about to ask Sandy if he'd liked Annabel, but thought better of it. What he had said about her relationship with the owner of the company had struck a familiar note. At college she remembered that an odd friendship had arisen between Annabel and one of their older tutors, a clever woman on the verge of retirement. The words 'teacher's pet' had been used by those unimpressed by Annabel's flamboyant personality.

As if reading her thoughts and as if in answer to her unspoken question, Sandy raised his glass. 'To Annabel,' he said, and they drank the toast with him. He put down his glass. 'I don't know about you two, but I think it's done me good to talk about her tonight. Her untimely death saddened me more than I can say. It's taken me weeks to even think about work again, and you must have seen when you came to the office how the others were only just beginning to cope . . .'

Somehow Dinah felt that a dangerous moment had passed, and Sandy knew it. 'Yes, I was touched by the way they wanted to console me because I'd been Annabel's friend, but it seemed to me that you people, who had known her so much more recently, were the truly bereaved.' As she spoke, she knew it sounded like a set speech, but it would bring the conversation back to where Sandy obviously wanted it: on a level that avoided any possible pitfalls. Not for the first time she wondered how close Sandy had been to Annabel, and later that night she raised the query with Franklyn.

By then Sandy Duncan had been seen off on the steps of

their hotel, refusing the offer of a cab. 'My flat's only a few streets away, and after your guid hospitality I could do with the walk. Mind you get in touch when you come back from Bute; you've got my number.'

Five

It surprised Dinah when Frank was able to answer her question without hesitation. 'No,' he said, 'Annabel and Sandy Duncan were never an item. Too like one another, and way too competitive. But Annabel did have a chap of her own. He's called Peter Mallen and he's a sports writer on the *Daily Record*.'

Dinah and Franklyn were in bed. She raised herself on her elbow and stared at him. 'How on earth did you get all this information?'

'You don't think it's only girls who gossip when they go to the loo, do you? I asked Duncan directly and he told me. He said he liked Annabel well enough as a colleague but that was all; he's got a girlfriend, anyway, who doesn't work in television – he prefers it that way . . .'

'Was he disappointed at not being sent to New York?'

'His feelings are overlaid, as it were, by what happened. But yes, I think he was. He told me how to get in touch with this Peter Mallen. Shall we have a word with him? If he's available this morning, we can easily get a later boat to Rothesay.'

'So, she did have a lover . . . Yes, I think I'd like to meet him.'

It was Franklyn who called in at the newspaper office the next morning and found Mallen not only willing but anxious to meet Dinah.

'She's back at the hotel,' Franklyn told him, 'having a lie-in. We were late up last night, talking to Sandy Duncan.'

'Oh, him . . .' Peter Mallen was pushing his arms into his coat; 'he's a canny one. You'd not get much out of him without a dram.'

Frank laughed. 'Perhaps you're right, but he did tell us that you were a particular friend of Annabel's, so we owe him that.'

They met Dinah in the hotel lounge, where she was drinking black coffee in the hope that it would clear her head. She liked the look of Peter Mallen, finding him unlike her image of what a sports writer should be: the build of a rugby player, a cropped head and the snappy tongue of a racing commentator. Instead, from his appearance he could have been a college lecturer, or even the headmaster of a progressive school. His black hair was longish but carefully cut, he wore glasses, and had a pale skin and remarkably soft brown eyes. Instinctively, Dinah knew that, if this was Annabel's choice of partner, then it had been serious.

'I wish I'd known about you coming,' he said. 'Of course I realize it would be ClydeSight you would get in touch with, and they don't know me there. Sandy Duncan and I were at university here in Glasgow, and we met again when I started going around with Annabel; but you couldn't call us friends . . .'

'Am I right in thinking that both he and Annabel were suitors for the hand of Mrs Adelaide Bristow, the Scottish celebrity?' Frank wasn't sure what note to strike with Peter Mallen; it would depend on how deep his attachment was to Annabel.

'At another time I would have laughed at that way of putting it, but at the moment I don't feel like laughing,' Peter answered in a low voice, his feeling so evident that Dinah shot a warning glance at Franklyn as if to warn him against flippancy. But Peter roused himself. 'It wasn't a secret,' he said; 'Sandy had been the favourite at ClydeSight until Annabel arrived, but her success and influence were so immediate – particularly with the Chairwoman of the company – that you couldn't blame him if he resented it. I don't think Annabel ever realized the impact she had on other people. I'd never met anyone like her before, and I don't lead a sheltered life. I was head over heels . . .'

Dinah poured him some coffee and he took the cup gratefully. 'I can't get over it,' he said, 'the gap she's left . . .'

It was obvious that he wanted to talk about Annabel, but he hadn't wanted to go to her colleagues at work. 'I think she

31

was a different person there than she was with me; she was so determined to make a go of it, become a full-time presenter, or become a name as the ruthless interviewer. With me she'd laugh about such ambitions, but I think in the office she was deadly serious, and never more so than with Mrs Bristow, whom she genuinely liked.'

He was interested to know that Franklyn and Dinah were going to Bute. Of course he had heard that Mrs Angus had died. 'Made a great splash in the papers – the double tragedy, and all that. I wish I'd met Annabel's mother but, as you probably know, they saw very little of one another. Annabel's father died some years ago and she'd never got on with him.'

Dinah agreed. 'I remember her split with her parents; it was one reason for leaving Scotland; she said she couldn't stand their cosy ways, their smugness.'

'Their Scottishness – that was it. I'm from New Zealand myself, and I don't mind admitting that I sometimes find that sort of comfortable complacency vastly irritating. Some folks up here – they wallow in trivial small talk like it was the butter on their scones . . .' He grinned. 'The phrase was Annabel's.'

'Oh, it's so good to talk about her,' exclaimed Dinah, 'and with you, I feel she's real. The other one, the TV personality – well, I never really knew her.'

'I think Annabel herself was just getting to know her. She told me she'd never realized how hard you had to be to get on in the media, and that she was delighted to find a streak like granite in her character. You find it in successful sportsmen too, who never knew they had it until they come up against the competition.'

Coffee time extended into an early lunch and even then Peter Mallen was reluctant to let them go. They must ring him as soon as they returned from the island, no matter how short their stay in Glasgow.

'He's been badly hit,' said Dinah, as they were clearing their bedroom, 'despite having only known her for a few months. I wonder if she would have stuck to him if she had become a real celebrity . . .'

'Well, at least we've found out the circumstances of her

going to the States,' said Franklyn briskly. 'One could write a whole philosophical discourse on the vagaries of chance,' he went on, rather more solemnly, 'and its effect on all our lives.'

For, according to Peter Mallen, it had been touch-and-go right up to the last minute as to which of the two, Sandy Duncan or Annabel Angus, should represent ClydeSight at the New York meeting. Sandy had been expected to be the choice, for he had worked on the whole series they were selling, whereas Annabel had come later; but she had already been sent to the States in the spring on another project of Mrs Bristow's and had made the proper contacts.

'Annabel made friends with some media people in Greenwich Village and stayed with them.' Peter had stopped suddenly at that point. 'Oh, I shouldn't have said that . . . Well,' he sighed, 'I don't suppose it matters now. The thing is, ClydeSight were of course paying all expenses of the trip – a good hotel and all that – but Annabel . . .'

'Would stay with friends, but claim the hotel expenses just the same,' Franklyn had interrupted. 'Happens in every trade or profession; lawyers are not immune . . .'

They had laughed, and Peter had looked relieved. He was having trouble with talking about Annabel in the past tense; to him, as to Dinah, the lost girl was still very much alive.

It had been with a certain diffidence that Dinah had asked him the inevitable question: when was the last time he had seen Annabel?

He had gone over it so many times in his head that to his hearers it sounded like the script of a play. Peter had been in Belfast – the big rugby match, Scotland versus Ireland – on Saturday 8th September, but was returning that night. He was sure he had told Annabel that he would be back some time on Sunday, dependent on sailing times, tides and weather.

Thursday had been the last night they'd shared together up in their flat at 41 White Street. No premonition then of tragedy . . . Annabel had been late in getting in, so it had been Peter who had cooked supper – pasta, he said, because it was easy. They had had a bottle of wine, talked, and gone late to bed. They had made love . . . That, he would never forget.

33

Annabel had been in a joyous mood. No, it was nothing to do with the American trip; Sandy Duncan was still the front runner there, so far as she and the staff at ClydeSight were concerned. What had thrown Annabel into seventh heaven was the invitation she had received for the Friday evening to attend a dinner party at the exclusive Bearsden home of her boss, Adelaide Bristow. 'Not issued to any but a select few,' Annabel had said; 'it can only mean promotion.'

It certainly had meant promotion, for it had been then she was told that it was she who was to go to New York, so that it was a very jubilant girl who had managed a phone call to Peter in Northern Ireland late on Saturday afternoon. It had been the last time they would talk to each other.

'If only I'd known . . .' Peter's voice had stuck at the words, and now, going over them together, both Franklyn and Dinah stopped too. There had been a silence then, as now – a silence that had filled up spaces in everyone's mind like a glimpse of deep water . . .

The call itself had been dislocated – Peter in a scrum of fellow journalists so that he could scarcely hear her, she in a furious hurry, so much to do, so little time. She had told him she had to get a briefing from Sandy in the office, then catch the Sunday overnight flight and be in New York on Monday, ready to meet the American sponsors on Tuesday.

She had been bubbling over with excitement, not simply about being sent as the firm's representative but because of some other project she'd been promised for the future. It meant, she'd said, working in the office right up to the last minute on Sunday before going to the airport. 'But she must have gone back to the flat at some time,' said Peter, 'to get her clothes and things . . .' His boat had docked late on Sunday morning because of storms in the Irish Sea; by the time he'd filed his story at the newspaper, and had a get-together with his fellows and a bite to eat, it was evening before he was home.

'Strange that Sandy Duncan didn't mention seeing Annabel in their office over the weekend,' Franklyn observed to Dinah as they stood at the rail of the ferry taking them to the island. 'Perhaps he thought his resentment would show. He must have been handed a right lemon on Saturday morning; or had Mrs

Bristow told him already that he wouldn't be going? It must have rankled.'

'Sandy is one of these bland Scotsmen who are good at hiding feelings,' said Dinah, thoughtfully; 'something to do with their colouring.' Sandy Duncan was in fact reddish-fair and, in her opinion, not bad-looking. 'I do still wonder about him and Annabel . . . Perhaps before Peter came on the scene. Between them, though, I now have a clearer picture of Annabel herself, and it has helped me. I can just see her rushing about over that weekend; she was in her element when something was going on with herself the centre . . .'

They were both quiet then, gazing out at the stretch of water separating Bute from the shores of Argyll, the water not exactly blue but hinting at it in the folds of waves as the crests caught the sunlight. It was a pleasant day with a chill wind and both Franklyn and Dinah acknowledged they were happy to escape from the city. A call to George McCready in Rothesay to enquire about accommodation had provided them with a bed-and-breakfast establishment on the front at Rothesay. 'It's no use going to the bigger hotels out of season,' he'd told them. 'You'd get more space but lousy food. Least, that's what the wife says.'

Obviously in the McCready household what the wife said was what George went along with. Franklyn had been told by Lennox Kemp back in the office that it was Grace McCready who held the reins. 'Just like she did down in Walthamstow at their detective agency. She would tot up the operatives' expenses in her head long before they got them down on paper: a shrewd woman. George was even then retired from the Met, so he must be getting on a bit.'

George McCready didn't look it. He was still upright and brisk in his walk, and though he talked of giving up the golf, he was obviously still proud of his game.

The English visitors called at the McCready bungalow as a matter of courtesy as soon as they had booked in at their lodgings – a solid red sandstone villa where their welcome had been so warm it was almost embarrassing. 'I feel like the Queen,' said Dinah, when they were finally left alone in a large bedroom overlooking the bay. She giggled. 'The way

35

Mrs Thing went on . . . I thought at any moment she'd drop me a curtsey.'

'She did come to Bute once,' said Frank, who had done his research on Bute before leaving Newtown. Wherever he went he liked to be forearmed with knowledge. 'Queen Victoria, I mean. She and her beloved Albert were touring the Western Isles in the royal yacht in 1841. But she wouldn't land on Bute because the Marquis had recently turned Roman Catholic, so the local burgesses had to row a boat out to pay their respects – which I understand Victoria was gracious enough to acknowledge. I bet she just stood at the prow and inclined her head.'

'Is that right, now?' Grace McCready said when Dinah took it upon herself to repeat the story to the McCreadys. 'Well, I never knew of it, but then I'm no one for the history. There's enough going on in the present day to keep me busy . . .'

Indeed she'd not sat down since they arrived, as she bustled about offering, and providing, trays of buttered scones, walnut loaf, shortbread and something she called 'fancies' covered in pink-and-white icing, reminding Dinah of sugar mice, which she'd hated as a child. George added to the plenitude by waving a hand at a sideboard display of every drink from aperitif to liqueur, and possibly back again, if you wanted the round trip. Both Dinah and Frank chose tea, which was good and hot and heartening. Only when they had eaten an ample sufficiency – her phrase – did Mrs McCready seat herself among them. She sank down on the sofa next to the tea-bearing table and slipped the cover on to the silver teapot. 'You'll be wanting second cups in a while,' she said, comfortably, looking much like a tea cosy herself with her good woollen dress, its frilly wee collar up to her chins. 'Now tell me about your friend that was lost in that awful thing in New York.'

Both she and her husband were good listeners. It would be part of the job, Franklyn was thinking, and what an astute pair they were! No wonder they had made such a success of that detective agency.

'That poor woman, Mrs Angus!' Grace exclaimed at one point. 'Of course there was a great stramash here in Bute over that. Folks couldna' understand how it happened the way it did. Nobody knew her that well, but those that did, they liked her. She came to that wee croft at Kilchattan after her husband died, I was told, because her people had come from there.'

Dinah told her about the holiday she'd had at the cottage with Annabel two years before, and how she had loved the place.

'Oh, aye,' Grace acknowledged, reluctantly, 'it's a fine view all right, but you'd be there in the summer. In winter, it's a bleak enough spot, and no neighbours for company. Give me the town with its bit of life . . .'

George and Franklyn agreed that there wasn't all that much life about Rothesay at any time of year. It was a town of ups and downs and at the moment mostly downs – Literally so, for soft red sandstone hadn't stood up well to the rigours of the weather and buildings had collapsed with depressing frequency, including a bank. 'Gave a new meaning to the term "falling profits",' said George, with some satisfaction; it hadn't been his bank. 'Folks had to cash cheques in the sweet shop next door,' added Grace. 'That's eighteen months gone by and they've hardly cleared the site.' She put a hand over her mouth. 'Oh, but I shouldn't be talking this way – not after those poor folk . . . and your friend . . .'

In the silence that followed Franklyn Davey found himself wondering how long it was going to be before that image faded, an image jerked into the mind by words that by themselves had no connection with it . . . Even George McCready looked slightly shame-faced about his little joke. He made a great fuss about getting up from his chair and going over to the sideboard. 'Have something stronger than tea before you go. It's cold out, and you've a bit of a walk back along the front.'

They didn't refuse, and resumed their talk, but in perhaps a more sombre mood. When they finally left, it was with a promise to return when they had seen Mrs Angus's solicitor.

'I hear he's a guid man, Dougal McFie,' said Grace, who seemed to know everyone on the island; 'took over when his father died. Ye'll likely get the proper story about Mrs Angus from Mr McFie; here in Rothesay we've got nothing but gossip.'

'On which our Gracie thrives,' Dinah remarked, as they fought their way through a whistling wind along the shore road. Just below them a high tide threw itself against the black rocks as if it hadn't a moment to spare.

'Long periods of inertia, and sudden bursts of hothead activity – that seems to be the way of Scottish history,' said Franklyn, who had been studying it. 'There'd be a time for gossip and a time for killing.'

'I blame the climate,' said Dinah, coming to terms with it.

Six

Lennox Kemp was thinking of George McCready as he parked his car at Walthamstow Town Centre – parking was easier than it used to be, but more expensive.

The detective agency had kept its former name when George had reached retiring age and sold the premises – along with the goodwill – to an eager City firm, and Kemp had expected something more palatial given the credentials of the London investigation bureau that now owned the building and whose services, from their own offices on Ludgate Hill, were used by all the best solicitors when secrecy was vital.

As he went in through the narrow doorway between the dry-cleaners and the betting shop, however, he reflected on what George had once said: 'People want to be seen going to a detective agency as much as they would if it was a VD clinic.' And George, of course, was right; the entrance had to be inconspicuous. The interior, however, had been given the treatment. Gone were the dusty old chairs, the worn rugs, the tattered curtains and the decrepit filing cabinets. All was now smoothly carpeted, gracefully lit and coordinated to raise the highest hopes of the clientele. Kemp did have a fleeting moment of nostalgia for the old musty smell, the unswept floors that creaked and the windows where dirt obscured the glass. He'd worked in the place at a time when only work could save him from despair, and he'd not forgotten.

This morning he was expected. George McCready's name still meant something here, and it seemed that Lennox himself had become a bit of a legend. That was exactly how he was greeted by the present head of the branch, Nick Freebody.

'Mr Kemp?' He held out his hand. 'You're a bit of a legend around this office.'

'Mr Freebody? For God's sake, you make me feel like a ghost . . .'

It broke the ice between them, but as both were in a business where time had to be paid for, Kemp wasted none of it.

'I want someone discreet – that goes without saying – but also someone with a good knowledge of German; an older man, for preference, and he must work on his own. This isn't a financial enquiry but one that goes back to the immediate post-war period in the British Zone, and possibly further afield.'

'When you rang, Mr Kemp, I immediately thought of the very man. He's on the verge of retirement and I've been easing him off a bit; But he's done enquiries before in Germany and speaks the language like a native. I only hesitate in recommending him because of his age. He's nearly sixty-five but sound in wind and limb.'

'I'm not in the market for a racehorse,' said Kemp, 'and if you recommend the man, I'll take him.'

'His name is Henry Pocket, and I'll have him round at your office this afternoon, if that will suit you.'

Lennox Kemp had an hour's gap between clients, and Mr Pocket arrived at three o'clock. If any witness had ever been asked to describe him, they would have been in difficulties. He was of middle height but somehow seemed smaller, perhaps because of narrow shoulders, and his whole appearance was undistinguished; there was nothing memorable either in figure or features to latch on to, if you wanted to remember him.

'It's Henry Pocket,' he said to Kemp, 'never Harry.'

'That's fine with me, Henry. Now this is what I want you to do . . .'

Mervyn Prentiss had provided some documentary evidence about the former Sieglinde Neumann, now Mrs Linde Prentiss, and the rather scanty results of his own searches, which did not appear to Kemp to have been conducted with any enthusiasm. All this he now placed before Henry Pocket.

'Not until fairly recently did this husband make any real effort to find his wife, so I'm hoping that you will be able to fill in the gaps in these reports.'

Mr Pocket studied them. 'Looks as if he just got one of his own men to make a few enquiries. Whoever it was went about it like an amateur. All the usual channels – employment, social services, credit agencies – he didn't try very hard, your client. He certainly wasn't spending much money on it. Talking of money, what was she living on all these years, this Linde Prentiss?'

'That's an interesting question, and I hope you can come up with an answer. He says he gave her a few thousand when she left, but that wouldn't last long.'

'She must have had something to live on – that is, if she's still alive . . .'

'I also have considered that other possibility. If she's dead, I don't think my client would be unduly upset.'

Henry Pocket thought for a moment, his pale-brown eyes looking round at Kemp's office furniture but never resting long in one place. If there was one thing about him that was remarkable, it was his total lack of expression. He could have been considering the client's lack of charity as shown up by Kemp's last words; he could have been thinking about supper.

He was skimming quickly through the papers in front of him. 'H'm . . . last known address Cromer; one before that Yarmouth . . . Seems to like the seaside, this lady.'

'She sent her husband postcards, apparently, from both these places, and others which he's lost. Then, after some years, nothing came. He thought she had jobs as a housekeeper, or what used to be called "companion" to elderly ladies – that, according to him, was about the height of her ambition.'

'And as she wasn't looking to him for any kind of maintenance, he just let things slide, as if she'd been a passing acquaintance with whom he'd lost touch?'

'That's right.' Kemp liked Mr Pocket's precision of language. Any criticism of the client's actual behaviour was naturally unspoken between them; it was the client who was paying.

'But now he wants her found?'

'He certainly wants to know where she is.' The reason behind Mervyn Prentiss's quest must, of course, not be disclosed; Mr Pocket was to know nothing of Alicia Simon, the law lord's daughter. Kemp had made his own judicial enquiries in that direction, simply to find out whether the prize was worth the money Prentiss was throwing at it. It surely was; Mrs Simon was a widow of means, her husband having died of cancer a few years ago, leaving her, it was said, desolate but with a small fortune to compensate.

'What about presumption of death after seven years of silence?' Henry Pocket obviously knew his common law – amazing how often it cropped up in detective work.

'I don't think the client would wish to rely on that alone,' said Kemp, carefully. It might well be sufficient for Mervyn Prentiss, but it would certainly not satisfy Lord Allen should things come unstuck.

'There is some urgency in the matter,' was all Kemp would allow himself to tell the enquiry agent, 'and, of course, discretion.'

Henry Pocket's features stirred, and a small disturbance appeared on his brow that settled into a frown. 'What do you take me for, Mr Kemp?'

Kemp grinned. 'I should never have doubted it, Henry. Any further information you need, phone me direct here in the office or at home. I'll give you my number. And when you do come to file reports, just send them here marked "personal" and they'll only be opened by me.'

'A plain envelope, if you please,' said Henry Pocket, rising. When he received it, he put the papers away carefully, and transferred the envelope to his briefcase, which Kemp could see contained nothing but a packet of superstore sandwiches and a carton of orange juice. It looked as if Henry Pocket travelled light and, like a swallow, took his meals on the wing . . .

They had discussed his going to Germany. 'It'll be a last resort,' Kemp told him, 'when all enquiries in this country have come to an end. Mr Prentiss himself said it was highly unlikely that his wife should have returned to her native country. Nothing there for her, he said. Myself, I wonder . . . Linde's mother, Lotte Neumann, was still with the elder Prentiss family when she died – I understand that was in the early eighties; Mr Prentiss is not too good on dates. The Colonel and his wife had been good to her even when she had become an invalid, and they paid for the nursing home in Brentwood where she died. Mr Prentiss says he had never heard of any German relatives and was vague about where the Neumanns came from. All he knew was that the *frau* had come into his father's household in Minden, where they were stationed.'

'Regular Army?' Henry Pocket had asked.

'I rather think it was the Control Commission,' said Kemp. Mervyn had been more than vague on the subject; even the word 'colonel' he had used with some hesitation.

'Charlie Chaplin's Grenadiers,' said Mr Pocket, without expression. 'That's what the Army called them. Well, it would have to be Minden, then, wouldn't it? It may, of course, be totally irrelevant, but the CCG do have records, and presumably this Frau Neumann and her daughter would figure in the arrangements when the Prentiss household returned to England. I shall bear in mind the possibility that the German connection might yield some answers. Linde Prentiss might well have gone back to trace where she herself came from, particularly once the Wall was down – the Neumanns could well have been refugees from the East. It's all open country now, anyway.'

As Kemp waited for his next client, he was surprised to feel a stab of envy for Henry Pocket. Once, when he himself had been in the detective business, the first steps in a case had always livened his mind, raised his spirits. The prospect of following so many half-obscured pathways, turning stones, opening networks in people's lives, unravelling things past – all these had used to exhilarate him. A fine curiosity was what he had called it; and it was still there . . .

And there was something more. This particular search for a missing wife intrigued him; was it the time-span – all those years of what could only be called indifference? – or was it the character of the client himself, a man who had callously taken over the life of a young girl – no matter if it was with the connivance of the mother – and then, just as wantonly, discarded it? He'd said he'd given her money, but Kemp suspected that money, in the sense that most people talked of it, had never been a problem for Mervyn Prentiss.

Kemp had been doing his own researches. The firm of Prentiss & Son was still on firm financial ground, as it had always been since being started just after the First World War, when the building trade had acquired much of the land fit for heroes and put houses on it. There had always been family to run it – uncles, when Mervyn's father had gone soldiering – and careful marrying had brought in wives of solid worth. Mervyn himself was only following tradition. From gossip around Newtown – particularly from the Town Hall – it seemed that the Prentiss men had never been popular, except, possibly, with women. The attitude of the firm itself, taken as the corporate body it was, reflected something of feudal arrogance, as if it had taken on the mantle of the old squirearchy. When the company gave to local causes it did so as patronage; when times were bad – as in the thirties – it built shabbier houses and cut wages. Even Mervyn's stint at present as Chairman of the Council was seen by many as a cynical ploy to get the firm as close as possible to the sources of power – in this case the Planning & Development committees.

It had always been Kemp's habit to take a long, hard view of a client; no one ever told their lawyer the whole truth – just enough to get the case going the way they wanted it. Time alone would tell whether more was needed. He had the feeling that if anyone could find their way back to the very point where Sieglinde Prentiss had vanished, it would be the inconspicuous grey sleuth-hound he'd set on the trail.

Kemp had great confidence in Henry Pocket.

Seven

The office of Robert McFie & Son was 'up a stair', in the words of the shopkeeper below, as Franklyn Davey and Dinah could have seen for themselves had they stepped back to the kerb and looked upwards. The firm's name appeared in gold letters across a series of windows that looked out on to Rothesay harbour.

'I doubt I'd get much work done with a view like that,' Franklyn remarked as they pushed at the street door, which creaked a welcome when it finally gave them access. He and Dinah had already spent some time leaning on the railings at the quayside while they watched a skipper and his crew bring a very old fishing boat alongside, a manoeuvre only accomplished after several trial-and-error attempts in a crowded space. Fortunately it didn't seem to matter what other hulls you bumped into in the process, as if car-parking without liability. The water in the harbour – what could be seen of it between sailing craft bobbing like ducks – was blue-green and choppy. It was a fine morning of bright sunshine, even if the wind was blustery and straight off some distant snowfield.

They had telephoned, and Dougal McFie greeted them warmly.

'Come in, come in . . .' His room, across the length of the building, was somewhat austerely furnished but none the worse for that, the grandeur of the windows needing no further embellishment. The lawyer's desk was set at an angle, which gave him the best outlook: a view of the pier, a stretch of water, and then, in fold upon fold of purple, the hills of the Cowal shore.

Franklyn said it again: 'I'd never do a stroke of work with that at my elbow all day!'

Dougal McFie seated them so that they could appreciate it. 'I'm used to it, of course,' he said. 'And remember that it gets dark early in these parts . . . I understand you're a solicitor yourself, Mr Davey?'

There was an exchange of such personal information as had not been already covered in Dinah's letter to the McFie firm and in telephone calls between them. It was, as they had suspected, a one-man firm, Dougal having taken over the practice on the death of his father.

Coffee and biscuits were brought in by the middle-aged woman who had shown them in. She had a fine, lilting voice as she enquired about their preferences for cream and sugar, and she put Dinah in mind of a parlourmaid rather than a legal assistant, but Dougal McFie informed them that Morag was what in England would have been a fully fledged conveyancer.

'She was trained in Glasgow, and worked here with my father for years. I kept her on because she's good at her job, and we do a lot of property business.' He laughed. 'I've no idea how old she is, and don't dare ask . . .'

It was with some diffidence that Dougal McFie finally mentioned their reason for being there.

'Ah, yes,' he said, bringing a folder from the drawer of his desk, 'a very tragic affair, and not without problems. She was Euphemia Kerr Angus – you'll know that in Scotland one can use either name – and her people, the Kerrs, had been on Bute for generations. None left now, I'm sorry to say, or things might have been easier . . .'

'You say there are still problems?' Franklyn enquired. 'Do they concern her estate?'

'Well, yes . . . Not from any monetary point of view, I hasten to add. There'll just be the croft – it's a bungalow now, though we don't refer to it as such. One of the only stipulations made by the Laird when folk modernize crofts is that outwardly the structure looks the same as it always did – whitewashed walls, slate roof – though you can do what you like inside. Mrs Angus didn't do much to hers when it came into her possession, she and her husband would only have his retirement pension, so they couldn't afford much in the way

46

of building work. But it's in a lovely position, and should sell easily. Trouble is, who is to get it . . . ?'

Frank thought for a moment. 'I understand that Mrs Angus had a heart attack when she realized that her daughter was in the New York tragedy. Is that correct?'

Dougal cleared his throat. 'Not quite . . . There is some doubt as to when Mrs Angus actually died; her body wasn't found until late on Wednesday night when a neighbour had to let the police into the croft with her key . . .'

'I hate to ask this . . .' Even as she spoke, Dinah hesitated. 'How did Mrs Angus come to hear about the thing in New York, and did she know then that Annabel was there?'

Dougal McFie coughed. He seemed to use clearing his throat and coughing as a shield. 'The answer to both these questions is that we just don't know. Mrs Angus didn't have a TV set, according to her neighbour, and her radio wasn't working properly – the batteries needed renewing . . .' His voice trailed off, and he gazed out of the window as if the view might help to solve his problem.

'Hold on a minute,' exclaimed Franklyn. 'Are you saying that Mrs Angus might have died earlier than Tuesday, and her heart attack have had nothing to do with her daughter's death?'

'I can't really say anything. We simply don't know . . . The local doctor – the one called in when she was found – couldn't put a time to it. The pathologist's report at the enquiry – that's like your inquest – was a bit uncertain as to exactly when Mrs Angus had died, but it wasn't considered important. It was only later that I found myself landed with the problem.'

Dinah had been remembering something she'd heard at the offices of ClydeSight. 'Annabel's firm wanted to break the news to her mother in the least distressing way. It was late on Tuesday evening when their New York colleagues confirmed that the meeting had been on the eighty-first floor of that tower. The Americans lost two executives and a stenographer. The other person who would have been present was Annabel. Everybody in the Glasgow office was terribly upset that night, but they were told that someone from ClydeSight would go down to Bute and see Mrs Angus. It was thought that would be the kindest way . . .'

'I know. I spoke myself to Mrs Bristow at the funeral; she was very distressed.'

'Mrs Bristow attended the funeral of Annabel's mother?'

Dougal McFie smiled slightly. 'There was a lot of publicity, a lot of outside interest by the press. You can understand. But Mrs Bristow's attendance seemed to me very proper. She told me the firm would have done all they could to look after Mrs Angus, and she also told me the efforts she herself had made that Wednesday to contact the old lady – first, by telephone from her office, to make certain Mrs Angus was at home.'

'That's what I heard at ClydeSight: they'd rung the Bute number but couldn't get a reply.'

'By that time Mrs Bristow was on the ferry. She got to the croft about midday, but there was no one in. She tried at the nearest neighbour to Glenhead – that's quite a bit away – but Mrs Cluthie was in Rothesay shopping. Mrs Bristow was a stranger to the area; she didn't know who to turn to. Annabel was, after all, just one of her employees; she knew little of her personal life. Apart from having her mother's address on their files, she knew nothing of Mrs Angus; and, as she explained to me at the funeral, her own time was limited; she had to get back to the Glasgow office that evening to get any further information from New York . . . To my mind she did the most sensible thing – but then you'd expect it of someone like Adelaide Bristow – she went to the police in Rothesay, and simply told them.'

'Sounds the right thing to do in the circumstances,' said Franklyn; 'it's often the police who have to be the bearers of bad news. Yes, it would be sensible.'

But not, it seemed, in Bute. Dougal McFie told them what had happened, but in the tones of one standing in the middle, a referee with leanings towards the home side. Mrs Bristow had approached the police headquarters in Rothesay for help in tragic circumstances. What she had forgotten – even if she had ever considered it – was that she was already known to that particular branch of the Scottish constabulary as the instigator of a documentary featuring the island in a satirical sketch of Clydeside holiday places called 'The Last Resort'.

'Oh, Annabel told me about that one,' Dinah interrupted. 'She said it hadn't gone down well with the natives.'

Franklyn gave her a look: her words weren't going down too well with this native either. Dougal McFie pursed his lips and was silent until Dinah, flustered, told him she was sorry about the expression, and asked if he would please continue with his story.

After Mrs Bristow had departed on the ferry, the sergeant to whom she had spoken had taken her message upstairs to his inspector, and they had both looked at the situation from all corners before deciding what to do. Neither of them had enjoyed the attention the television item had brought to their island and, even allowing for the terrible tragedy across the Atlantic, they were suspicious of anything that might again bring the media to their shores. So they had proceeded cautiously, and slowly.

By the time they had reached the croft, Glenhead, it was almost evening. They had left their car at the road end – for although the lane was metalled, it was heavily overgrown – and made their way on foot. They had found the little house all closed up, but a dog was barking intermittently as they waited at the door. They had had no excuse to break in; Mrs Angus might simply be out shopping, or perhaps had gone to Glasgow for a few days; they had no means of knowing . . .

After some time had passed, while they debated what to do next, Inspector Scott had sent the constable across the fields to the nearest neighbour, Mrs Cluthie at Killour Cottage, but she was not at home. The two men had then returned to the road end and sat there for another hour until the sound of Mrs Cluthie's car alerted them to the fact that, at last, here was somebody who could help. She had been all day in Rothesay, then to a nursing home to visit her sister with whom she'd had supper before returning home.

After that, events had moved fast. Mrs Cluthie had assured them that Mrs Angus could not be away: she never left the dog for any length of time without arranging for Mrs Cluthie to walk and water it; and there had been no mention of such a thing. Yes, Mrs Cluthie had a key, so there was no need to break in . . .

'That was when she was found?' said Franklyn.

'Yes,' said Dougal bleakly. 'And even if the inspector had acted quicker it would have made no difference,' he added, defensively; 'Mrs Angus had been dead some time. Her body had been lying there when Mrs Bristow knocked at the door, and when the police arrived earlier. It might well have been there since Monday. She was last seen by Mrs Cluthie on the Saturday morning when she called with some eggs. They had a cup of tea together and chatted for a while. Mrs Angus said she had felt a cold coming on and so didn't plan to go out except to give the dog his walk in the afternoon.'

'The telephone operator at ClydeSight said there was no reply when they tried to get Mrs Angus on the phone on Wednesday morning to prepare her for a visit from Mrs Bristow,' said Dinah.

'Oh, she was dead by then; the path. report is sure on that point. It's just that they still can't say how much earlier.'

'And that's your problem,' Franklyn observed. 'I don't envy you. Let me get it straight: if Mrs Angus died before Annabel, then Annabel's estate gets the croft, and Annabel is dead . . . If she died after Annabel, then it's her estate, and who gets that?'

Dougal scratched his thick mop of dark hair. 'The will Mrs Angus made with us leaves everything to her daughter; there's no one else. As to other relatives – well, that's my job to find, I suppose.' He didn't appear to relish the prospect. 'And as there's no money apart from the house, then it'll have to be sold to pay all the expenses.'

'Cheer up,' said Franklyn; 'at least you'll get your fees. If there's no blood relatives, it would be going to the Crown anyway. Do you think the little property will sell even if it is in such an out-of-the-way spot?'

'Oh, it'll be taken as a holiday home. There's still quite a demand for such things, even if we are the Island of Last Resort.' He gave Dinah a lopsided grin as he said it, and she decided that Dougal McFie was not as dour as he looked.

'But you'll be wanting to see it.' He got up hastily and went

50

to the door. 'Morag,' he said, 'I'm away out to Kilchattan with these folks. Be about an hour. Hold the fort.'

They were hustled down the stairs and out into the street in no time. Franklyn decided this was very much in the Scots mode: progress by fits and starts.

Eight

'Its not very big,' Dinah observed, standing in the kitchen of Glenhead Cottage, 'but that view is perfect.' The window was deep-set in the thick wall of the former croft, and needed no curtains. It looked out upon green fields and hedges, a strip of sandy shore and then the Clyde, blue with cold this winter afternoon. Across the water there were small islands and a further coastline, pale gold as it caught the sun.

'Aye,' said Dougal, sounding more Scottish in the rural environment, 'beats mine. You can watch every ship that's in or out of the Clyde from this window.'

Although it had been modernized, the cottage still felt like it must have done when a working croft. Dinah remembered Mrs Angus telling her all about it: 'That was the byre,' she'd said, 'where the cows stood and got milked, and there was the drain in the floor. Up above was the loft where the hens got in the wee window at the top of their ladder, and behind the kitchen there's the dairy. I mind as a child seeing the butter made in the churn, and the pans standing on the bench with the cloths over them to keep out the flies. There'd be just the one bedroom, but of course there'd be the recesses off the kitchen – whit they called the holes in the wa' – for other beds; and the lads of the family, they'd likely be up in the loft . . .'

Mr and Mrs Angus had obviously used the outbuildings to extend the croft so that it was now, in effect, a modern bungalow, with a double garage, garden and a fine outlook. Franklyn agreed with young Mr McFie that it would probably fetch a decent price as someone's holiday home.

'But not for the winter,' said Dougal. 'It's a good half-mile over the fields to the nearest neighbour, and that drive from the road end has to be kept in proper repair or your car gets stuck. It's a lonely place out of season, despite the scenery.'

Walking through the rooms, Dinah was sharply reminded of her friend. 'What a dump,' Annabel had called it. 'God knows what made the parents buy here.'

Dinah could see why: she had more feeling for the country than Annabel, who was City or suburbs born and bred. Yet now Dinah ached to hear that voice again . . .

'How tidy everything is,' she exclaimed as they stood about in the bedroom; 'it's as I remember it: so neat. I suppose someone has been in?'

Dougal coughed, and cleared his throat. 'It wasn't untidy when the police got in, nothing out of place, and Mrs Angus lying on her bed – not in her nightclothes but . . . perhaps, she was about to undress.' He stammered slightly as if out of embarrassment at the intimacy of the scene. 'I . . . er . . . arranged for a cleaner since then, just to keep the place in order, but it's hardly necessary. We don't get the dust, you see, like in the towns.'

'What happened to the dog?' Franklyn asked. Almost on cue there was the sound of barking at the back door, which was thrown open to admit a black Scottie dog that had a stout woman in tweed coat and headscarf on the end of its lead. 'Oh, it's yourself, Mr McFie. I saw the car and wondered. My, but it's cold. I don't come this way often, but if I'm in the top field, Chummie's off to the croft and there's nae stopping him. Here's your dish, Chummie, and I'll get you the water.' As she kept up the run of talk, she went to the sink and filled the dog's bowl. She put it down on the floor. 'It's as if he'll no forget, like. But he's good as gold, Mr McFie, when he's with me, and it's a wheen better than going to that dogs' home. If there's nobody else as wants him, I'll be glad to have him, Mr McFie, deed I will . . . And you've got visitors, I see; would they be prospective buyers?'

It was obvious that Dougal McFie knew how to stem this tide. 'Miss Prescott and Mr Davey were friends of Mrs Angus's daughter, Mrs Cluthie,' he said, very firmly. 'They are not interested in the property as such. It is good of you to take on Chummie, and, yes, I think I can say with some certainty that he can stay permanently with you, if you would be so good as to have him.'

'There now, I said I'd have a home for you, Chummie, didn't I?' Mrs Cluthie stopped and patted the little dog, who licked her hand. It seemed that at least one small item of Mrs Angus's estate had been conveniently disposed of.

'I think I remember you, Miss . . .' Mrs Cluthie was peering into Dinah's face. 'Didn't you come here on holiday with Annabel one summer?'

'Why, yes, I did . . . There was a little tea party. Of course I remember you, Mrs Cluthie.' Dinah, in fact, could not have told apart any of the tweed-clad, grey-haired matrons who had come to Glenhead one day for tea and whist while she and Annabel had been staying, but she now realized that Mrs Cluthie had been one of them. 'I'm sorry it is on such a sad occasion that I meet you again.'

'Aye, it is that . . . I shall miss Effie Angus. She was a rare woman – never pushy, ye ken, never put herself forward. I only wish there were mair like her. Oh, it's a sad day for Glenhead . . . I depend on you, Dougal McFie' – she gave him a fierce look – 'to see that I get decent folk as neighbours. None o' they London types that'll be here one minute and gone the next with their big cars and their screechy voices . . .'

'We will have to take whatever comes, Mrs Cluthie,' Dougal responded somewhat stiffly, 'and it's more likely to be a holiday home than not. As executor, my firm has to get a fair price.'

'Aye, I ken all that . . .' She switched the subject as if it had already been well covered. 'Oh, there's that wee wireless of hers.' She pointed to the Roberts radio sitting at the back of the dresser as they trooped into the kitchen. 'Did she ever get the batteries for it, I wonder?'

'May I?' said Franklyn, lifting it down. He turned it on, and a flood of music filled the cottage. 'Well, it's working all right now. Didn't you say something about batteries, Mr McFie?'

Dougal looked discomfited. 'Someone said her radio wasn't working. I'm afraid I didn't try it.'

'No reason why you should, I suppose,' Franklyn assured him. 'But I wonder if the police gave it a thought.'

'She had it by her bed; it was there when they found her.' Mrs Cluthie spoke more slowly now. 'And it was me that said about the batteries. Effie told me the week before that she needed them and I offered to get them, but she said no need – the shop at Kilchattan has them, so she must have got them herself. She was independent that way.'

'In that case,' said Dinah, 'Mrs Angus could have heard about the tragedy on the radio on Tuesday afternoon when the news first came through.'

There was that uncomfortable silence again, no one knowing quite what to say until Dinah broke it. 'Is it right that she didn't have television, Mrs Cluthie?'

'Oh, she'd the television, but it was away into Rothesay for repair. They'll not come out here in the winter time, you ken. She took it in herself the week before and they'll still have it.'

'But even if she did hear about the attack on the radio, it wouldn't have affected her personally unless she knew that her daughter was in New York,' said Franklyn, reasonably. 'Would Annabel have told her mother about the trip she was making?'

Dinah shook her head. 'I asked the girl who did all the arrangements at ClydeSight for Annabel's airline tickets and hotel bookings if Annabel always let her mother know where she was going. The girl – she was also a personal friend of Annabel's – said definitely not; in fact, nobody in the office knew anything about Mrs Angus, apart from her name being on Annabel's file as next of kin. Even though her father had died – and he was the main reason for her split with the parents – Annabel seems to have cut her mother right out of her life. Or, if that's a bit hard, she was simply too busy to bother . . .'

They had been standing about rather aimlessly for some time, and their feet were cold. Something of the old croft's dampness was already rising through the rooms, despite modern tiles and fitted carpet, as if to re-establish the building on its original bedrock of ancient stone and soil.

'If there's anything in the way of a memento you'd like to take, Miss Prescott . . .' said Dougal, diffidently. 'Or perhaps you would prefer a small item of jewellery . . . I have taken

55

those to our office, of course, and I shall be letting her friends know they can come and choose. You, too, Mrs Cluthie,' he added hastily.

Dinah shook her head. 'I wouldn't presume. After all, I scarcely knew her. But perhaps a book of hers . . .'

'There's the one she was reading,' broke in Mrs Cluthie eagerly. 'It was by the bed. Well, it had fallen beside her when she was found, so it must have been on the bedside table . . . Funny, though, because she'd read it before; I know that for a fact. Neil Munro's it was: *The New Road* – him that wrote the Para Handy books; but it's no like that, it's historical. Effie said it was a favourite of her husband's.'

'Is it still there, in the bedroom?' asked Dinah, 'because, yes, I would like to have it, if that's all right with you, Mr McFie?'

The lawyer went and brought the book back to her. 'It would only be sold with the rest of the stuff,' he said, handing it over. 'And I've looked through all the other books here – Mr Angus was quite a reader – and there's little they'll go for. So, please, take it.'

After Dougal McFie had carefully locked the cottage, and Mrs Cluthie was striding across the fields to her home with Chummie bounding beside her, Franklyn and Dinah were glad of the warmth of the car taking them back into Rothesay. Before leaving the road end Dougal had emptied the post box, a battered tin affair almost hidden in the thorn hedge. 'Just the usual circulars,' he said, tossing them into the glove compartment. 'At least it's slowing down. In the first few weeks that box was crammed with letters of condolence which I sifted through so that they could be answered where necessary.'

'Now there's a point . . .' said Franklyn. 'As to the time of death – just when did Mrs Angus last open her mail box?'

The blurred lights of the town were just coming through the cold mist as Dougal McFie steered the car down the steep slope from the moor. 'Well, the postman gets to Glenhead around ten in the morning – there's only the one delivery – and she'd collected it on the Monday, for there were letters in the kitchen postmarked 8th September; that would be the Saturday. But whether she cleared the box on the Tuesday after the postman had been, we'll never know. When the police opened it on the Thursday evening, there was accumulated mail; it could have come Tuesday, Wednesday or Thursday – there's no telling. I have it in the office.'

It was to the office they were going, tempted by the offer of a warming tea. Morag produced a treat almost to rival Grace McCready's, and it was only as they sank back replete that Franklyn once again brought up the subject of the timing of Mrs Angus's death.

'Is there no way,' he said, careful not to impinge on the duty of executors, 'to establish more closely the actual time?'

'Naturally I took that question up with both Dr Macauley, who was first on the scene, and the pathologist who carried out the autopsy. But there is still doubt . . . and in a way, Mr Davey, it hardly matters. There is so little in the estate, apart from the croft itself – sorry, the bungalow – that amounts to anything more than a few thousand – at the most, perhaps, thirty . . . I suppose, if there were relatives pursuing the matter . . . but, as you know, there's nobody.'

'Mrs Cluthie did confirm at least one of my own impressions,' said Dinah, 'about Annabel's relations with her mother. Things might have gone better if it hadn't been for that documentary on the Island of Bute that was produced by ClydeSight and in which Annabel had more than a hand. When it was shown, some time last year, Mrs Cluthie says her friend Effie Angus was embarrassed because Annabel's name was on it as assistant producer. So it wasn't entirely Annabel's fault that she never came to see her mother after that – apparently Mrs Angus wouldn't have her near the cottage, said it would only spoil her relations with the neighbours . . .'

Dougal McFie was fiddling with the paper clips on his desk. 'It did make an impression,' he said slowly, 'which perhaps you from England do not understand. This is a very closed community in the off season when there are no tourists. Most of the island people have been here for generations; they don't boast about belonging – they don't hold with all this ancestor stuff you see on the television – but in their hearts they love Bute whatever its economic circumstances. They'd be hard-pressed to say so, of course, and they were tongue-tied when those so-called experts came to interview them. So they came out as incoherent yokels . . . men and women who knew their family backgrounds right back for three or four centuries, the farms they rented, their hold on the land, the very names that had run through them since the fifteenth and sixteenth centuries. They knew, but they couldn't say . . . The Scottish background, Mr Davey, is one of extreme reticence; you do not show your feelings. But that does not mean that feelings are not deep – much deeper, if I may say so, than the shallow here-today-gone-tomorrow ethos of most television programmers.' The rebuke implicit in Dougal McFie's words was softened by the gentle manner of his delivery, but both Franklyn and Dinah felt admonished.

As if to let them off, Dugal produced a file of the letters that had been in the mail box at the road end of Glenhead Cottage when the police had opened it. The only item of interest was the letter sent by ClydeSight Television when Mrs Bristow had returned there on the Wednesday evening after having failed to get a reply at the cottage, and after she had informed the police and asked them to convey her terrible message. Her letter spoke of the high regard in which Annabel had been held in the firm, of her own very personal interest in the girl and the very great affection she had felt for her. It was a kind letter, and obviously from one deeply distressed by the event that had effectively removed Annabel both as a member of Mrs Bristow's company and as an only daughter. It regretted the writer's inability to gain entrance to the cottage and promised that, as soon as possible, Mrs Bristow would call again to comfort and commiserate.

Dinah was much impressed. Obviously Annabel had become more than simply a member of the team at ClydeSight; she had caught the attention and secured the affection of its influential Chairwoman. Annabel would have had a brilliant future ahead, the rising-star simile had been no illusion, its trajectory need have had no fall. Events over which neither she nor her mentor had had any control had overtaken them both, and the star was gone, leaving only its afterglow . . .

Nine

The temperature in Scarborough was no warmer than in Scotland, but Henry Pocket was used to being out in all weathers and, as he stood looking down on the wet sands from the promenade, he gave no thought to the chill wind. For him it was tempered by the warm glow of achievement beginning to fill his whole being, which he recognized from past experience as the reward for work well done, at the moment when a case started to break and open out.

He smiled to himself, thinking of Miss Miles – Maureen. She was a spinster of indefinite age and quietly contented with her lot in life. Henry, being himself a bachelor from choice, admired that attitude – her acceptance of a state many would have found as bleak as those winter sands. She had been running the Arcade Employment Agency for some years, since the former owner had died and left her the business. 'We do domestic,' she'd told Henry, 'so we're a bit old-fashioned; but the hotels and boarding houses seem to find us reliable, and that's a good thing nowadays, isn't it?'

Henry Pocket had agreed with her that reliability counted for more than incompetent computerization, and was pleased to find not only that Miss Miles had worked at the agency for nearly thirty years, but that she had never thrown out a record. 'Folks think it silly,' she'd said, 'but there's a great basement to this place, and storage shelves, so I just left them there.'

She had led him down steep stairs to the lower depths, switched on the bare bulb hanging from the ceiling and shown him the range of grey filing cabinets – probably not their original colour, but now the same as the bundles of tattered paper they held. 'If only you had a more definite date for the lady you're looking for,' she'd said, as they shook off the dust and went back to the office, 'but, as it is, I'm afraid there's little chance of finding any record of her that we might have.'

'I have all the time in the world, Miss Miles,' Henry had said, taking off his overcoat and laying it carefully over the back of his chair. He had begun to roll up his sleeves. 'I don't suppose you've got any overalls?'

Maureen Miles had been happy to enter into the spirit of the enterprise. 'As a matter of fact, the handyman who does jobs in this block leaves his working clothes out the back. I'll fetch them for you.'

This had occurred at eleven that morning; it was now dusk. Henry had not left the basement in all those hours, but had been brought a hot dinner and afternoon tea on a tray by his hostess. Half an hour ago he had found what he was looking for, and on the strength of his success he was taking Miss Miles out to dinner at the Imperial Hotel that evening.

'I would call it a miracle, Mr Pocket,' she said now, 'if I had not seen you down there taking those files apart.'

'Henry, please . . . It's work I'm used to, Maureen, and I don't mind how dirty I get doing it.' He smiled at her. 'There's a metaphor there, isn't there? People say it's dirty work that I do as a private investigator, but I've always kept my own hands clean.' He poured her some wine.

'I'm sure you do, Henry. And, of course, I won't ask what you found about Linde Neumann, the name she used when she was on our books all those years ago. In my business, too, we have to be discreet. You didn't have to wine and dine me to make sure of my discretion.'

'Just as you didn't have to feed me when I was doing the job. Asking you out may have been simply my way of saying thanks, but it has given me great pleasure to have your company tonight.'

The words might have been banal, but they came from his heart – an object that colleagues used to say Henry Pocket didn't possess. Perhaps it was just that he was feeling good at the breakthrough in his investigation, or it might, as he said, have been the pleasantness of her company; but when he took her home he kissed her, and said he'd be in touch. Whether she believed him or not – he sensed a scepticism in her cool response – he did mean it at the time. Over dinner she had asked him outright why he had never married. He had spread his hands, palms up, on the tablecloth in front of her. 'Look at my job,' he said. 'What woman would put up with it? – the long absences from home, the odd hours, the very nature of the stuff I have to dig up and that can't be discussed . . . It's worse than being in the police, and we've seen enough television dramas where the officers' wives head for the divorce courts after maybe five years of it.'

'They should know what they're in for when they marry,' she'd retorted, but gently, as if she could have some sympathy for them. She had made no reference to her own single status beyond saying, no, she had never considered marriage. She had looked after both her parents in their declining years, and only had recently lost her invalid mother. 'I'm perfectly happy as I am,' she'd said, and laughed when he made the gallant but well-used remark that some man out there didn't know what he had missed . . .

Henry spent almost another week in Scarborough, but the days had been too busy to call back at the Arcade Agency. While he was at last driving down the Al to London he wondered about that; it was not usual for him to admit regret, even to himself. Ah well, he thought in the end, like good wine, she'll keep . . .

By the time he was reporting to Lennox Kemp at the solicitor's office in Newtown, Maureen Miles had become a faint figure at the back of his memory.

Henry Pocket took it from the start; and that was a matter for complaint. 'I was frustrated,' he told Kemp, 'by having to go over ground already well trodden by Mr Prentiss's own man, Mason. Any idiot could have come up with the same old facts: Linde Prentiss had never been employed, had a bank account, drawn social services benefits, or had a medical record. So far as bureaucracy was concerned, she didn't exist. Her husband gave her a few thousand, she never asked him for more, and all she sent him were postcards for a year or two, then nothing . . .'

'He says some letters came but he can't remember where from, and he never kept any of them. He was satisfied she was well, so he didn't bother looking any further – till now, of course . . .' Kemp watched Henry's face, which gave away nothing of his opinion of this behaviour.

'Right. And any sources of correspondence he'd had were investigated – if you could use the word – by his man, Mason. All those seaside resorts – Folkestone, Brighton, Worthing, Cromer – where she's supposed to have stayed produced zilch. It was a waste of my time, Mr Kemp.'

Kemp noted the phrase: not a waste of client's money, but a waste of Pocket's time. Pocket was the sort of investigator who liked to make his own way, open up his own lines guided by instinct and experience, rather than follow trails laid down by others.

Henry was still complaining. 'I felt I was being led, Mr Kemp. Stepping stones put in front of me to jump on so's I'd get nowhere. It's not the way I work.'

'I'm sure it isn't, Henry. But Scarborough was yours. How did you get on to it?'

The agent brightened, a shallow smile rippled across his face and he spoke with subdued pride. 'It's all in my report, Mr Kemp. Partly luck, partly the old nose . . .' He laid a finger against that feature to emphasize the point. 'I went back where Mason hadn't been – well, he wouldn't, would he? working for Mr Mervyn as he was . . .'

The house where the young son of the firm and his new bride had begun their married life was in Chigwell – the new post-war Chigwell being hurriedly built on by Prentiss & Son, Builders. Between the suburb itself and Epping Forest there had been stretches of woodland ripe for development and on one of the estates Henry Pocket had found Aspen House.

He had surmised that, if you have a building firm in your family, you don't buy your new semi from competitors; you get one built for you. A friendly solicitor, a search of the Land Registry and there it was: Aspen House on the Prentiss Estate, first owners Mervyn and Sieglinde Prentiss, no mortgage. Well, there wouldn't need to be, would there? Either Dad or one of the uncles would have forked out for the place.

The estate – now simply called The Woodlands – had

weathered, which suited the mock-Tudor red brick; the garden shrubs were luxuriant and in the best possible modern taste. Aspen House was at the end of the row and backed on to the forest. Careful local enquiries had produced the name of Spencer as the present occupants, but they had no knowledge of the history of the house; they had been resident some ten years and, although they knew the name of Prentiss as the original builders, they could tell Pocket nothing useful. As he left, however, he saw a van delivering fertilizer and compost – obviously food for a garden already suffocating under a surfeit of rich plant life – which advertised the local garden centre. However varied the human lives that had come and gone since the Mervyn Prentisses had set up house, nature would require cultivation and restraint if it wasn't to eat up the lot and return the land to virgin savagery. Henry popped into the garden centre just down the high road to Chigwell.

Brian Stocks ran the place and was not averse to answering polite questions about The Woodlands estate, since it had been responsible for much of his business over the years; but he shook his head over the first owners of Aspen House. 'I'd be only a kid then,' he said, 'but my dad, he'd remember.'

A courteous question, a note changed hands and Henry Pocket had the address of Bill Stocks, a small terraced house off the main road in the older – and less posh – part of the town. They were a friendly couple, Bill and Betty Stocks, and on a winter afternoon only too ready to welcome a visitor and talk about past times.

'Why Bill was a gardener at that place you're asking about, Aspen House, weren't you, Bill?'

When her husband was eventually allowed to speak for himself and Betty went off to make a cuppa, as she called it, Mr Stocks was a gold mine just waiting to be plundered. Henry sat, entranced. It was the first time, as he afterwards told Kemp, that Sieglinde Prentiss had come out of the paper world, and into his.

For Bill Stocks had come back from the War without employment to return to; he had taken up gardening just for something to do, and ended up loving it. Laying out the gardens of Aspen House and looking after them for

63

years had been only the beginning of a successful horticultural career.

'She got me to call her Linde when I'd been working there a few months. I reckon the girl was lonely, stuck in that monster of a house with hardly any furniture. She was supposed to choose it, and all the curtains and stuff, but she'd no idea . . . So she'd come out of the big French windows – as they called them then – and talk to me.'

'Did she go about much?'

'Hardly ever. He'd take her over to her mother for the day. That would be to the Colonel's place, top of Mott Street on the other side of the Forest. Then, when her mother got ill, she was in a nursing home in Brentwood, and Linde spent a lot of time with her.'

'Did they entertain people here at Aspen House?'

'You must be joking. No one came. It was as if he was ashamed of her – Mr Mervyn that is. I never liked the man, I don't mind telling you, not then, not now . . .'

'Were you still there when Mrs Prentiss – Sieglinde – left?'

'Never knew she'd gone, did I? I got the chance of a course to go on and was away six months. When I came back to Chigwell and asked about her, folks were vague, but it was clear she'd gone. I never got the chance to say goodbye and wish her well. I'd have meant it, Mr Pocket.'

'He would,' his wife affirmed, as she arranged the tea tray. 'Right smitten with her, he was.'

Bill Stocks shuffled his feet. 'I was sorry for her, that was all. I wasn't surprised she left him: he'd no time for her – it was all business with Mr Mervyn. I don't think he cared whether she lived or died.'

'She must have talked to you, Mr Stocks, more than to anyone else.'

'Reckon that's so . . .' Bill sighed. 'There wasn't anyone else. I can see her now coming out on the terrace in those little schoolgirlish frocks she wore, with her hair on her shoulders – reddish hair that gleamed in the sun . . .'

Betty Stocks gave Henry a look. 'What did I tell you? He was right gone on her. Funny thing is, nobody round here –

even them that goes back a long way – they don't know she ever existed. Then Aspen House was let for years, and finally sold. I've heard all about how high up Mervyn Prentiss has got himself, and I've heard folks say he was never married.'

'She was only a child,' Bill muttered, away deep into his memories of the sunlit terrace and the girl who had talked to him. 'I'd been stationed in the part of Germany she came from and knew a little of the language. Sometimes we talked in German; I think she liked that . . .'

'Do you think that's where she might have gone when she left Aspen House, Mr Stocks?'

'No, I don't.' Bill's tone was firm. 'When we talked about Germany, Linde was certain of one thing: she would never go back. I think all the revelations that came out after the War made her turn away from what was her native country. Sad, in a way, specially after her mother died and she had nobody . . . No, she would never go back. She said there were no relatives she'd ever want to see. It was the only time she spoke harshly about anyone, so I let it alone, and talked about the countryside, the River Weser "deep and wide" . . .' The old man chuckled. 'She liked that . . . so I had to get her the whole poem of "The Pied Piper" . . .'

'She sent you a postcard, didn't she? Have you forgotten that, Bill?'

Mr Stocks roused himself, struggled gamely to his feet. 'Glad you reminded me, Betty. I'll let the gentleman see it . . .'

It was that postcard of a promenade, a stretch of sand and a cold-looking North Sea that had taken Henry Pocket to Scarborough. The postmark was clear – 1973 – and so was the handwriting: 'I like this resort as well as any. Perhaps I'll take a place here.'

'I just thought she was on holiday up there, and mebbe she and her husband were buying a place by the sea. I didn't know then that she'd gone for good. Truth to tell, I didn't take much notice. By that time Bet and I were married, and had busy lives . . . It's only now, when you come here and talk about Sieglinde Prentiss, that she comes back to me, and I wonder what did happen to her . . .'

'And it's my job to find out,' said Henry Pocket, without, of course, telling them why. They were not inquisitive people – they had their own lives and their own problems; but Henry had learned a lot from them that afternoon as well as wakening old memories – and perhaps old yearnings – in an agreeable elderly man.

When Linde Prentiss had written about a 'place' in Scarborough Henry Pocket thought she was using the word in its old-fashioned sense, meaning a situation, and it was this reading of her postcard that had led him to the Arcade Agency, and his meeting with Miss Miles. Naturally that meeting had not got any great coverage in his report to Lennox Kemp.

Ten

In any event, Lennox Kemp was far more interested in the
nuts and bolts that Henry's report put down in detail so
clearly that, although Sieglinde Prentiss could not be expected
to walk into the office tomorrow, at least she was closer to
reality than the ghost-figure from Mervyn's non-too-reliable
memory.

In January 1974 she had taken up a post as housekeeper/
companion to a Mrs Farley of Eastleigh, Sea Road, Scarborough.
It was noted by the Arcade Agency that Sieglinde Newman – as
she called herself – had no references, but Mrs Farley had made
no objection; and that was the last the agency had heard of Miss
Newman who, in their short memo when she was interviewed,
merely noted that she had no previous experience but a family
bereavement had made it necessary for her to earn her living by
the only attributes she had: an ability to cook and clean. These
qualities must have been more than sufficient for Mrs Farley,
because Sieglinde had still been with her when she had died
some twelve years later.

Henry Pocket had not only checked up on the old lady's
will, but he had also interviewed Mrs Farley's son George,
who was still running his father's old-established engineering
business. That had not been a difficult trail to follow, once
Henry had the name Farley, for it was a name well known
in the town. Sitting in George Farley's office, Henry had
somewhat diffidently stated the reason for his call – that he
was interested in Mrs Farley's housekeeper rather than in the
family or its business.

Henry had been fortunate the day he had called on the
Farleys, because George's wife, Shirley, had been in the office
at the time – she did part-time bookkeeping for the firm.

When George realized what Mr Pocket wanted, he called her in.

'It's about Siggy,' he told her. 'This man's looking for her.'

'Oh, I do hope nothing's happened to her,' Shirley Farley had exclaimed. 'I don't know what we would have done without her looking after Mother all those years. When people say that someone's a treasure, that's just what Siggy was . . .'

Apparently, Miss Newman – 'Siggy' to the Farley family – had become the mainstay of the elder Mrs Farley's life, particularly in her declining years. 'She wasn't an easy invalid,' George had explained, 'and the only person who could handle her was Siggy.'

'So you weren't surprised when your mother left her the house – Eastleigh?'

'Your ma was a cantankerous old witch, George, and well you know it.' Shirley had a strong Yorkshire accent that lent weight to her words; 'she'd seen the back of scores of housekeepers before Siggy came along.' She turned to Henry. 'Of course, we were only too glad that Mother had the good sense to leave it to her.'

'The family were well pleased for her to have the house, Mr Pocket; there was plenty for us without it – as you probably saw when you checked the will . . .' Henry vowed never to try to put anything over on a Yorkshireman; the Farley family had indeed been left a tidy sum.

'I do wish Siggy had kept in touch,' said Shirley, 'but she was so independent. We tried to make her more one of the family, but somehow it didn't work. She wasn't at ease in company, and she was never a chatty person. She kept to her position, if you know what I mean – though that attitude's gone out with the tide, hasn't it? I mean the old servant–mistress thing's dead as the dodo, but Siggy held on to it . . .'

'Oddly enough, it didn't suit her, being mistress of her own house,' said George, 'so for a while she did bed-and-breakfast during the season, which brought her in enough to live on; and I was all for doing up Eastleigh so that she could take in more. But she wouldn't have it – liked the place as it was.

She was a wonderful cook, got quite a reputation – she could have opened a restaurant.'

Shirley shook her head. 'She was too shy for that kind of thing. Odd that she'd made no women friends . . .'

She suppressed a giggle. 'Shall I tell him, George?'

Her husband looked a bit uncomfortable, but he nodded.

'Our Siggy was a great favourite with the men,' Shirley said, smiling behind her hand. 'People who called on Mother, like her doctors – she had a lot of these – or her solicitor, would often stay and talk to Siggy. They seemed to find her – how shall I say? – attractive . . .'

'Well, she was,' said George, rather gruffly.

Shirley raised her eyebrows at Henry Pocket. 'You see, though women didn't see anything in her, somehow the men did – even George . . . And when it came to taking in visitors for bed-and-breakfast – it was noticed that it was mostly single men.'

Henry Pocket was fascinated by this new aspect of his quarry. He recalled how Bill Stocks had remembered the girl on the terrace at Aspen House and how, after all the years, the old man had still been moved by the memory.

'And how attractive was she?' he asked George Farley, outright.

'Difficult to say . . .' George Farley turned red and was flustered, not helped by his wife's amused glance. 'Don't look at me like that, Shirley; to me Miss Newman remained what she'd always been: my mother's splendid companion and nurse. But I've heard that she was much admired by men of a certain age . . .'

'Perhaps it was the uniform,' said Shirley; 'she always kept on wearing starchy aprons and pale-blue blouses. A mixture of the schoolgirl and the French maid that men of a certain age – as George so delicately put it – are said to go in for . . . And, of course, she was German. You read about these things in the papers, don't you?' She made the last remark as if to dissociate herself from any such peculiar practices. 'Anyway, it was no business of ours what Siggy did at Eastleigh before she left . . .'

'And that was . . . ?'

George answered, glad to get away from nebulous speculation. 'She asked me for advice about putting the house on the market . . . Let me see, it must have been five or six years ago.'

'Longer than that,' Shirley interrupted. 'More like seven years. I met her in the town one day just before she left and I had Toby in the pram at the time. Yes, definitely seven years ago. She didn't say where she was going. She said she'd let me have an address when she was settled, but she never did. It was as if she disappeared.'

Sieglinde's disappearances were something Henry Pocket knew about; when they happened, they were complete; she left no strings behind. Even in Scarborough, where she had lived for so long, where she had prospered – George had been pleased with the amount she had got from the sale of Eastleigh – and where she could have remained . . .

'Would she have gone back to Germany now that things were better over there?' he asked Shirley.

'Absolutely not. She was adamant about that. Never would she go back, she said. I asked her about relatives in Germany that she might visit, but she scorned the very idea, said she'd no time for any she might have: "They'd only be after my money" – that's what she said; and it was unlike Siggy to be so harsh about other people.'

George had confirmed this particular trait in his mother's companion. 'She said she hated Germany for what it had done; she would never set foot in that country ever again despite having been born there. She was the most stalwart Anglophile . . .' He laughed. 'Perhaps that side of her appealed to her middle-aged clientele – they'd be most of them Tories of the old school on whom the sun of Empire had never set.'

'Farleys do a lot of business in Europe,' explained his wife, as if in apology for her husband's unexpected burst of rhetoric. Henry Pocket was more taken up by George's word 'clientele' . . .

'You think she was running a brothel?' Lennox Kemp asked on Henry Pocket's second visit to the office.

Henry put his head on one side like a bird scrutinizing a seed. 'If she was, it would be very genteel, and would only welcome careful drivers . . . But I ran out of further information in Scarborough. That's why I'm back awaiting orders.'

'The client was very interested in the Scarborough episode, and has his own ideas about where his wife went from there. We'll come to that in a minute.'

Kemp had delivered the anonymous envelope containing Mr Pocket's report – factual, concise and bereft of all conversation, speculation and guesswork – directly to Mervyn Prentiss at his home on the outskirts of Newtown. They had discussed it in the property developer's study, but even there Mervyn had made sure the door was locked and Kemp had heard him give orders to his staff that on no account was he to be disturbed.

'Well, all I can say is that I'd absolutely no idea she was in Scarborough. But the fact that she got herself a job, and then a house, explains why she never came whingeing to me for money . . . And you say these Farley people are to be trusted?'

'I trust Mr Pocket's judgement,' Kemp had said. 'He asked that his visit to them be kept confidential. The Farleys run a reputable business; they're used to dealing with enquiries that call for privacy. You've no need to worry on that account.'

'If you say so . . .' Mervyn had sounded disgruntled. 'Your man should've contacted me before traipsing up to Yorkshire.'

Kemp had tried to keep anger out of his voice. 'And you would have told him she'd never been in Scarborough, Mr Prentiss. Then we'd have had no idea what she'd been doing for nearly twenty years without money.'

'For God's sake, Kemp . . . I'm not criticizing you or your man. It's just – well, this thing's weighing on me. I want to go ahead with the wedding. I can't keep Alicia waiting much longer; and anyway, I've found something that makes all that Scarborough stuff irrelevant. It was among my mother's things when her house was cleared after her death. I'd not had the chance to look at them till now . . .' He had opened the drawer of the desk at which they were seated, and produced a small slip of notepaper. 'It's the address of Frau Neumann's brother in Germany. My mother must have written it down when the housekeeper was in a nursing home before she died. My parents were very concerned when she

71

became ill and they must have wanted to know if there were relatives.'

Kemp looked the piece of paper on which was written an address in Rinteln, Westphalia. The writing was faint and in German script but readable: 24 Joshua Stegmann Strasse.

'And that's where he wants me to go?' Henry Pocket was unenthusiastic as he folded the slip of paper, and it was quickly absorbed into his folder of the Prentiss case, which was thin: Henry kept notes only in his head. 'Why did he not come up with this sooner?'

Kemp shrugged his shoulders. 'Says he had never really looked at the contents of his late mother's bureau – she only died last year. And he wouldn't have found it now if he hadn't been selling the little desk. Someone told him it was a rather good antique and should fetch a fair price at auction. I must admit that sounds just like Mervyn Prentiss. Anyway, he came across this address.'

'Very timely is all I can say.' Henry was not impressed. 'Surely he must have talked about his wife to his mother, particularly once she had gone . . .'

'He didn't go into the intricacies of the Prentiss family lifestyle,' said Kemp, 'but it sounds as if each member of it went their own way without reference to the others. The elder Mrs Prentiss wouldn't speak to Sieglinde when the young couple were living at Aspen House, nor was she in the least bit interested when she chose to disappear. It was always the Colonel who was concerned about Frau Neumann and ensured she was well looked after until she died. By then he and his wife had separated – officially, that is. According to their son, they'd lived apart for years anyway.' Kemp looked keenly into Henry's face, where expression was scarcely visible. 'I sense some mistrust in you, Mr Pocket . . . Do you think this discovery does not ring quite true?' Kemp was interested in the other man's opinion, since the same suspicion had crossed his own mind.

'I think it's true that I went to Scarborough and he didn't like it.'

Kemp had received rather the same impression, but did not say so. Instead he merely remarked that, as the client seemed anxious for the investigator to go to Germany, then to Germany he must go.

'Do you know the area, Mr Pocket?'

'Fairly well. I've been there before. Rinteln is merely a small town on the Weser but near the spa of Bad Oyenhausen, which, back in the immediate post-war period, was the headquarters of the British Army. And it's also close to Minden, which was the base for the Control Commission, so it's not altogether surprising that Frau Neumann should come from that part of Germany.'

'She was a refugee,' Kemp informed him. 'I did some checking of the Colonel myself through Army records. He was stationed in Minden for about four years; Frau Neumann was in his household when he left and travelled to England with them, bringing her little girl. Eventually the Colonel took out the proper papers for her so that she could stay. There's no record of either her or the girl returning to Germany.'

'Did Mrs Linde Prentiss have a passport?'

'Mr Prentiss says he did get one for her, but she never used it while she was living with him. However, she did take it with her when she left. He's convinced that she will return to her homeland at some time, particularly now that Germany's prosperous and leading the field.'

'Whereas from what I've heard she says she would never go back . . . The trouble is, Mr Kemp, that after Scarborough I've run out of leads.'

'My client has happily presented you with one,' said Kemp, with only a hint of sarcasm in his voice. 'So, for you, it's off to the cruel wars in High Germanie . . .' Kemp hoped that the line from an old ballad might bring a touch of humour into the conversation, but Henry wasn't having any.

'I think it was Bavaria they meant in those days,' he said reprovingly. 'North Rhine Westphalia, the region Mr Prentiss has given us, is on a lower plain, if you'll forgive the pun; but I'm sure its wars were just as cruel.' He sighed deeply, but not, it seemed, at the thought of distant battles. 'I'm not happy, Mr Kemp, not happy at all . . . I feel like I'm being led, and I don't like it. It's not the way I work.'

'I understand your feelings, Henry, but we all have to work

the way our clients wish us to – up to a point. I think you should go to this address and see what you can get out of Herr Dieter Neumann – if he's still alive, that is.'

'And not done a vanishing trick like his niece. I'm assuming from his name that if our Frau Neumann was his sister, she had kept her . . . er . . . maiden name. The fact that she was called 'Frau' doesn't mean anything – if she was the cook in the Prentiss household, she'd automatically be called that. It would be like *Upstairs, Downstairs* . . .'

'And our Siggy seems to have retained the same sense of class, from what they said about her up in Yorkshire. You know, Henry,' he confided. 'I've begun to like her enormously after reading your reports and talking to you.'

If Kemp had hoped to propitiate Mr Pocket by this show of camaraderie, he was disappointed.

'Looks as if Sieglinde can attract men of a certain age even when they've never met her.' Henry swept the folder into his briefcase beside an apple and a carefully wrapped pork pie, and left Kemp's office, still grumbling . . .

Eleven

Franklyn and Dinah were spending their last Saturday evening on Bute at the McCreadys'. There had been a splendid dinner, and afterwards the four of them ringed a blazing fire in the front sitting room. It was a room furnished to flout every canon of good taste; the beige, gold and brown theme would have set any decent interior designer's teeth on edge, while the assemblage of objects from family photographs to Dresden shepherdesses clinging for dear life on to every inch of level surface would have brought tears to the eyes of modern minimalists. Yet, as Dinah sank into the corner of a deep sofa under a framed woodland scene of startling banality, she breathed a sigh of pure bliss. The wind and rain outside the storm windows seemed locked in some titanic battle to beat the hell out of the little island; within, the atmosphere was full of sleepy contentment. Dinah thought of caves, of cliff dwellings, of primitive people's desperate desire for shelter, as she accepted tiny glasses of Drambuie and crumbly shortbread. She half-listened to Franklyn being fascinated by George's talk of an earlier Lennox Kemp.

'When I took him on at the agency in Walthamstow, I had me doubts he'd stick it for long. I mean, him being a lawyer even though they'd thrown him out. Most of my men, see – they were a pretty shady lot; they'd knowledge of the criminal courts all right, but some of them from the wrong side. I'd come across a few in my job at the Met. Some had been grasses. But I'll say this for Mr Kemp: he never looked down on them. It was more like as if his fall from grace, as he put it, had made him their equal.'

'I liked him from the first,' said Grace, stoutly, 'because he could be trusted, and we couldn't have said that about all our operatives, could we, George?'

All this, to Franklyn Davey, was a new aspect of the man he worked for. Although Franklyn had been with Gillorns as articled clerk and now associate solicitor, he was still rather in awe of his boss – as he thought and spoke of him. Lennox Kemp seemed so ordinary, an unassuming man with nothing to speak of in the way of appearance – he'd been described as looking like a well-worn teddy bear – though he could be sharp when occasion demanded, as Franklyn had found when his own professional behaviour had been at fault. It was a revelation to learn in what high regard Kemp was held by the McCreadys, and what a reputation he'd had at the detective agency. 'He'd a nose for the job,' said George; 'that softly-softly approach of his can be deceptive. It never mattered whether he was talking to a managing director or a wee typist in the pool, Mr Kemp could wheedle out folks' lies like a fisherman tickling a trout.'

Grace caught the end of that, and her voice crackled louder than the sound of the burning logs. 'Don't be wearying the young man with fishing tales. He'll get plenty of those when he meets Dr Macauley tomorrow.'

Franklyn raised his eyebrows at George.

'I thought, as you're interested in the death of Mrs Angus, you might like to meet the man who pronounced her dead. Ian Macauley's no great friend of mine, but we're both golf club members, and like myself he's a keen angler. I've arranged for you to meet him tomorrow at lunchtime up at the club. All I said was that your fiancée was a friend of Mrs Angus's daughter . . .' George paused.

'And where do I come in?' asked Dinah.

'You don't,' said George; 'Dr Macauley has no time for women . . . In fact, he's been known to be very rude to them.'

'He has been heard to say of his women patients – and that'll be well over half his practice – that they're nothing but guzzling, girning, greedy gossips . . .' said Grace.

'He's good at alliteration,' said Dinah, 'and obviously a misogynist.'

76

'He's a brute of a man,' said Grace, succinctly; 'I'm just thankful he's not my doctor. In any case, Dinah, I've made other plans for you.'

It seemed that both the McCreadys had been busy. After church the next day, George was to take Franklyn to lunch at the golf club, where he would meet this disagreeable Doctor Macauley, while Dinah was to be taken out to afternoon tea at Big Kilcrag, the farm down the road from Glenhead Cottage.

'Annie Semple was a good friend of Mrs Angus. I only found out about that yesterday when I met her at the church – we're both on flower duties this week and we got talking. I told her about you being a friend of Annabel's and she said she'd love to see you before you left the island. You'll not mind me taking you out there tomorrow? Let the men get on with their own things. George only goes to the kirk to please me; he'd be a lot happier at the golf.'

Franklyn and Dinah exchanged glances from either side of the shining brass fender. They were being manipulated, there was no doubt, but as each in their own way was still immersed in the twofold tragedy – the horror in New York and the lonely demise of an elderly resident here on Bute – they would allow themselves to be carried along such paths as the McCreadys seemed to have chosen for them.

By morning the weather had changed yet again. The storm in from the Atlantic had passed through, gone to torment the eastern shires, and the sky was a radiant cloudless blue. At three o'clock Mrs McCready called for Dinah and drove her out along the shore road to Kilchattan. At the road end to Mrs Angus's cottage Dinah asked if they could stop for a moment. She got out and leaned on the old wooden gate.

'I remember, when I was here that summer, Annabel and I would leave the car here, and walk down to her mother's. The smell of honeysuckle in the hedge – I can't forget it. Perhaps I would have done, in time, if this hadn't happened . . .' She was near to tears.

Grace came and put an arm round her. 'You'll never forget, lassie,' she said, 'and maybe that's the way it was meant to be . . . You'll keep the both of them in your heart, your

77

Annabel and Effie Angus; they've become a small part of you. You'll remember them when your life's at its deepest . . . and in the valley of the shadow of death. But come away, now.' Grace got back into the car, and Dinah followed after a last look down the track to where the grey slate roof and chimney of Glenhead could just be seen above the hedges. She had the feeling that at some time she would return. There was something unfinished here; it was as if the old croft itself was crying out. It was such a strange sensation that it kept her quiet until the car drew up outside the grey stone house that was Kilcrag Farm.

'I've a call to make at the nursing home in Kilchattan,' said Grace McCready at the door, 'so I'll just introduce you and leave you with Mrs Semple. I'll be back for you at five.'

'There's no need for introductions, Mrs McCready.' Mrs Semple had come out to meet them. 'I remember this young lady. Didn't you stay at Glenhead a few years ago? You were with Annabel.'

Oh, that tea party . . . Dinah felt ashamed at not remembering all those ladies she had met that day. She knew why: Annabel had been so scathing about them – the cosy talk that went on endlessly, the sameness of their clothes. 'They sit there like a row of turnips,' she'd said. But as individuals they would all have been different, just as she, Dinah was different from Annabel.

She ought to have remembered Annie Semple, for the farmer's wife was years younger than, say, Mrs Cluthie – was an attractive woman with an educated voice and none of the Scottish 'verbal felicities' (Annabel's sarcasm) that had characterized the others. Annie was, in fact, English.

'It was Mr Angus that I knew first,' she explained to Dinah, 'because we used to meet in the Rothesay Library, both of us great readers – not exactly a common species here on Bute!'

Gradually a friendship had built up between the retired couple in Glenhead Cottage and the farming family at Kilcrag, despite the age difference – not so much in the case of Neil Semple, for he was some twelve years older than his wife.

'I don't think Effie was exactly lonely when Mr Angus died, for she had friends here and she went to the Women's Rural, and of course the kirk, and she too read a lot. We've a busy life on the farm and I've not much spare time, but I would go and see Effie at least once a fortnight. She was contented, in her way . . . Of course, she would have liked to see more of her daughter, but Annabel's few visits this last year or two have been disastrous . . . Oh, I didn't mean your holiday, but afterwards.' Annie Semple was busy with the tea things on a trolley wheeled into the front parlour. The room was pretty – or would be in the summertime – but chilly and probably not much used in winter. Dinah would have preferred to stay in the large, homely kitchen, where a fire blazed in the chimney corner and an Aga filled the rest of the room with warmth and the smell of baking; but she was a visitor and must be entertained in the appropriate place.

'I knew Annabel had fallen out with her father years ago when she chose an English college to go to – he'd wanted her to stay in Glasgow.'

'Effie told me all about that split . . . but I think she hoped that after Gordon's death she could be reconciled with Annabel. It was just unfortunate about that film that was made. Word had got about that Mrs Angus's daughter was on the production side. People here didn't know much about how these so-called documentaries are put together, but of course there was great excitement when the TV crews arrived. I'm afraid I'm not much of a one for television myself, and Neil never watches anything but the news and the weather.'

'I should think your life is far too busy – back in Ireland all the farmers' wives say the same.'

'It's the beasts, you see. There's the feeding in the winter, and the milking; it doesn't do it by itself despite all the mechanization, and there's got to be time for the vet . . .' Annie broke off, and laughed. 'Sounds a tale of misery, doesn't it? But I wouldn't have any other life. My own family are farmers in North Yorkshire, so I knew what I was letting myself in for when I married Neil. Oh, here are the young yins . . .'

Dinah too had heard the sound of feet clumping in the kitchen, and now the owners came round the door, hesitant at the sight of a visitor.

Annie had spoken about the boys, so Dinah knew their

ages; Andrew was nine and Hamish seven. They stood in the doorway, shuffling their feet and staring at Dinah.

'If you're coming in here, leave your boots in the hall.' Annie cut more slices of sponge cake as the boys retired noisily and returned, their eyes on the trolley.

'Sit down a minute and be polite,' said their mother, handing out plates. 'This is Dinah, who I met once at Mrs Angus's. Say hello . . .'

'Hello,' they both said at once, wide grins on their faces.

'Are you from Glasgow?' asked Hamish, licking jam and cream from his fingers and holding out his plate for more.

'Further away than that,' said Dinah. 'I'm from London.'

'We've been to London,' said Andrew; 'we went in a coach.'

'Took hours and hours and hours . . .' his brother added.

'How'd you know? You went to sleep on the coach.'

'That was a sensible thing to do,' remarked Dinah, passing another plate to Hamish. 'And what did you see in London?'

Hamish thought about it. 'Not the Queen,' he said. 'She wasn't home . . . Big buildings, like in Glasgow.'

'Not like Glasgow, silly, much much bigger.'

Annie explained that they had gone in a coach with other farmers from the mainland connected with the Countryside Alliance, but she confessed it had been more of an outing for families than anything political. The boys agreed it had been great. Dinah noticed that both spoke with strong Scottish accents but did not use the vernacular in the way she'd heard in the streets of Rothesay. Perhaps that was the influence of their English mother, but when she mentioned it to Annie, she laughed.

'You should hear them when they're in the school! They go to the one in the village, and then it'll be on to the Academy. We're lucky here in Bute with education. Folks down South would say we've little choice, but we don't need it – the village schools are good, and the Academy will get them both to university; it's got a fine record.'

Bereft of their boots, the boys took it as an excuse for a roll on the chintz sofa and a pull at the cushions. In the way of children, they could not let a matter drop until they'd wrung it dry.

'Big Ben's bigger than anything in Glasgow . . .'

'No, it's not.'

'Glasgow's not got skyscrapers.' Andrew pushed his brother into the pile of cushions, and silenced him temporarily. 'We saw that one – what's it called, Mum? Canary something . . .'

'Canary Wharf,' said Dinah, adding, to appease Hamish, 'but it's not really a skyscraper.'

'Not like them in New York,' Hamish piped up, as he punched cushions on the sofa, 'and fire coming out of the tops . . .' Both boys started arguing as to which of them had seen the television pictures first, while Annie Semple explained quietly to Dinah that it was difficult to keep anything from children, even in remote areas. Dinah agreed. 'They would see it in Tonga; they would see it in Finland . . . What do they make of it?'

'Fortunately, perhaps, there is so much horror on television anyway that it all seems to merge. I don't think they draw the line we do between fact and fiction. Maybe that's just as well. When we got the news that Effie's daughter had been at the World Trade Center that awful morning, we couldn't take it in at first; and it was the end of the week before we heard that Effie herself was dead.' Annie had been talking in a low whisper, but not low enough for Andrew, who had given up fighting his brother.

'Johnny Boag saw that lady,' he announced.

'Mrs Angus, Andrew? You mean Mrs Angus?'

'No, the other one . . . the one Dad said should never set foot on Bute again.'

Annie Semple went red. 'Oh, he didn't mean anything – well, personal . . .' She turned to Dinah. 'It was that film; none of the farmers liked it. I'm sure it wasn't your friend Annabel's fault that they emphasized all the wrong things . . .'

'Is that what you meant when you said Annabel's visits lately had been disastrous?'

'She only came once after the film was shown. Effie had one of her tea parties for her, but nobody went. We were away in Islay at the time, so I got out of that one. I was sorry for Effie; she depended on her social life here and that film spoiled it for a while till folks forgot. And of course it meant that Annabel herself refused to come down to her mother's from Glasgow, even though it wasn't far.'

Andrew was standing rubbing one stockinged foot against the other. 'But Johnnie did see her . . .'

'When she came that time last year?'

'No.' Andrew looked at his mother with scorn. 'Everybody knew she was here then. But Johnny Boag saw her yon other day on the bus.'

Dinah leaned forward. 'When was this?'

'It was his birthday, so he got the money to go to the pictures in Rothesay. I wanted to go with him, but you wouldn't let me . . . It was *Raiders of the Lost Ark* . . .'

'But you'd already seen it, Andrew.'

'I wanted to see it again. It was great, and I wanted to go with Johnnie, but you said I couldna . . .'

Dinah hastily tried to smooth what seemed to be a rough spot between mother and son. 'Do you know the date of Johnnie's birthday?' She asked.

It was Annie who replied. 'Well, yes, as a matter of fact I do. Johnnie's the son of one of our men on the farm; the Boags have a cottage on the road, and Johnnie's round here a lot. He's fifteen, and a good lad. He's a bit of a hero to my two, but I must admit he's been a great help to me with them. I've always given him something on his birthday – the Boags don't have much to give – and this year was no exception: Neil and I got him a bicycle.' Annie became aware of Dinah's small fidget of impatience. 'His birthday's the eighth of September.'

Dinah turned to Andrew. 'Is your mate Johnnie Boag sure he saw Mrs Angus's daughter on the bus that Saturday? He wasn't mixing it up with the year before?'

'Johnnie Boag's no daft,' said Andrew, looking at Dinah as if she was. 'He saw her get off at the road end for Glenhead. She'd a big hat on like she didn't want to be seen.' He grinned. 'Johnnie said she'd as well not be seen for what folks might do to her: she'd get lynched . . .'

'Oh, come now, Andrew . . .' said his mother helplessly. Then she said to Dinah: 'Is it important to you that Annabel was here that weekend, the weekend before . . .' She stopped.

Dinah was thinking furiously. It wasn't possible; there must be some mistake . . . Annabel had been in her Glasgow office scrambling material together for the American trip, or at the flat taking clothes from pegs, packing a suitcase, rushing around . . . Could there have been time? And why didn't anyone know?

'Mrs Semple . . . Annie . . . could you do something for me? I've already taken up so much of your Sunday afternoon, I hate to ask.'

'What is it? I think I'm beginning to be intrigued by all this.'

'Could I possibly see this Johnnie Boag? Just to make sure . . .'

It was Hamish who first padded to the door. 'I'll get Johnnie for you,' he shouted. 'He's only oot in the yaird.' Excitement fractured the niceties of language.

'Bring him into the kitchen.' Annie Semple got up and began pushing the trolley out of the parlour. 'He'll be more at ease in there,' she added to Dinah. 'And you do the asking; I'm no good at this kind of thing.'

The boy who came in, finally, towed like a prize bull by both Andrew and Hamish, was long and thin, with bony wrists and ankles jutting from a dark suit – possibly his father's – put on for Sunday.

'You wanted me, Mrs Semple? I was efter a clockin' hen. She's away in yon far corner by the barn – got a rare wee nest and twa eggs in it.'

While they had been waiting, Annie Semple had said Dinah might find Johnnie's speech a bit difficult. He went to the public school in Rothesay rather than the Academy – an explanation Dinah found more inexplicable than the boy's words. Typically Scottish, she thought afterwards: the public school wasn't Eton; it simply meant a school for everyone and free – the description was accurate, unlike the English one.

Now Annie explained, sotto voce, that Johnnie had been looking for a hen that was laying away from home, but she couldn't tell Dinah where the word 'clocking' came from . . . Anyway, Dinah at the time had more important things on her mind.

'Andrew and Hamish tell me that you saw somebody get off

83

the bus at Glenhead road end on the Saturday of your birthday this year, Johnnie. Do you mind telling me about it?'

Johnnie Boag came up to the fire, and held out his hands to it; they were blue with cold. 'I wis at the pictures, and I got the bus hame. It would be near five o'clock it leaves the Square. There weren't many folk on it, but there wis a leddy at the back I niver saw properly till she got off at Glenhead.'

'And you'd seen her before?'

'Aye. I saw her when yon TV people came first and gave that wee talk doon at the hall at Kilchattan. I thocht there'd be jobs goin', so I went with my dad.'

'I remember that, Johnnie,' said Mrs Semple. 'I think a lot of people thought there might be jobs in it, but they were disappointed. Are you sure this lady on the bus was Mrs Angus's daughter?'

'Sure I'm sure. I'd seen her picture in the *Buteman*, too. It was all ower the front page efter the film got shown on the TV.'

'Did she have any luggage with her, this person who got off the bus at Glenhead?'

'She'd one of these wee travel bags you see folks carryin' on airlines. She'd a long coat – one of these light-coloured sort they call camel; it looked expensive – and this hat pulled down on her brow.'

'But you saw her face?'

'Oh, aye, the wind caught the hat as she stepped doon, and I saw her face, plain as I see yours.'

'Why was nothing ever said about this?' Dinah's mind was so confused she forgot her usual courtesy and spoke sharply.

Johnnie Boag looked puzzled. 'Naebody asked me,' he said, and went on rather sullenly, 'How wis I to know it mattered that the leddy was on the bus? I just thocht, she's here to see her mother and she'll not want the whole island to know.'

'I'm sorry, Johnnie . . . Did it occur to you later – when the other tragedy happened in New York – that you'd seen Annabel Angus on that Saturday just a few days before . . .' But Dinah couldn't finish her sentence.

Annie Semple handed a package to the boy. 'There's some scones and cake for the weans, Johnnie, and tell your mother

I'll be round to see her in the morning. I know she's not been well.'

'She's not been well since the summer, Mrs Semple. Thanks all the same, and I'll tell her you'll be in.' He turned to Dinah. 'I can only say what I saw, miss. I did give it a think, efterwards . . . it being so sad, like, when the old leddy died when she heard aboot that awfu' thing away in America . . . But it wisnae for me to say onything, and naebody asked.'

When Johnnie Boag had gone, the youngsters clattering at his heels, Annie sat Dinah down by the fire. 'Well,' she said, 'you'll not doubt the lad. It must have been Annabel Angus he saw that Saturday afternoon. She would be off the last boat, gets in just before five.'

'Why'd she not take a cab?'

'Cabbies remember folk; she'd maybe be the only fare that day. A bus would be safer, if she didn't want it known that she was here. And is it so surprising she should visit her mother before making that trip? It would be the natural thing.'

Dinah shook her head. 'Not for Annabel. She'd made plenty of trips before – to America, to the Far East – and I doubt whether she'd even bother to send her mother a postcard.'

'That's true. Mrs Angus never really knew where her daughter was, nor what she was doing.' She sighed. 'A sad situation for a mother. She didn't even know whether Annabel had a boyfriend – she used that old-fashioned term about it.'

'Annabel had a boyfriend; they shared a flat in Glasgow. He's a very nice man, and I think Mrs Angus would have liked him . . .' As she spoke, questions were piling up in Dinah's brain. Why hadn't Peter Mallen known that Annabel was coming to Bute that weekend? That new cashmere camel coat – it was Annabel's all right. Peter knew she'd taken it from the flat; he'd described it to Dinah when she'd asked about the clothes that were taken. Annabel had bought it only the week before . . . Dinah closed her eyes, and saw the field of debris under the fallen towers . . .

85

Twelve

W hile Dinah had been in the pleasant company of Mrs Semple at Kilcrag Farm, Franklyn Davey had not been so fortunate. On the drive home from the golf club he told George McCready: 'I've met some nasty-looking men at times, and some nasty-natured ones, but never the two together in one man until today.'

George chuckled. 'Ian Macauley couldn't have been much to look at when he was young, and age hasn't improved him.'

'Seems he's worked at being the worst-tempered doctor in the country to match those scowling features he must have had even as a child. I gather he was a brilliant student; that, too, he must have worked at. And the end result is an ego the size of a mountain. There's no talking to the man.' Franklyn stopped in disgust.

'People round here used to say that his bark was worse than his bite, but they've stopped saying it, because it's just not true. He certainly got his bite into you when you queried his timing of Mrs Angus's death . . .'

'And I was pretty mild about it,' said Franklyn, still fuming. 'I only suggested vaguely that there must have been difficulty in determining the exact time, in the circumstances.'

'I should have warned you. When Macauley was first called in by the police, he refused to give them any hint as to the time she'd died; but when the pathologist gave his somewhat ambiguous report, Macauley was furious – said that from the start he'd known she'd died the Tuesday night, she'd heard about the events in America . . . A heart attack brought on by the shock.'

'How could he be so certain, in the face of what the pathologist had said?'

86

'Search me. Professional jealousy, probably. Nobody on Ian Macauley's list dare ask for a second opinion – he just won't hear of it, and he browbeats his patients till they stop asking.'

'I wonder he's allowed to go on practising . . .'

'Oh, there's been plenty of complaints, and there's been moves to get him shifted, but nothing's come of them. He's near retirement age, so I reckon the powers that be have just hoped he'll take it early. Some hope. He's got his wee empire going and he'll not give it up.'

'His patients must all be masochists.' Franklyn thought for a moment. 'He really had a go at me when I suggested that the funeral of Mrs Angus took place rather quickly . . .'

'That really got his dander up. A lot of folk thought the same, but of course no one would say it to his face. The whole island was so stunned by recent events that they tended to close in on themselves and keep quiet.'

Franklyn was remembering the fury in the doctor's eyes when he had mentioned the funeral of the old lady.

'Show some respect, young man, before you talk of things you know nothing about. There were ghouls like you arriving by the boatload agog for sensation. Make the front page – Huh! If I'd not insisted on the burial when it was, they'd have been taking pictures of the coffin. There had to be dignity, a word these pressmen never heard of . . .' His voice had risen and several people in the hotel lounge had looked across. Seeing who it was, however, they averted their eyes. 'I will not have it said by anyone that there was not proper reverence for the dead. And I'll be damned if I answer any more of your impertinent questions, Mr . . . whatever your name is.'

'I'm sorry if I've got you in wrong with the man,' said Franklyn; 'you have to live here in Rothesay and I don't.'

'No skin off my nose,' said George. 'Grace and I aren't in his practice, and every one of us at the golf club has been hectored by Macauley at one time or another. But what he got angry with you about interests me. He's blaming sensation-hunters, for instance, and yet he was in thick with Mrs Bristow at the funeral. She was the chief mourner, as it were, and the whole thing was arranged by her.'

'Why was that? She didn't know Mrs Angus.'

George thought about it. 'Maybe she thought that being seen to care was good publicity, and it was. There was plenty of what we call press interest, and you can see why.'

'Hm. Perhaps Mrs Bristow hoped her presence would placate the islanders who'd resented that television programme "The Last Resort"?'

George shook his head. 'She always distanced herself from that one: it wasn't made by her company and she hadn't liked the way it portrayed the island.'

'Yet she took on Annabel Angus, who had been part of the production team.' Franklyn shrugged. 'Well, I suppose that would be OK in her business. She saw talent and went for it. In any case, the slant taken in the film might not have been Annabel's fault . . .'

From what Dinah had told him about her friend's attitude to the islanders, Franklyn knew otherwise. 'Well, I hope I never have to meet that beastly doctor again,' he told George as they arrived back at the McCreadys' bungalow.

Crossing the Firth the next morning, Dinah and Franklyn took refuge in the saloon out of the rain and a tearing wind from the south-west that had the ship's crew clinging to the railings.

'I simply don't understand.' Dinah had heard herself say it so many times since yesterday, because there didn't seem anything else to say.

Franklyn was more analytical. 'The trouble is that we don't know enough. We're only holding the ends of things, the bits people tell us, and none of them fit.' He had a trained, logical mind, and liked to see patterns in events and occurrences that one could understand. 'Here,' he went on, 'even the times seem awry. Could Annabel possibly leave Glasgow say about midday on Saturday and be on that bus by five o'clock? I suppose she could, but I don't know the timetable of the boats . . .'

'I don't see why she had to visit her mother at all. It was out of character . . . particularly when there was so much to do. She had to be in the office at ClydeSight for her briefing on the New York trip, which she'd only just pinched from Sandy

Duncan; then she had to get to the flat to collect clothes and stuff . . . Was there really time for all that?'

Franklyn hated to be without information when he needed it; he decided the first thing he'd get hold of when they landed – if they landed at all, he thought, as the ferry rolled helplessly in the churning waters – was a timetable. That would at least give him something to work on.

'It could be done,' he said, when they were safely on the train to Glasgow. 'There was an afternoon ferry on the Saturday she could have got if she left her office before twelve, rushed round to the flat and packed that airline bag your wee laddie Boag saw her with. It's not the kind of thing he'd make a mistake about . . . Then, on Sunday, there's a restricted ferry service, but Annabel could still have got to either of Glasgow's airports – Renfrew or Prestwick – in time for the night flight to America. It would all be rather a hectic rush, but it could be done.'

Dinah could see that he was pleased to have fixed those nuts and bolts, but what interested her more was why? 'I'm glad we're seeing Peter Mallen again. Maybe he can explain why she never told him she was on Bute when she made that last telephone call to him.'

'We don't know that she didn't. Remember, he said the line was bad, and he was in the middle of a scrum of fellow reporters in a pub.'

'Why'd she not phone him at the flat on Sunday, then? Or from the airport before the flight took off?'

'I've no idea. As I said, all we're getting is bits and pieces that don't fit. There's something not right about this whole thing.'

Out of the rain-splattered windows Dinah watched a fleeting landscape. The clouds were grey, the hills were grey, the Clyde was a steely silver like the roofs of the tenements on the other side of the river. It wasn't the weather that was making her miserable; she had brought Franklyn to this hard country in order to find some solace for incoherent feelings, a desire – and a selfish one, she thought now – to forgive herself for the neglect of her friend . . . It had helped at first – she acknowledged that; but the visit to Bute had brought its own

89

problems. She could see that Franklyn had become involved, not in any emotional sense but on a practical level, with those last days of Annabel. For herself – Bute had unsettled her. Perhaps it was the going back, the contrast between then and now at the Glenhead croft, the sunny window with a pale curtain blowing the day Mrs Angus's ladies had come to tea, and the chilly emptiness of that bedroom where she'd died . . .

The train was running into the smoke of the city. Looking out at its buildings, she was reminded of the Semple boys' childish argument, and the innocence of Hamish's face as he mentioned '. . . fire coming out of the tops'. Would people ever forget, she wondered, or would the events of their own lives, so much more personal, so much more precious, finally overlay those pictures in the mind? Unless, of course, there had been someone they knew in those towers . . .

She phoned Peter Mallen's newspaper office as soon as they arrived at their hotel, where they had booked in for one more night. Fortunately he'd been doing the home matches on the Saturday, so was not on his travels. She said nothing on the phone about what they had discovered on Bute. Mallen was eager to see them and would come round for dinner.

The hotel receptionist had a message for Dinah: 'Mrs Adelaide Bristow,' she said, in a tone of some awe, 'has been trying to get in touch with you. She left her private number for you to call.'

'You must have caused quite a stir at the offices of ClydeSight,' said Franklyn. 'You don't imagine you're being head-hunted, do you?'

'How did she know where I'd be?'

'Television has its spies everywhere. I should think Sandy told her which hotel we were staying at, and she guessed we'd be back here before leaving Scotland.'

It was a starchy voice that answered when Dinah phoned the number she had been given. Yes, Mrs Bristow was most anxious to meet Miss Prescott. Could she possibly come into the ClydeSight offices tomorrow morning, at a time to suit herself, since Mrs Bristow was aware that Miss Prescott would be returning to England later in the day?

'We don't have to leave till late afternoon,' said Franklyn. 'You go off and see this wonder woman. I've been reading her up in the local press – she's quite a tartar. Sniffs out sleaze like a hound-dog: she's already got one Scottish minister out for fabricating his expenses. She wants *her* parliament – that's what she calls it – to have clean hands from the start. And she's popular with the people who are fed up with fat-cat salaries in industry and politicians out for the quick buck.'

'She's got money herself, from what I hear,' Dinah protested.

'Ah, but Adelaide's a sole woman fighting in a man's game, and she gets the credit for earlier struggles when she hadn't a bean.'

'Well, thanks for the pen picture; I'll be sure and wash my hands before meeting her. I've said eleven o'clock, if you don't mind doing the packing up and checking out . . . Oh, Frankie, how I long to be back in London. There's something here weighs on me; it lowers my spirits.'

'I think I know how you feel. There was something on Bute that I didn't like, either. Maybe it was that beastly doctor with the beetling brows . . . I could sense how, in a small place, someone in his position could become a raving bully and be difficult to shift, the people cowed by his profession and too scared to complain. You said that Annabel complained of just that docility – everything nice on the surface but seething underneath.'

Dinah nodded. 'Lace curtains in the parlour, murder in the kitchen; gentility covering mayhem. In some ways Annabel was right, even if she did cause unrest among the natives. If it hadn't been for that, she might never have had to be so secretive about visiting her mother.'

When she voiced this theory that evening to Peter Mallen, he disagreed vehemently. 'I just don't believe she was there,' he said. 'That boy you talked about – he's mistaken. Annabel would have told me if she was going down to Bute. In all the months I'd known her she hardly mentioned her mother. It was me who wanted to visit; I wanted to get to know Mrs Angus. You two simply don't understand. Annabel and I were serious; she was going to come out with me to New Zealand next year

91

to meet my folks. I told her over and over again that I'd like to meet her mother, who was only a few miles away, but she was always vague about a trip to Bute . . . I began to wonder if her mother really was the archetypal witch of legend.' Peter wiped his brow; he was tremendously worked up. 'I'm sorry,' he said, 'but I just can't take it in . . .'

They were in the lounge bar, having drinks before dinner. Dinah was suddenly overwhelmed by compassion for the young man: what they had told him hadn't helped his memory of Annabel; rather it had roused feelings that would have been better left at rest.

Franklyn also sensed that Peter's denial of Annabel's presence in Bute that weekend in September had more to do with a certain resentment that she had kept things from him. Yes, he eventually agreed, it was possible to do that trip in the time; she could have finished at ClydeSight earlier on Saturday, taken the afternoon ferry, gone to her mother's cottage and straight to Renfrew airport on Sunday night.

'But she would have phoned me. She would have got me on my mobile, or she could have contacted me at the paper . . .' He brushed his hand over his face. 'Even without this tale of her being on Bute, I had wondered why she didn't get in touch with me before she left for America. I hadn't wanted to worry her, if she was working that Sunday at the studio – I knew from her excitement on the phone just how busy she was going to be – so I didn't get in touch with her. Now I don't know what to think . . .'

'You mentioned Renfrew. Was that the airport she would be flying from?'

'They told me that when I went to their office on Tuesday, after we'd had the terrible news. Yes, she was booked on the ten-thirty flight from Renfrew. If she had been to Bute,' he added, grudgingly, 'it was an easy journey from the ferry at Wemyss Bay. she would have taken a taxi from there, as she didn't have the car . . .'

Dinah asked him again about the coat. 'Yes, a cashmere camel she'd bought the week before in McDonalds. When she told me on the phone that she'd been picked to go to New York, I remember she made a joke about how impressed they'd be by the coat, Scottish cashmere being a big hit over there.'

'Those friends she had made in Greenwich Village—' said Franklyn, 'do you have their address?'

'It was in the address book we keep at the flat. And of course I rang them as soon as I knew . . . but they hadn't seen Annabel. I had asked her if she would be staying with the Greensmiths – that's their name – and she said she'd contact them when she arrived; but they hadn't heard. Of course, they were terribly upset when I told them her meeting had been at the World Trade Center . . .' His voice trailed off.

'I'm sorry to keep harping on timing,' said Franklyn diffidently, 'but I'm finding it hard to make things fit. Annabel went to dinner with Mrs Bristow on the Friday; would she be late in getting back to the flat?'

'I wouldn't know,' Peter replied, 'I was on the Irish boat crossing to Belfast. She may even have stayed over in Bearsden that night, if she and her boss had things to discuss. All I know is that Annabel came back to the flat at some time over the weekend to collect her clothes . . .'

He paused. 'I'd taken it for granted she slept there Saturday night . . . Now I don't know. She hadn't made the bed, but that would be Annabel in a hurry. As to going to see her mother, I just can't believe it.'

Dinah changed the subject. 'Mrs Bristow wants to see me,' she said. 'There's always the possibility that Annabel told her she was going to Bute. After all, it was at that dinner party she learned she was to go on the New York trip, so she may have said something . . . Anyway, I can always ask.'

Dinah found, however, that it was not altogether easy to take a personal line with such an adroit politician as Adelaide Bristow. Even after a short introductory conversation designed, Dinah felt, to put her at her ease, she could not help being so impressed that words died on her lips.

Mrs Bristow was a tall woman with only the slightest suspicion of elderly hunched shoulders and the stiff walk of an arthritic. She shook Dinah's hand warmly and sat her down in a comfortable chair before taking up her own position behind her desk. She turned large amber eyes of great calmness on her visitor and enquired as to whether the Scottish weather had not deterred Dinah and her friend from going to Bute. When Dinah replied that it had not, Mrs Bristow asked if they had visited the bungalow where Mrs Angus had lived, and agreed that it was indeed a lonely spot in winter.

These were simply preliminary remarks before Mrs Bristow came to the real reason for wanting to meet Dinah – her friendship with Annabel. At the end of some ten minutes Dinah felt she had been under the spell of an expert interviewer. Everything she knew of the dead girl, from their moments of girlish fun at college to more serious discussions they had had on careers, hopes and ambitions, was wheedled out of her by this engaging woman, who said she wanted to share in the life Annabel had lived before she had met her.

Coffee and biscuits were brought in, and dispensed by the assistant Dinah had already spoken to in the office. 'Thank you, Beth,' Mrs Bristow said. 'We are talking about Annabel. I have had to be so brave, you know, because just after it . . . happened I could not bring myself to talk about her at all. In fact, I was quite ill for days, wasn't I?'

Beth handed Dinah a coffee cup. 'Oh, you were, Mrs Bristow. I don't know how you managed to speak to the press, but you did. You saw us all through it.' She seemed simply to breathe the words so quiet were they, but Dinah could not detect even a flicker of insincerity.

In all the people she had met in the offices and studios of ClydeSight she had found this same response when they talked of their Chairwoman: a subdued kind of awe and a more overt genuine affection. Dinah had expected a different kind of woman, harder perhaps and more worldly than this kindly person who wore her soft brown hair, only lightly streaked with grey, tied back in an old-fashioned bun and who crooked her little finger as she held her cup. She could be anyone's Granny, she thought; perhaps that was the attraction for Annabel, who had rejected her own mother. And it was easy to see how the attraction played on the other side.

Beth left them. Dinah finished her coffee, ate a biscuit and looked at her watch.

'Of course, my dear,' Adelaide Bristow said quickly. 'You

have a journey to make. I shan't keep you. You have been such a consolation to me today. Hearing you talk about your friend brought her back to me so vividly. It was good of you to come.'

Dinah wasn't sure the compliment was deserved; she had, in fact, come out of curiosity. Feeling a little guilty, she had to return words in the same vein. 'Good of you to see me, Mrs Bristow. And it was you who made Annabel so happy since she joined your firm. She was overjoyed at being chosen to go to America.'

'How do you know that?'

The sharpness of the question took Dinah by surprise. 'Peter Mallen . . . she phoned him when she knew . . . She was very excited about it.'

'Oh, you mean the sports writer? I don't think he was going to last long in Annabel's life; she had a great future before her . . . Yes, when I told her I wanted her to go to New York rather than Mr Duncan, of course she was pleased . . .' Mrs Bristow had half-risen from her chair, but now she slumped back. Her voice shook as she went on: 'If only I hadn't taken that decision . . . But I couldn't know – how could anyone have known? But every day I blame myself for having sent her. It was my fault she died.'

The soft, heavy features were flushed now and tears clouded the great, lambent eyes. All Dinah's caring instincts were roused. She crossed the desk and took the elderly woman's hand. 'It wasn't your fault, Mrs Bristow . . . You mustn't blame yourself.' Even as she was speaking, Dinah knew that whatever she said was useless. Somehow, when this kind of situation arose, all one could do was prattle, she told herself angrily; one tried to cover up the unspeakable by throwing petty words over it . . .

How she wished she had Franklyn with her; he would have known what to say, the proper words to use – something low-keyed, practical, to get away from the horrific, and all this talk of the wonderful future Annabel had had . . .

'She was so pleased to be asked to dinner with you, Mrs Bristow, that Friday evening – that was what she said. Did she stay over, or go back to her flat?'

'What?' Mrs Bristow was looking at her as if she hardly knew who she was. Then she seemed to give herself a shake. 'I'm so sorry, my dear. I was quite overcome there for a moment . . . My Friday dinner party? I think she enjoyed it. Annabel was always marvellous company. She could have stayed the night, but when I told her she was to go to New York, she said she must return home to pack a case; and, of course, she had to be in the office in the morning. Fortunately one of my friends, Bill Erskine, was going into town and they decided to share a taxi. It was kind of him. That's Lord Erskine, you know . . .'

Dinah didn't, but at least the piece of trivial talk had got over the sticky patch, and Mrs Bristow seemed to have recovered her composure, so Dinah was able to say goodbye on a less emotional note.

All the same, when she passed Beth in the outer office, she asked for the washroom to give herself some breathing space before facing the rest of the staff. The interview with Mrs Bristow had been more painful than she had imagined, and it had left her with a feeling of disquiet, as if something had been left unsaid that could have put things right.

Dinah went the round of farewells to those in the office who had spoken to her so kindly of her friend. Only with one young woman did she linger. Stella Burns had done the bookings for the New York trip, and yes, she told Dinah, it had been a bit of a bother on the morning of Saturday 8th September to have to phone the airline and explain that, instead of their Mr Duncan travelling on the ten-thirty plane from Renfrew, it would be Miss Angus. But such changes had happened before, she said; there was nothing to it . . . Maybe now, in the months after the 11th, things might be different, but all firms make sudden alterations in their bookings . . . As for the New York hotel – well, Annabel had assured Stella that once she'd arrived there, she would do her own explaining. Of course, the American firm had been told that Miss Angus would be taking the place of Mr Duncan, and as they already knew Annabel, of course, they would be only too pleased to welcome her . . .

This was another language, thought Dinah, the language of the business world: arrangements being planned, changed, cancelled or carried out to the letter. At least Franklyn would be pleased with her; she had done all she could to tie up his loose ends . . .

But there was one she had missed.

'Did Mrs Bristow tell you why Annabel went to Bute that weekend?'

Dinah felt as if she had failed an exam. 'I forgot. Halfway through our meeting I had it on the tip of my tongue several times, but nothing came out. The island, in fact, was only mentioned once, I think, when she agreed the croft was in a lonely spot. We scarcely talked of Mrs Angus except in connection with Annabel's relations with her parents . . . Oh, damn! Somehow I had the feeling I was being led through the conversation, and then she had that emotional break . . . I was getting there, truly I was. I did ask about the Friday night, and she told me, no, Annabel went home – in a taxi shared with one of the other guests . . . At that point I did feel that our Adelaide was simply making trivial conversation. And of course I couldn't ask about what Annabel was doing on the Saturday, because that was clearly office business, and it would have seemed like impertinence. Now I know I should have mentioned it – that Annabel went to Bute.'

'Perhaps Mrs Bristow didn't know.'

'She didn't sound too keen on Peter Mallen – seemed to think he was unimportant in Annabel's life. I think that was what put me off any more enquiries. It was like an interview with a rather nice headmistress; you didn't want to raise any issues that might show you up. I didn't want to seem like an interrogator. It was bad enough her being tearful at one point.'

Their little holiday was over, and they were on their way back to England. Dinah still could not get rid of the unease she had begun to feel on their visit to Bute, and her last call at the offices of ClydeSight had done nothing to settle it. She would have liked to see Sandy Duncan again, but he had been up at St Andrew's, where there had been a likely story about the heir to the throne. However, he had left a message for them: he expected to be in London in the near future; he had Franklyn's number and would call him.

'I hope he does,' said Franklyn. 'I don't like things that don't fit . . . Maybe he can answer some questions.'

'I don't see why you worry about details like time and place, darling, when there isn't anything more we can ever know about how Annabel spent those last two days . . . And does it really matter? The awful thing is that she's dead, and nothing can alter that.' Dinah knew that her words were as bleak and unhopeful as the fact. 'There must have been many in the World Trade Center that morning who left unfinished business when their lives just stopped . . .'

Thirteen

Henry Pocket prepared his ground well before approaching the address he had been given in the small medieval town of Rinteln. He had been in Germany many times before – in fact, he had for a short time attended a college in Heidelberg; but, booking into the only listed hotel in the centre square, he pretended to have little knowledge of the language. All the better to hear you with, he told his ears, knowing that speech would slow down for him and sometimes voices would be raised – it happened in other countries than England when foreigners were addressed.

He had a map, and studied it as he paused on the fine bridge above the icy waters of the Weser. Joshua Stegmann Strasse wasn't far; in fact, it formed part of the old walls built to protect the citizens in the Middle Ages – not that such timid earthworks would have been much good against the maurauders of Tilly, Wallenstein and Gustavus Adolphus as each in his turn galloped the land in pursuit of ever-changing aims in Germany's catastrophic Thirty Years War. *Der Dreissigjahrige Krieg* – he rolled the harsh syllables round his tongue; it had ridden its rough and wayward course many times through this region, and Rinteln an der Weser must have suffered more than most, being by the river and on the edge of the great North-West German Plain. He wondered just how often its weary people had dug themselves out and started to rebuild all over again.

In the bar room of the hotel the evening before, Henry had posed as neither tourist nor commercial traveller – just a visitor to the region, he had smiled, and asked, in uneasy German, did anyone know a family called Neumann who lived on Joshua Stegmann Strasse?

'Next the stonemason's yard?' someone asked, and was told

it was the Neumann's business, and had been for years. An old man told Henry the Neumanns had been refugees from the East at the end of the War, like so many others flooding into Westphalia, and no more welcome than refugees anywhere. What was surprising was that they seemed to be still unpopular. 'Stuck-up', he heard one comment, 'always going on about being Berliners . . . Why'd they not go back there? I'd say . . .' 'Got more money than sense, that Ilse woman . . .' 'Always got the latest in cars, Klaus Neumann – what's he need posh cars for in his business?' Such remarks were, of course, muttered behind beer glasses, hand to mouth, and were not intended for the ears of the stranger passing through, who had bought a round of drinks and in return was given guidance as to how to reach the Neumann house. 'It is in connection,' he said, haltingly in tourist German, 'with a family matter. Is Dieter Neumann still living? I understand he had a sister who went to England . . .'

However, they were all much too young to know anything about the elder Neumanns. Even the old man grinned at Henry and said he wasn't anything like as old as Dieter. 'He must be well over eighty, the old skinflint,' he said. 'I'm sorry – I hope you're not a relative.' It was a bit late for an apology, thought Henry, and assured him that he wasn't even a friend but was pleased to know that Herr Dieter Neumann was still alive.

Word seemed to get around as fast as in an English village, and next morning Henry was not altogether surprised to be gently quizzed by the lady proprietor. 'I understand you are visiting the Neumanns in Joshua Stegmann Strasse,' she said to him after breakfast. 'Ilse comes in here sometimes after shopping, but the family tend to use the larger hotel up near the Schloss.'

'It is Herr Dieter I wish to see,' said Henry. 'Did you know he had a sister who went to live in England?'

Frau Wedler shook her head. 'I've never heard talk of any sister,' she said. 'My parents used to talk about the old man, but they never mentioned any other relatives. When Dieter Neumann came here first, he worked as a boilerman in that house on the Joshua Stegmann Wall; it belonged to a doctor who died and the relatives took Dieter on as caretaker. He worked at the stonemason's next door, and in no time he'd made it a thriving business and had enough money to buy the house.'

'He rose from the lower depths, so to speak,' Henry commented, but not in German. 'He is not liked?' he asked Frau Wedler, who shook her head.

'I only know what I hear,' she said. 'His wife is dead now, and he is looked after by his son Klaus and his daughter-in-law, Ilse, who have two children.' She gave a little shrug. 'I do not know why he is disliked – perhaps simply because he rich. Is it the same in England?'

Henry agreed, rather tepidly, not wishing to cast a slur on his country.

'And Berliners,' went on Frau Wedler, 'they think themselves so clever . . . They look at us as if we're country bumpkins. And we've had to put up with all those folk pouring in from the East, taking our jobs or living on our welfare. That's twice it's happened: once when they fled from the Russians and now . . .'

Henry gave a small laugh. 'I'm afraid my German isn't good enough for a discussion on politics,' he said, thinking he'd heard all this before in some faraway Midlands town, where the issue was black and white rather than West and East. Same complaint, though: the invading hordes . . .

Mid-morning seemed a good time to call; it was a Saturday, so perhaps both the Neumann menfolk would be home. No point in telephoning first, though he had checked their number in the directory at the hotel; it was in the name of Dieter. Henry preferred the face-to-face approach.

The house was newly painted a pale ochre, like the others in the street, thereby showing up their shabbiness. The use of the old-fashioned bell pull beside the door brought a sonorous peal from somewhere far indoors, and eventually the door was opened by a small woman in a dark-blue dress and apron.

Henry explained in halting German that he wished to see Herr Dieter Neumann, if he was at home. 'I am English,' he said; 'I have little German.'

She made no response in his language, but said she understood him well enough and asked if he was expected. He said he wasn't but would appreciate some of Herr Dieter's time, and he gave her one of his cards – he carried many connecting him with various trades, but this was simply Henry Pocket's own name. She hardly glanced at it, but at least she asked him to step into the house.

She showed him into what was a small parlour adjacent to the front hall, a typically German room – dark furniture too large for the space, heavy curtains obscuring light from the window – but a stove on the hearth gave off a pleasant warmth and when she gestured that he should sit, the chair was cushioned and comfortable. 'If you will wait,' she said, 'I will tell Herr Dieter Neumann that you are here.'

A little pale sunshine was filtering through the drapes, the tiled stove softly hummed to itself, and there was a smell of burning wood: the atmosphere was soporific. A little longer and he might fall asleep . . .

The door creaked slightly as it opened, and there was the sound of a rubber-tipped stick on the polished floorboards. Henry got up and faced the old man who entered, the woman hovering uncertainly in the background.

'Herr Pocket?'

'Herr Dieter Neumann . . .'

The ritual was almost a drill without the clicking of heels. The greeting over, Dieter Neumann settled himself into a large winged armchair beside the stove and asked the woman in the apron – it sounded to Henry more like a command – to fetch coffee for himself and his guest. When he turned and spoke directly to Henry, he said his English was rusty; how was Henry's German?

'Not good, I'm afraid but I can understand the basics. I must apologize, Herr Neumann, for coming unannounced, but I was passing through this district and was reminded of an old connection.'

From the first moment he had seen Herr Dieter Neumann, Henry had been bothered by a problem that is all too prevalent in these days of television and film: seeing a likeness to some actor or another and thereby either prejudging a complete stranger, or going through a bewildering struggle to get that actor out of one's mind . . .

For Herr Dieter was Peter Vaughan on a particularly bad day, and to Henry Pocket – until he could get rid of the illusion – this meant that the man was a soft-spoken, devious, crafty old shark who was capable of unmentionable evils and never to be trusted. In appearance the elderly Dieter was large of frame, though shrunken by age; he had cavernous features that might well have been handsome in youth, when his complexion would have been a healthy red instead of the yellow of ill health. But his eyes were shrewd, almost black in colour and set so close together that one got the impression of converging arrow points.

For all their sharpness, however, the old man could not have been more polite as he listened to Henry's farrago of truth and lies. The explanation for his call was interrupted by the domestic – too old to be a maid; the word domestic seemed to fit – bringing coffee and a certain kind of sugary biscuit, of which Henry was extremely fond. He scoffed several as he went on with his tale of having met Sieglinde Neumann while working in Yorkshire – he did not specify exactly where – saying that he had wanted very much to continue the friendship only to have his hopes dashed by his being incapacitated for months following a road accident. When he had recovered, he had sought out Miss Neumann, but had been told she had left the district and there was no forwarding address. That, Henry explained, had been a few years ago . . . Business had brought him now to Hanover, and he remembered that she had once told him her people came from a small town on the Weser called Rinteln. So here he was, having found the name Neumann and the address in the local phone book. He apologized, yet again, for the intrusion, and said he was most grateful for the courtesy with which he had been received. Tourist German, with just a hint of commercial use, made the tale sound almost plausible, even to Henry's own ears.

Herr Neumann had asked him several obvious questions, to which Henry replied as if he was laboriously translating to himself, and then answered in the same halting fashion, searching for the words in a limited vocabulary. Yes, he was a representative of Ward & Company of York, who dealt in office stationery and were seeking a market through a firm in Hanover. No, this was Mr Pocket's first time in Germany. He simply hoped it would be his good fortune to have found relatives of his lost friend Sieglinde, with whom he wished to renew acquaintance.

Henry's diffidence and his hesitancy over the language added something of a *romantisch* element to the narrative, in the German meaning of the term, and it seemed that Dieter was affected by it, for his face softened as he listened.

He put down his cup unsteadily on the side table, and leaned forward towards his visitor.

'And it is to the right place you have come,' he said. 'This Sieglinde Neumann was my niece.'

Henry gave an exclamation of delight, although he had noticed the tense. It took him a moment to recover. 'Did you say she *was* your niece? Does that mean . . . ?'

'I am sorry, Mr Pocket, truly very sorry . . .'

Henry's downcast look was not put on. 'Sieglinde is dead?'

The servant at that moment entered and gathered up the coffee cups, set them on the tray and was about to withdraw when the old man addressed her in rapid German. There would be a guest today for *mittagessen*, he told her; and would she ask Klaus and Ilse if they would join him in the sitting room as soon as convenient . . .

When she had gone, he turned a sad countenance to Henry.

'Yes, she is dead. Over ten years ago. We will tell you about it; that is why you must meet my son, Klaus – he was there, you see.'

'So I did get the right family?'

'Oh yes, Mr Pocket.' Dieter, out of a certain courtesy, addressed him in the English fashion. 'Sieglinde's mother was my sister, Lotte. She worked for an English family in Minden and went to England with them, taking her little daughter, Sieglinde.'

'But you kept in touch?'

Dieter shook his head. 'I rarely heard from her. You must understand how it was. I hardly knew Lotte. We were separated when we were very young. She got out of Berlin with other *flüchtlingen* at the end of the War. They came to Westphalia and many of the women like Lotte were taken on by British families here. I stayed on in Berlin. I came out later when it became too dangerous to stay.' He grimaced. 'I was lucky to get out before the Wall went up. I came to Rinteln because a mate had friends here and got me a job. When I was settled, I went to your Control Commission at Minden to find out about Lotte. They gave me the address of a Colonel Prentiss in England and I wrote. We exchanged letters for a while, but you must understand we had little in common and Lotte was much older than I was; our experiences had been different. Then I got a letter saying she had died in a nursing home – I think it came from the Colonel's widow. I wrote back, of course, but I heard nothing more. There was no point . . .'

'And Sieglinde?'

'I believe she married the son of the house.' Dieter's lip curled, and for the first time since he had got over the Peter Vaughan image, Henry felt dislike of the man. 'So she did well for herself, yes? Over the years we might get the odd postcard from some of your English watering places, so we gathered she'd joined the idle rich . . .' He stopped and groped for his stick, hung over the back of his chair. Henry rose to help him.

'This room is too stuffy. We will go and meet my son, Klaus, and you will stay for a meal, will you not?'

With the story only half-told, Henry eagerly assented. He held the door open for the old man and followed him to the rear of the premises, into a large sitting room where the double windows gave on to a pleasant garden and orchard. On their way they had passed what were obviously the offices and working areas of the business. As the old man walked slowly, Henry took time to look out of the side windows at the tidy mason's yard, the stacked stones and extensive sheds. The original dwelling house must have looked out on to this very yard and one couldn't blame the present occupants for adding an extension with a happier prospect, rather than suffering a daily view of gravestones.

They were instantly welcomed by a burly man in his forties and his slim, smart wife, who rose from the overstuffed sofa at their entrance. She wore a high-necked silk dress, brightly patterned and rendered even more eye-catching by gold chains, earrings and jangling bracelets. This was the Ilse about which Frau Wedler's comments had been tepid – 'more money than sense', someone in the bar had said . . .

Klaus Neumann was cut to the same pattern as his father. He had broad shoulders, an invisible neck and plenty of jowl; but he lacked the hardness – the bedrock as it were – of the old man. He greeted Henry Pocket in fair English – he had studied it at business school in Hanover, he said, and was proud of his proficiency. Ilse simply shrugged and said she'd forgotten any English she'd learnt at school, but she could read all the fashion magazines. This Henry could well believe. He resigned himself to the conversation being widened by Klaus's knowledge of English, but he himself was stuck with tourist German; it would still enable him to catch the undercurrents, the whispered asides and the throwaway remarks they might not be able to resist making in their own language.

There were photographs all round the room of Ilse and Klaus with their children, Irmgard and Viktor, but unhappily Herr Pocket would not have the pleasure of their company; they were with Ilse's parents for the day.

While Henry had been looking at the photographs and admiring the garden, which, even for winter, appeared to be well tended and neat with carefully laid-out shrubs and small trees, he heard Herr Dieter telling his son and daughter-in-law the reason for Herr Pocket's visit. Both reacted according to character: Ilse, almost with tears in her eyes, took Henry's hand and told him how sad it was that his search should end so tragically. She hadn't known Sieglinde Neumann, because she had only been married to Klaus for the last seven years, but she had heard about the poor lady's death, so tragic . . .

As Henry was still in ignorance of the facts, he could only stammer that it was indeed unfortunate that Sieglinde was dead, he had so hoped to see her again. Ilse was looking at him with wide, wet eyes, as if he was some forlorn hero of opera . . .

Her husband and father-in-law were still deep in conversation but broke off to enquire whether Herr Pocket would have a beer, or would he prefer wine? Having taken his order, as it were, for the latter, Klaus turned to him and said he would give him all the details about Sieglinde Neumann's death when they were all sitting comfortably over drinks. Airing his English in the meantime, he spoke of economic matters, asking Henry's opinion on various issues of the moment. He and Klaus had sat down in adjacent armchairs, Dieter had been guided into what was obviously his personal seat by the stove, while Ilse spread herself to best advantage on the sofa.

Wine was poured by the woman in blue, who had entered unobtrusively with a tray of glasses and several bottles of red and white wine. The room was excessively warm. Henry guessed it was Herr Dieter who chose the temperature of the house; as an invalid, he would feel the winter chill.

'Be good enough to inform Herr Pocket of the circumstances of my niece's death, Klaus. I have not yet done so. As you are at home today, it would be better for him to hear it from you, as you were with her at that sad time . . .' It was a complicated sentence, involving several tenses, and would have made a good example for a German language examination paper.

'You don't mind, Mr Pocket, if I use German, so that my father understands and can correct me if I go wrong?'

'I think I shall be able to follow you if you speak not too fast, Herr Neumann. I am only too anxious to hear . . .'

'She came for a short holiday. It would be in the autumn of eighty-nine. We had not heard from her in years, but then travel was more difficult. My father had received postcards from time to time, but we knew nothing about her. She wrote and said she wanted to visit the place where her mother had come from, and she would like to stay with us for a few days.'

Herr Dieter Neumann seemed to find fault with his son's narrative ability and kept up muttered interruptions in rapid-fire guttural German, as if to keep the story on the right lines. 'It was not autumn, nearly winter when she came. It was Berlin she wanted to see, not here . . .'

'Yes, it was to Berlin she wished to go,' continued Klaus. 'She had asked if there were still relatives of ours in the city, and my father told her he had a distant cousin there . . .'

'Tell him she was Berta Meyer. She had a shop in the Gendarmenmarkt, and was still there then under the Communists, but she was old, and now she too is dead . . .' The

107

old man continued as if he was a stage prompter every time Klaus hesitated.

'You understand, Herr Pocket, things had eased by then between East and West Berlin. I did business in both, and had the proper permits to go into the Eastern Zone. We were negotiating contracts for stone from state quarries in the GDR . . .'

'It is not of business we speak,' rasped Dieter, 'but of my niece. Our visitor isn't interested in stone quarries, Klaus . . .'

Klaus proceeded unperturbed. 'As it happened, I had to visit East Berlin while my cousin was staying with us and my father asked if I could take her with me. It was not too difficult for me to get a permit for her to visit an elderly relative because I had my commercial credentials in any case. So I arranged to take her in my car. She was most grateful.'

'And so she should have been . . .' Dieter sounded disgruntled.

'Klaus went to a great deal of trouble, particularly in view of her health. Tell Herr Pocket about her illness . . .'

Herr Pocket contrived to keep his face impassive during the old man's outbursts, which he guessed he was not meant to understand. It was Ilse who helped out at this point.

'Was poor Sieglinde not well, then, when she came from England, Klaus?'

'She suffered with her heart, I was given to understand.'

Dieter made a gesture of impatience. 'You remember, Klaus, she told us a doctor in England had warned her not to travel . . . Yet she came, against his orders.'

'I had forgotten that, Papa.' Klaus turned back to Henry, and resumed his story. 'She was breathless from time to time but told me that was normal, and that there was nothing to worry about. We put up for the night at my usual hotel in West Berlin, and in the morning we drove through to the East.'

'The date, Klaus, the date . . .' Dieter again interrupted. 'You have forgotten to tell him the date.'

'I was coming to that, Papa. It was the evening of the ninth of November; do you know what that meant, Herr Pocket?'

Herr Pocket knew very well but, retaining his ignorant persona, he shook his head.

108

'A momentous time for us,' said Klaus, and even Ilse sat up and smiled. 'It was the night the Wall came down . . .'

'Of course. I should have known. As you say, a momentous occasion, a very joyful occasion,' said Henry, 'and from where I was in England, totally unexpected. Was it like that in Germany?'

Klaus was eager to show off his particular knowledge of this piece of recent history. 'One cannot imagine,' he said, 'what it was like. It was almost by accident that it happened. Of course we'd known in the weeks before that thousands of Germans from the GDR were flooding into the West through Hungary and Czechoslovakia, but in Berlin the Wall was still in place. I suppose the party chiefs in East Berlin got so concerned at stopping the chaos, all those refugees getting the hell out – if you'll pardon the expression – they fumbled an announcement on the evening news and said people could get travel permits on demand so that they could use the border crossings between the two Germanies. That was enough for the Berliners; they were there in their thousands within minutes of hearing the news, demanding to be allowed through the checkpoint . . .'

Klaus was laughing now, with such genuine enjoyment that Henry joined him. 'Quite a farce,' he remarked; 'someone had blundered . . .'

'Oh, I don't know,' said Klaus, more seriously; 'it was bound to happen in the end. But that night the border guards hadn't had any orders, and didn't know what to do, so they did nothing . . . Myself and my cousin – we saw it all: the Easterners pouring through the crossing, on foot, on bicycles, in those little two-stroke Trabant cars, which were all they had over there . . .'

'Herr Pocket does not need a history lesson, Klaus,' snarled the old man. 'It was all in the papers. There were tourists from other countries. Get back to my niece . . .'

'We just stood and watched,' said Klaus, solemnly. 'We became part of that great party of people cheering and singing. We stayed up nearly all night, and in the morning there was no trouble driving through to the East, and finding Frau Meyer's shop. I had been to see her before on one of my business trips, but this was so different . . . She could not take in what had happened at the Wall . . . She was old, of course, and set in her ways under the Communist regime.'

'She was terrified of the Stasi. Tell him about the Stasi, Klaus.'

'He doesn't need to know about the Stasi, Papa . . .' Klaus dismissed the interruption, and refilled Henry's glass. 'There was such excitement in East Berlin – crowds of people on the streets – it took us some time to reach the shop; but we did so at last. I think Sieglinde was quite overcome to meet another relative, and in such circumstances . . . It was supposed to be only a short visit, you understand, but Frau Meyer was very emotional, and Sieglinde became unwell. She suffered a heart attack that evening. The doctor said it was the shock. It had all been too much for her . . . She died almost immediately. I am so sorry to have to tell you this, Herr Pocket.'

'I did not know she had heart trouble,' said Henry, truthfully.

'I could see it when she came,' Dieter growled. 'She was not in good health. She should not have insisted on going to Berlin.'

'You must have had a difficult time,' said Henry to Klaus. 'What happened?'

'Poor Frau Meyer was in hysterics when her doctor was called and said that Sieglinde was dead. And I could sympathize. The dead woman was in her house; she was afraid of what might be said . . .'

'Of what the neighbours might say?' Henry prompted, and got a faint smile from Klaus. 'More serious than that. She hadn't understood what was going on in the streets, she was old, and yes – Father is quite right – she was afraid of the Stasi. The dead woman was from the West: there would be questions asked. You must understand, Herr Pocket, Frau Meyer had lived under the regime all those years, and all she wanted was to keep out of trouble. And the doctor she had called was the same: he didn't want anything to do with the death. "Take the body back to the West," he said; "it'll save a lot of trouble for Frau Meyer." So, that's what I did. We put her in the car and I drove out of East Berlin with hundreds of other Ossis – that's what they were called, those coming to the West.'

110

'What a sad story,' said Ilse, wiping her eyes, 'but happy, too, for the poor lady to be brought home in the end to Rinteln.'

'She is buried in the local cemetery, Herr Pocket,' said Dieter Neumann, this time in English. 'We will this afternoon take you to the grave.'

'That is good of you,' said Henry. 'You have been most hospitable to me today.'

The woman in the blue dress had discarded her apron when she announced the meal was ready, and they filed into the dining room.

The food was delicious. As he was a surprise guest, Henry thought that if the Neumanns ate like this every week they were a fortunate family. The soup, fish and even the inevitable veal escalopes were of a delicate flavour, and better than Henry had ever tasted in German restaurants or hotels. The meal was served by the woman in blue, assisted by a young country girl with bright-red cheeks who fumbled the dishes and was sharply rebuked for it; she was obviously being trained in the serving arts. When Henry congratulated Ilse on the quality of the food, she raised her well-plucked eyebrows and said she had nothing to do with the kitchen; along with her husband and father-in-law she was a director of the company and, as the mother of Irmgard and Viktor, she had quite enough to do. Were women not like that in England, also? Henry hastened to agree with her, and said to himself that obviously *Kinder, Kuchen* and *Kirche* were out, as far as the modern German female was concerned.

Brandy was produced after the *apfelstrudel* with whipped cream, and Henry protested he was by now replete as to food and drink. If he further indulged, he would not be able to walk to the cemetery, as Herr Dieter had proposed. He was assured that it was but a short distance, and in any case they would go by car.

A very fine car it was, too – a Mercedes, brand new and gleaming with care and attention. As Klaus brought it from the garage, Henry saw that it had not been alone there; a Volkswagen and a family saloon were visible, both highly polished and ready to go . . . Was there so much money to

111

be made in the craft of stonemasonry? But Klaus had hinted they were now part of a larger concern, although they kept the original firm in Rinteln.

Henry remarked that it was a charming small town, which seemed to please Dieter. He had said he no longer drove himself, but there was little need for it; although he had officially retired from business he still ran the workshops and supervised the men in the yard. He said they needed a firm hand: they were lazy – nothing like the workmen of former days. 'We rebuilt West Germany,' he went on, as if it had been a personal triumph, 'brick by brick, stone upon stone. We worked with our bare hands, day and night. Now men are too soft; they don't want to dirty their hands. Lazy . . .' He used a German expletive with which Henry was not familiar. He decided he would not have liked to have Dieter Neumann as a boss, now or at any time . . .

The cemetery was close to the river; in the quiet afternoon they could hear it rolling swiftly beyond the raised bank. 'The River Weser deep and wide, Washes its walls on the Southern side,' thought Henry; but that was Hamelin not Rinteln . . .

Fourteen

'And was there a grave?' asked Lennox Kemp, looking up at Henry, whose report he had been reading for the past forty minutes. Points had been raised and answered, discussions on the various characters had taken place, and now Kemp was on the last page.

'Oh yes, there was a grave all right, complete with tombstone. Some ornate Gothic script told that Sieglinde Neumann Prentiss lay beneath this stone – a stone like nearly all the others in that small town graveyard – and she had lived from 1950 till 1989.'

'And why did this Dieter Neumann and his son not inform Mr Prentiss in England of the sad death?'

'It seems that young Klaus Neumann was not so efficient then as he undoubtedly is now. When Mrs Prentiss visited Germany at that auspicious time, she brought a travelling bag and her handbag. In the unfortunate circumstances of her sudden illness and death, and with the task of getting the body into the back of his car, Klaus forgot the handbag, and her travel bag contained little except cosmetics and clothes. I think Father Dieter gave him a right ticking-off for the lapse. As he explained to me, Sieglinde's passport and home address were all in her handbag. Klaus endeavoured to get in touch with Frau Meyer and would have gone back into East Berlin, but Frau Meyer by that time had shut up shop and gone into a home for the elderly. Within months she was dead. Klaus confided in me that the old lady was pretty gaga anyway, and she'd probably burnt the handbag as soon as she found it in case the Stasi searched the shop. Fat chance of that, he said (or the German equivalent), as it wasn't long before the state police buildings were themselves ransacked,

113

and papers strewn about the streets. He said it was a time of great confusion . . .'

'I'm sure it was,' Kemp agreed. 'Well, you've done a good job, Henry. I shall report to my client at once. He will be delighted at the outcome.'

'Not so fast, Mr Kemp.' Henry Pocket had been eating an impromptu lunch at a corner of the desk. Now he tidied away his paper napkin, being careful not to spill any crumbs, and from his suitcase he produced another envelope.

'These are my own jottings, and other material,' he said. 'I was most impressed by what I heard about in Germany, but I have my own methods; I go my own way . . .'

As he had done on that last evening in Rinteln. The Neumanns had returned him to his hotel, deplored the fact that he must leave in the morning and expressed their regret that they would no longer have the benefit of his company. In turn, Henry had thanked them for the trouble they had taken, and asked them to convey his compliments to Ilse and his good wishes to all the Neumann family. Farewells by heads of state after a summit conference could not have been more elegantly phrased.

The hotel dinner had been early and only just within Henry's capacity after his ample lunch, so that when he had risen from the table he'd still felt full, and in need of a walk. He'd taken the path along the river, which led eventually to the cemetery; he might as well get that inscription correct: there had not been time while he stood with Klaus at the graveside. Dieter Neumann had remained in the car, saying his old legs were too stiff these days for much walking.

Actually, the graveyard was nearer by the river path, which was just as well for Henry, because it had begun to snow. There had been that soft, waiting air in the afternoon, as if snow was not far off, and now large feathery flakes came silently out of the grey night sky. He had walked down between the tidy rows of graves, each with its almost identical stone and shaven square of grass, till he'd reached the one in the corner by the hawthorn hedge.

He had taken out his notebook and a torch, and begun to copy the Gothic lettering as accurately as he could. Like most

114

of the other tombstones in the cemetery the letters were incised deeply and not easy to read. Henry had bent down, fumbling with his notebook and pencil, and lost his footing on the turf, which already had a faint sprinkling of snow. He had dropped his torch as he put out a hand, grabbing at the stone to keep himself from falling.

The stone had moved.

Henry was not an imaginative man – in his line of business it didn't pay – but he was susceptible nevertheless to sudden shock. The touch of something that should have been firm as rock slipping under his fingers, the darkness of the scene now the torchlight was gone, the snowflakes landing soft and wet on his cheeks, the stillness of the air, had all made him acutely and fearfully aware that these were graves surrounding him – that he was in the presence of the silent and unseeing dead . . .

'I scrambled to my feet pretty quick, I can tell you, Mr Kemp. I did not run back to the hotel, but I did not linger in that place. Only long enough to figure out that the stone was loose, and the others round it were firm enough, so it wasn't the soil.'

He had stumbled into the hotel like a white ghost, according to Frau Wedler, who had taken him to the fireplace, where logs were burning, and plied him with schnapps and comforting conversation. With a little guidance there had been talk of the Neumanns. Frau Wedler had been impressed that Henry should have lunched with them; in her opinion they were too snobbish to have much to do with ordinary folk in Rinteln. 'Arrogant,' she'd said, 'like all Berliners.' She'd sniffed. 'They came from nothing, but now they have money . . .'

Tentatively, Henry had spoken of the events of November 1989, and mentioned that Herr Dieter Neumann had lost a niece who was buried in the cemetery there in Rinteln.

'Must have been a very small funeral,' Frau Wedler had said; 'I'd not heard of it . . . It would be about then they built on that extension to the house. It's always the way, is it not? – money goes to them that's got it. Maybe she left them something. Over ten years now since the Wall came down; to think of it . . . All I can remember is that it was a time of great confusion.'

'That was as much as I was going to get from that quarter,'

said Henry, sitting back and giving Kemp a bland stare. 'Now, are my personal findings going into your report to your client?'

'You're hinting it's unfinished business, Henry. Are you up to something?'

'When I got home, Mr Kemp, I had some mail. It is my practice, when on a case, to cast my bread upon the waters, if you take my meaning, and await results. I give a card to people and ask them to get in touch if something stirs their memory. Nine times out of ten I get nothing, but the tenth time – ah, the tenth time . . .'

'You hit the jackpot?'

'I get a lead,' said Henry stolidly, not liking Kemp's term, with its connotations of gambling. 'And this one's a cracker . . .' He paused in order to lengthen the suspense. Kemp felt like telling him to get on with it, but Henry would neither be hurried nor led – that had been his ongoing complaint about the Prentiss matter.

'I had a letter from George Farley – a bit shame-faced, I'd say. He enclosed a postcard that he'd had from Sieglinde some years ago. Didn't like to mention it in front of his wife, she'd only tease him etc. etc.' – Henry folded his lips primly – 'and perhaps worse . . . Anyway, he thought the postcard might be useful in my search for his mother's companion.' Henry suddenly sat up straight like a conjuror about to produce a white rabbit, and slid an envelope across the desk.

Kemp drew out the folded letter and set it to one side. Then he looked at the postcard: a picture of the pier at Southend-on-Sea under a bright-blue sky. He turned it over and saw the postmark: July, three years ago. And the signature: Siggy Prentiss.

'Well, well,' was all he could say to Henry Pocket, sitting there with a smirk on his face.

Fifteen

It was some time since the partners and staff of Gillorns had met for one of their Friday night after-work sessions. Christmas was always pretty horrendous: clients and their removal vans converged disastrously on sparse working days of the festive season; split families bickered over where the children should go in the holidays and sought help from those who had originally shepherded them through the courts; the criminal lists had to be dealt with at the double, so that clients could be either in or out for their Christmas dinner.

By the end of January calm was restored. Even the dreaded audit had taken place, with no fault found, so that Lennox Kemp was able to congratulate the office and tell them to relax. The usual discussion took place over general issues that might have cropped up in the holiday season – fortunately, as Parliament had also been on vacation, there had been no political storms involving the legal profession, and the somewhat hastily drafted legislation arising from the events on 11th September was in the process of being happily diluted.

Mike Cantley was talking to young Franklyn about the difficulties that the Scottish lawyer had to contend with over the death of Mrs Angus. Mike said he didn't know much about Scots law, but it sounded as if the little estate might just come under the rules on intestacy and, in the end, fall to the Crown. Would that be the same in Scotland?

Kemp caught up with the conversation when Franklyn was explaining that, unfortunately, they could be sure of the actual time of the daughter's death, but not the mother's. Mike quibbled at that. 'No one can know just when Annabel died,' he said. 'Nor can it ever be actually proved that she did die . . .'

'Oh, come on . . .' exclaimed Franklyn. 'You can't say that.'

'Just for the sake of argument,' said Kemp, 'I agree with Michael. We have no proof that Miss Angus was at the World Trade Center that morning.'

'But she left Scotland with the intention of being there,' Franklyn expostulated; 'the airline was booked, the meeting with the American firm was all arranged – Dinah even saw the correspondence when she was at the ClydeSight office.'

'That still doesn't mean her friend Annabel actually turned up for the meeting.' Kemp was being stubborn; he knew Franklyn Davey had no experience of criminal trial work and its standard of proof, just as he knew the discussion was a purely hypothetical one – a sharpening of wits, maybe, but nothing more. 'I don't suppose you checked with the airline, did you?' He asked Franklyn, simply to take the matter a stage further.

Young Davey might not yet have stood up in a court of law to argue a case, but he had a good brain and was not to be put down. 'As a matter of fact, Dinah did speak to the girl in the office who was responsible for arranging the flight. There had had to be a last-minute change, because it was a man called Sandy Duncan who should have made the trip.'

'Lucky Sandy,' murmured Sally Stacey. 'I bet he feels good about it now.'

Frank agreed, but came back to Kemp's question. 'I don't see that either Dinah or myself had any reason to check with the airline.'

'You would have had to have a legitimate reason,' said Sally. 'And in any case, wouldn't it have been a time of great confusion on both sides of the Atlantic for the airline? They would have had a deluge of calls . . .'

'What did you say, Sally?' Kemp spoke to her rather abruptly.

'That they'd have been deluged with calls,' she said, puzzled.

'No, before that . . .'

Sally thought back. 'I think I said it would have been a time of great confusion.'

'Thank you, Sally. The words just reminded me of something . . .' Kemp dismissed the sense of déjà vu, and turned to Franklyn. 'I'm sorry,' he said. 'I was only taking the discussion to the furthest edge. D'you want the other half?'

Drinks were bought, and enjoyed, the conversation shifted; but as he left the Cabbage White, Franklyn Davey felt he should have done better in the argument. It was much the same kind of feeling he'd had when he returned from Scotland. The visit had done Dinah good – he was sure of that. She had talked with Annabel's colleagues and had visited the island. She said herself she now understood her friend better, caught something of the ambition that had fired her, and was more inclined to be reconciled to the death.

It was Franklyn himself who was not satisfied. He had been left with a sense of unfinished business and, as one who liked to draw final lines beneath assignments, this bothered him. On a sudden impulse he ran and caught up with Lennox Kemp, who was walking home, but in the opposite direction.

'Did you mean what you said – that I should have checked with the airline?' he said breathlessly. 'Because, you know, I very nearly did that, but I didn't want to upset Dinah.'

Lennox Kemp realized that the young man was serious.

'Is Dinah expecting you home?'

'No. She's got some kind of shindig on at the college – somebody's leaving party.'

'Then come to supper with us, and you can fill me in with the Scottish story.'

Franklyn grinned. 'It's hardly *Macbeth*,' he said, 'but I wouldn't mind talking it over with you. Yes, I'd like to come to supper – so long as Mary won't mind.'

'Of course not. Mary's not the conventional kind, and it's not the first time I've brought her an unexpected visitor.'

He knew Mary had a liking for young Davey, and she showed it by her welcome. 'You've both been drinking at the pub,' she said, 'at what Lennox calls an after-work conference, but I know is only an excuse. So I've got the babe in bed and the meal on the table. Come and eat, and tell me, how's the lovely Dinah?'

It wasn't until the coffee stage that Franklyn spoke about

his Scottish visit. He assured Mary that it really had done Dinah good to meet, even for a short time, the people Annabel had worked with. He hesitated to say more, and it was Mary herself who was quick to see why Lennox had brought him to the house.

'You two go into the study while I animate the dishwasher, and then there's likely to be a wee howl from upstairs. I can see you've things to discuss.'

'It's not that I don't want to talk about it,' said Franklyn, when he and Kemp were alone. 'It's just that I feel a bit of a fool . . . I may be worrying about nothing, and I don't like the idea of people thinking I'm imagining problems when there aren't any.'

'Tell me the whole story of your visit to the North, and why it's got you concerned, because you *are* concerned, and I don't think you're the kind that imagines things.'

It was not too difficult for Franklyn to relate the facts; already he had gone through them in his mind many times. Now his narrative was straightforward, although he could not repeat verbatim the various interviews and conversations he and Dinah had had while in Scotland.

'Of course, at the time I didn't think I'd have to remember exactly what people said. And even when we came back, I began to think I was making something out of nothing – until we had a visit from Peter Mallen two days ago. He'd rung to say he had business in London and could he come and see us. In fact we put him up for the night.'

It had been a long night for, after Dinah had gone to bed, the two men had sat up talking into the small hours. Franklyn had guessed that, although it was nearly five months since Annabel's death, her partner was still deeply distressed by his loss. What he could not put out of his mind was those last days . . .

'Why didn't she let me know where she was?' he'd kept saying. 'If only that phone call on Saturday afternoon hadn't been so disrupted . . . And how was it I couldn't get her on her mobile on Sunday when I got back from Belfast? I took it that she was busy in the office – she'd said there would be so much to do before her flight . . .'

120

He'd explained that they both realized their individual careers put a certain strain on their relationship, and each tried not to interfere in the other's working arrangements. 'There were times when I had to be away, and the same went for Annabel. She kept out of my job, and I had never been to the ClydeSight offices until that Tuesday – and yesterday . . .'

He had gone to see Sandy Duncan – not as a friend, for they had never been close; but Sandy might have been the last person to see Annabel before she left. Sandy had been evasive and not particularly helpful. He had admitted to being angry at the time when he was told by Mrs Bristow, on the Saturday morning, that she had chosen Annabel rather than him for the New York trip.

'The old bat had the nerve to tell me on the phone – didn't even have the guts to say it to my face . . .' he'd told Peter, but added that he no longer felt any resentment. 'I should have guessed earlier on that she would give the assignment to her new favourite; they'd become such chums, you know.' Peter ignored the sidelong look and the innuendo; even at college Sandy Duncan had had a penchant for prurient gossip.

'Anyway,' Sandy had gone on, 'I didn't see why I should give Annabel any help that morning. I just told her, as she'd got the job, she might as well get on with it on her own. Being Annabel, she as good as told me to get lost. So I took her at her word and walked out of the office. I didn't go back in till Monday.'

Peter had questioned other members of the staff, but had been unable to find anyone who had worked with Annabel on the Saturday. One of them had said there wouldn't have been any need; she'd only had to collect papers already prepared, and she could have been out of the office by midday. And there had been no one working on the Sunday. Of course, she'd had her own set of keys, had she needed to be there, but the security chap on duty had shaken his head; he had not seen her.

'Peter's a journalist,' said Franklyn; 'he knows the right questions to ask, and he has access to all kinds of people: but what he's coming up with is negative answers.'

'And all you've got is a supposed sighting by a farm boy.'

Kemp was trying to keep the matter at a low level, and not fuel further anxieties. Already he was rather regretting the tone he had taken with Franklyn at the meeting – Kemp had only meant it as an exercise, not as an endorsement of the young man's doubts.

'What does Dinah think?' he asked.

'She feels she was bamboozled by Adelaide Bristow, and can't forgive herself for being overawed at that interview.'

'Hm . . . She shouldn't blame herself; Mrs Bristow is quite a personage and in danger of becoming an icon to the Scottish Parliament – a combination of Margaret Thatcher and Mary Whitehouse.'

Franklyn shuddered, then remembered Dinah's word – 'Kindly,' she'd said. 'She seems to appeal to people more than either of those two. Peter would like to have talked to her. After all, there was that dinner party on the Friday night at her house – possibly the last time Annabel was with other guests. But Mrs Bristow doesn't give interviews to mere sports writers and, from what Dinah gathered, she didn't think much of Peter Mallen as a partner for Annabel.'

'That's reasonable, if she did have that certain type of feminine fondness for the girl. She was grooming her for stardom: Peter might just have got in the way. But we're losing the point here. The question still remains: if Annabel went to Bute that weekend, why does nobody know about it? Why did she tell no one? And, of course, why did she go at all?' Kemp thought for a moment. 'I wasn't being serious when I asked if you'd checked the airlines. Now I'm not so sure . . . Peter Mallen could do it.'

Franklyn nodded. 'He's going to try. We'd talked half the night away, when we both thought of it together. We were reluctant to mention it because of the implications . . .'

'Which are grim. I don't think any of you want to take your doubts that far. And yet . . . If Peter has no luck with the airlines—'

'Which I'm sure he won't . . . We must not forget that it was a time of great confusion.'

'So everyone keeps telling me,' said Kemp testily. 'But there will be records. Anyway, I have a better idea. Here's

Mary with the coffee, and I'm sure she'll agree with me.'
He turned to her as she put down the tray. 'My dear, I'm
thinking of putting some work in the way of our old friend
Bernie Shulman.'

Sixteen

Bernard Shulman was explained to Franklyn by Mary. 'He's a private eye, New York style,' she said. 'Lennox used him when he was finding me,' she added, as if it simplified matters, which, to Franklyn, it didn't. 'Well, that's not quite true . . . Let's just say that, at the end of the story, Lennox and me, we met and we got married.' She and her husband exchanged glances, and Franklyn knew that nothing further was going to be revealed on what the office of Gillorns had always regarded as a mystery: how had this strange Irish-American woman come to marry their boss? She was nothing to look at; she was well over thirty when they had married, and it was rumoured the New York Police Department had been only too glad when she had left their city . . .

'I'll get on to Bernie right away,' said Kemp, briskly. 'I know he's still in business. What I'd like from you, Franklyn, is the date and time, exactly, of Annabel's flight from Glasgow, along with its expected time of arrival in New York, the name and address of these people in Greenwich Village – did you say their name was Greensmith? – and anything else that you and Dinah found out at ClydeSight that might be relevant. Got that?'

'And do tell your Dinah exactly what you think, and what you're doing,' said Mary Kemp, earnestly. 'I don't know the whole tale, of course, but if you're keeping anything from Dinah, don't.'

'She speaks from experience,' said Kemp, with a wry grin, 'so heed her advice. Put your two heads together on this one. You say you haven't spoken of your doubts because you don't want to upset her, but I think your Dinah is more likely to be upset if you keep things from her.'

124

'That's what they both said, Dinah,' Franklyn told her that night. I'm only sorry I didn't do it before.'

'Didn't you realize, you fathead, that I was just as worried as you were? I don't try to make things fit, as you do, but I do have an instinctive feeling when things are wrong, and ever since we were on Bute I've known something is wrong . . . Now that we've talked to Peter Mallen, I'm more convinced than ever that all we've got is other people's stories and not the true facts. I've argued with myself that perhaps it doesn't really matter. Annabel is dead, and all we're doing is prolonging the agony of coming to terms with it. But other times I think over all we've heard and, just like you, I come up with things that don't fit. And then there's this book I've been reading . . .'

'The one you got from Glenhead? I saw you were deep in it. What's so special about it?'

'Nothing I can put my finger on, but it's way out from my usual reading, so I'm intrigued by it. It's a plain tale, beautifully written, about a young lad schooled on the Continent and back in his native Scotland, trying to come to terms with two aspects of it: the romantic Highland myth of mountain mists and brave hearts, and the sober reality of the New Road being cut by General Wade through the countryside to divide the clans and civilize them by bringing trade and money . . .'

'Ho-ho,' said Franklyn, laughing at her, 'I scent sociology and global politics – America selling her way into peace between nations . . .'

'Don't be naive; this is around 1730, when they'd never heard of sociology . . . There are Gaelic-speaking characters and English, and of course there's no need to tell you which come off best – it makes the writing like shreds of another language.'

'It's certainly kept you up at night. 1730, now – that's between the 1715 and the 1745. It would be a turbulent time . . .'

'The lad's father was at Glensheil when the Jacobites lost, and part of the tale is concerned with his disappearance: was he drowned? did he die an exile in France? or did he never leave Scotland?'

Franklyn was struck by her seriousness as much as by her

words, and was quiet for some time. Then he said: 'Are you thinking of our problem, too?'

'About his never leaving Scotland?' Dinah said, slowly.

'Yes, I think I was finding some sort of parallel . . . It's an ugly thought.'

'And you haven't finished the book?'

'No . . . and it's too like a detective story to even take a peek at the last page.'

'Well, we shall know one way or another . . .' Franklyn still shirked the actual words. 'Either through Peter's efforts at the airline, or Mr Kemp's friend in New York . . . Then we can, perhaps, face an entirely different set of circumstances.'

Within a few days Peter had phoned them; he had had no luck with the airline that had booked Annabel's flight. They were as certain as they could be that all the seats had been taken, but of course their records weren't as clear as they were meant to be – after 11th September there had come new regulations: more work for their staff, more checks on travellers. They could only give what information they had, admitting it might not be completely accurate; after all, as they said, it had been a time of great confusion.

When Franklyn related this piece of information – or rather the lack of it – to Kemp, verbatim, he was greeted by a surly: 'That bloody phrase again. It's going to be used for all kinds of mischief in the future. Have you got those details about the Greensmiths?'

When he had handed over the address and telephone number that Peter had taken from Annabel's address book, Franklyn nipped out of the head partner's office rather smartly. Obviously it didn't do to linger when Kemp was in a bad mood, as he seemed to be this morning.

It wasn't anything to do with Franklyn Davey, actually. What Kemp couldn't make up his mind about was Mervyn Prentiss – how much to tell him, how much to hold back, how much to trust him . . . Well, that was easy; Kemp didn't trust him at all. Still he was a client and he was paying well over the odds.

In the end – and conscious that he was procrastinating – he decided that he would simply telephone Prentiss and say that he had achieved a result, and perhaps it would be better if he reported it personally – at a time convenient . . .

Kemp was lucky. Mr Prentiss's assistant informed him that his employer was away for a few days, but Mr Kemp's message would be e-mailed, and an appointment would be made for the following week. Kemp had already said the matter was not urgent; what he didn't say, of course, was that Mr Henry Pocket might need a little time to take in the sea air at Southend-on-Sea . . .

In the meantime, Kemp must contact Bernard Shulman, private investigator, New York City, and he was delighted to find that Bernie was indeed still in business. After an exchange of pleasantries during which Kemp relished the terse idiomatic usage and strong Brooklyn accent of his friend, he gave a short account of the problem and what he wanted from Bernie.

'Laycock and Peabody,' he said, giving the name of the American company that Dinah had learned from ClydeSight; 'I understand the meeting with them was to be on the eighty-first floor. They lost some of their people, so you'll have to tread softly . . . Miss Angus should have been staying at the Taft, but she may have gone to the address I've given you in Greenwich Village for the Greensmiths. They are apparently very distressed . . .'

'Ain't we all?' Bernie's response was laconic but heartfelt. 'What goes for missing persons, these days, eh? I gotta half-dozen cases . . . Reckon they'll go on for years . . . Yeah, I'll take up the Angus one, put the word out. Might take a week or so. Hey, how's that Mary of yours? A great little lady, that one. It's not every day someone gets the better of the NYPD.'

Kemp assured him that Mary was well and more taken up with her little daughter than with settling old scores with New York's finest – though she had spared them a thought and a few tears when the Twin Towers came down, so strong yet was her bond with the City where she had spent her youth.

'Yeah, that was a bad scene . . .' Bernie coughed, and Kemp realized that even Yankees can run out of words. 'I'll do what I can with this Angus case of yours. Bill you, as before?'

'Right. Thank you, Bernie. Yes, account to me.'

There was no client to meet the expenses, and no fee for the firm either, Kemp thought as he came off the phone. Perhaps it was time he got on with the proper work of Gillorns and earned the money to allow for indulgences such as tracing the last steps of Annabel Angus.

At least the disappearance of Linde Prentiss would bring in a fee – though not as large as Mervyn had first offered; Kemp was too scrupulous for that – which would cover what he called Henry's pocket expenses . . . though possibly not all of his time. Where was he now, for instance? Well, the operative's meals wouldn't figure largely on the bill. Nibbling sandwiches at a corner of the desk, indeed. Did the man never eat a proper meal?

Nothing was heard of Henry for some time, but Mervyn Prentiss was in touch before Kemp was ready for him. Damn e-mail, he thought; it's much too fast. Mr Prentiss had received the message; would Kemp simply forward the report to his home address by personal messenger. He saw no reason for an interview; he was much engaged in public affairs.

Well, if that's the way he wants it . . . Kemp took the work home, and carefully compiled a report, essentially a résumé of Henry's German visit and the sad facts of Sieglinde's death. He did not mention the moving stone nor any of Henry's own comments and, for the time being, he omitted any mention of the postcard or Southend-on-Sea.

Sally Stacey, Gillorns' tax expert, lived not far from Mervyn Prentiss, and it was she to whom he entrusted the envelope containing the report, together with his account. She joked about the size of the lettering PRIVATE AND CONFIDENTIAL, and asked if it contained salacious memoirs or pornographic prints. She was told it was neither, but must be put directly into the chubby hands of Mr Prentiss himself; in fact, on handing it over, she was rewarded by a glass of sherry in the Prentiss library.

Mervyn was a man of quick action when it suited him. Next day, by Special Delivery, a letter from him landed on the solicitor's desk.

Lennox Kemp opened the envelope, held the cheque for a moment between finger and thumb, and thought of the phrase 'filthy lucre'; then he laid it on his desk, and read the handwritten accompanying letter. The gleeful satisfaction of Mervyn Prentiss oozed from between the lines: '. . . such diligence . . . a great job of work . . . I am so relieved that, thanks to your efforts . . . etc., etc.'

The actuality of Sieglinde's death played no part in the missive save for a bare: 'Naturally, I regret her death. Her heart, like her mother's, was never strong. Being back in her own country at a time of great confusion etc., etc.'

That bloody phrase yet again! Kemp couldn't think why it so grated on him, as Mervyn's words also grated despite the fulsome praise, the overdone gratitude, the reference to an announcement of wedding plans.

Only in a postscript did Mervyn show his true colours: 'I enclose cheque in payment of your very reasonable bill. Don't you wish you'd accepted my first offer?'

Kemp took the cheque through to his cashier, thinking he'd better get it banked before he had second thoughts and tore it up. After all, Henry had done all that was required and the report that had been duly sent to Mervyn Prentiss was properly drawn up, and detailed every step Henry had taken. It did not include the postcard sent to George Farley, nor the fact that the gravestone had moved. Nor did it contain anything of the doubts lingering in the minds of both Henry and Kemp himself, for nothing might come of them. The assignment had been to find Sieglinde Prentiss, dead or alive and, for the moment, as far as the client was concerned, that mission had been accomplished.

He guessed where Henry was now, and reflected that any further expenses on this one would have to be on the house.

'You've got an e-mail from New York,' his secretary told him later that day; 'it's quite long.' She knew that Kemp was still getting used to electronic communications and only used them when their content was neither personal nor private. 'Solicitors have to be careful,' he told the office staff; 'you never know when your utterances, written or otherwise, are going to end up in a bundle tied with pink tape.'

As he expected, Bernie Shulman revelled in electronic mail. His notepaper heading alone was a medley of infinite joy in the lingo of dot.com symbolism. Kemp sighed, and read.

Seventeen

S outhend-on-Sea on a sunny day in February looked very much like it did on the postcard: the buildings shone with a lick of fresh paint here and there, and the sea looked cold but magically blue. Henry had never been to the town before, which lent some credence to his pose as a bemused visitor.

'Is it always like this?' he asked the girl in the lightly staffed tourist office.

'Good Lord, no,' she replied. 'It's just your lucky day. You could have a storm down from the North Sea, or a fog thick as porridge . . . Are you staying long?'

'Only a few days,' Henry said, and hoped it was true; he felt this was now or never for Sieglinde Prentiss. 'I'm convalescing after an illness.' Henry never looked robust anyway, and the way he hung his head now made it look as if it hadn't been long off the pillow.

'Poor you . . . Now, do you want a hotel – it's out of season, of course, so they come cheap – or would you prefer bed and breakfast?'

Henry would have liked to spend Mervyn Prentiss's money right up to the Hilton, but he didn't think they'd have one and, in any case, hotels were not to his purpose. 'Oh, I think a nice quiet B and B would suit me nicely. I shall be taking the sea air most days, like my doctor said.'

The girl handed him a brochure. 'What you do now, sir, is go and have a coffee somewhere – there's a good café on the front by the pier – and then come back, and I'll ring up for you when you've made your choice. Or you could always just call at one of the places you fancy; they're not likely to be busy, but some of them shut up for the winter and they forget to let us know.'

Henry sat in the window of the café and checked out the list of establishments that catered for the transient holidaymaker. He seemed to be surrounded, both in here and along the promenade, by people of his own age and above, walking sticks to the fore, wheelchairs in full cry, or leaning on one another like trees in a gale.

He chose three likely places to put his head down and went back to the helpful girl in the tourist bureau. 'I'd take that one nearer to Leigh-on-Sea,' she said; 'a nicer district, and quiet.' She rang while Henry studied the posters round the walls, which promoted the town as something between Monte Carlo and Las Vegas with an additional blast of youth culture thrown in.

'Will you be wanting supper?' The girl asked him, holding the phone.

'Oh, yes, please.' said Henry, aghast at the thought of being let loose in the evenings in this place of disco dancing and high-priced gambling joints . . .

'And it is an old-established business?' he queried, when she came back to him. Several had boasted longevity in serving visitors to the town, but Rosebarn with its: 'under personal management for over forty years' had attracted Henry above the others.

'Oh, yes; Mrs Purvis and family have been on our books a long time, and been highly recommended. Now, I've booked you in, Mr Pocket; you just go along and I hope the place suits you.'

Henry got into his car, which he'd parked out front, and took his time driving to the Leigh end of the town, where he saw that the roads were cleaner, the gardens larger, and the houses had a respectable – if not quite a Victorian – air of quiet prosperity. On a corner of two avenues stood Rosebarn, secure in its opulence of bay windows and a conservatory large enough to house a family – not that, even in the busy season, that would ever have been conceivable. Somehow, Henry was reminded of a similar extension to a house in Germany. There had been money spent at Rosebarn, and the place reeked of it . . .

He made himself known to Mrs Purvis, a lady of such indeterminate age that he felt ashamed of even trying to gauge it. She showed him a room on the first floor, complete with bay window from which there was a distant view of the sea. Henry made the right noises, assumed the right attitude and tone of voice, so that his hostess, if she was of a sympathetic nature, might take to him. It had worked before, and it worked now. She was sorry that he had not been well; his doctor was right to prescribe sea air, and where better, within reach of the capital, than Southend? Would he be a vegetarian? Was he on a special diet? Either of these conditions could be met by the cooking at Rosebarn. Henry assured her that he could eat almost anything; all he required was good sea air, and plenty of rest. He congratulated her on the room furnishings, and the size of the adjoining bathroom, and told her he felt fortunate in having found such a haven. When she left him to unpack, he knew he had made a friend by the way she smiled and relaxed her landlady-type demeanour enough to wish him a pleasant stay and, as there were few other guests staying, perhaps he would care to join her for a drink on the house after supper. Henry was in . . .

In the afternoon he strolled into several estate agents' and said that he and his wife were looking for suitable retirement property. He was met with responses enthusiastic enough to inflate the whole town like a gigantic balloon; he was showered with leaflets extolling houses, flats and bungalows in language ranging from fulsome to hysterical. To each and every agent Henry promised to return – words they must have heard often, and despaired of every time . . .

The evening meal, shared with about half a dozen other diners, was insipid, but then Henry had not expected haute cuisine. Nor, it seemed, had his companions, for all muttered, 'Very nice, thank you,' when asked by the plump serving girl if everything was all right. There was a retired couple who had run out of connubial conversation years ago, and two younger sets who might well have been on honeymoon or, more likely, unmarried holiday breaks.

Later, in the lounge, which was empty except for themselves, Henry blessed the instinct that had led him to Rosenbarn, for Mrs Purvis was an encyclopaedia of knowledge of the bed-and-breakfast business in the whole of Leigh and Southend.

Not for nothing did she advertise that this had been a family-run establishment for over forty years; in fact, her parents had set it up in the fifties, and she had taken over when they died. Nothing was said of Mr Purvis, except that she was a widow.

They shared coffee, and an exceptionally good glass of port together, while Henry pumped her gently on newcomers in the field, persons who might have started up such establishments as hers in the last fifteen years or so. Mrs Purvis relished the opportunity to expound on the shortcomings of her competitors without quite getting into slander, her remarks offered more in sorrow than in anger; but no name cropped up that, to Henry's ears, might have given a hint of Sieglinde Prentiss. He finally excused himself on the grounds that his doctor had advised early bed, but he hoped that Mrs Purvis would again give him the pleasure of her company – perhaps the following evening?

Upstairs he once again shook out of its envelope the postcard from Southend sent to George Farley. All it said, in a good, firm hand was: 'I am settled here. It is like Scarborough but warmer and there's not much sand. I hope you and Mrs Farley are well.' And it was signed 'Siggy Prentiss'. Despite the inclusion of his wife's name, George had not, in fact, conveyed the message to her, and Henry noted the postcard had been addressed to the works . . .

The postmark had been clear to both Henry and Kemp: 5th July, 1997 – some eight years after Herr Dieter's niece had perished in East Berlin and been buried in Rinteln cemetery. Or so he had been told . . .

Henry twisted the card in his fingers, and became pensive. For all these last weeks he realized he had thought of little else but Sieglinde Prentiss. Gradually he felt that he had come to know and like her, and on that afternoon in the graveyard by the Weser he had experienced bitter diappointment, a feeling too deep to be merely the end of an investigation – it had been more a sense of personal loss.

The following night's adventure had brought shock, yes, but also a rising of his spirits. Nothing pleased Henry Pocket more than to be told what he thought of as a pack of lies and then to find his instincts correct. There had been something about that tale of Klaus Neumann's with old Dieter in the wings prompting his every utterance. Did they take him for a fool – he, Henry Pocket? How easy for them to fix a gravestone – their yard was full of them – and pay one of their underlings to incise a name. Requiescat in Pace, indeed!

He would not let himself be downhearted by failure to benefit from Mrs Purves's exhaustive knowledge; there was always tomorrow . . .

After breakfast he studied the mass of estate agents' particulars that had been thrust upon him. They were only a means to an end – a good excuse to keep their office staff chatting about properties, and how often they changed hands. But he saw the name 'Eastleigh', and stopped. He must not make too much of it. There was Leigh-on-Sea close by, and there would be an East and West to it. Yet he sought out Mrs Purves, apologized for troubling her: did she know this house in which he was interested?

She knew of course that this nice Mr Pocket was considering retirement to her town. She got out her spectacles and looked at the estate agent's flier.

'Oh, I thought it wouldn't be long before that house came on the market. Silly name, of course, because it's more in Westcliff. But I hear it's a good property. Are you going along to see it?'

Henry looked at the picture. 'It would be a bit large for me and the wife,' he said, 'though the family will visit, I suppose. Is the price about right? I value your judgement.'

Mrs Purves took pleasure in the phrase. 'It's a nice property for that end of town, and I think they'd take less than the asking price.'

'Why do you say that, Mrs Purves?'

'An executors' sale, isn't it? Must be. The poor lady died just before Christmas; it was in the paper.'

'Were you acquainted with her?'

'No, I didn't know her, though those that did say she was a nice person, and everybody was sorry when she got killed in that accident. I can't remember her name, but the paper said she'd lived here for many years. I'd say that would be a good house to buy, Mr Pocket; you nearly always get a bargain when it's an executors' sale, and the agents want it off their hands quick.'

'That sounds excellent advice, Mrs Purves. I think I might just take a walk that way.'

Walking in Southend-on-Sea – though he now found that he was, in fact, in Westcliff – Henry disagreed with Sieglinde: the place was not like Scarborough. Whereas in that town of the northern ocean houses were built to keep out the weather, here they gladly welcomed it in with windows open wide-eyed to the sun, ironwork balconies and glazed patios where you could lounge and take in the mildest of sea breezes. Even in February one could sense the difference those few degrees further south could make for the tourist trade. Of course, Southend was supposed to be common, but as far as Henry could gauge by the size of the cars and the clothes of the residents, the epithet was outdated. He gathered from the brochure, which he read as he went along, that the gambling and strip joints – his own words not those of the tourist office – were away up at the other end of the town.

He came across Eastleigh sooner than expected, in a tree-lined road a short distance from the promenade. It was quite large, and he saw what the estate agent's particulars meant when they said 'well presented'. It stood four-square in a tidy garden, and said plainly, 'Here I am, look at me,' and was indeed worth the look. The asking price was just under £300,000 freehold.

The garden was well tended but not large. Henry proceeded past the wall of the property to the next corner, where he was rewarded by finding a shop that supplied provisions, newspapers and wines to this exclusive neighbourhood. Henry went in and bought a local paper, and complimented the proprietor on the district.

'Thinking of retirement?' The query was enough to loosen Henry's eager tongue. After a short résumé of the tale about him and his wife looking for a place – the more Henry spoke of it, the more he was coming to believe in it – he hesitantly produced the leaflet from the estate agent. 'I wonder if you know anything about this one? It's just down the road . . .'

136

'Of course, Eastleigh – Mrs Newman's property. It's about time it went on the market. We were beginning to wonder if there'd been a private sale. Ivy?' The man called to someone moving about in the room off the shop.

A small, beaky-nosed woman popped through the door. 'Yes, what is it?'

'This gentleman is interested in Eastleigh. An estate agent's got it at last.'

'And about time too. Poor Mrs Newman . . . I can never go past that house without thinking of her.'

All Henry had to do was stand there with raised eyebrows and a half-smile. Nothing showed of the tumult that word 'Newman' had stirred up within him.

It was a slack time of day for business in the corner shop, and both John Smith and his wife Ivy were happy to talk to this very respectable gentleman, who might well retire to their district and become a customer.

They had been here six years, Ivy told him, and Mrs Newman at Eastleigh had been there when they came. 'Folks say she'd been in that house a long time. Very well liked, she was – a widow and comfortably off.'

Henry remarked that the house was large for someone on her own.

'Oh, but she had family and they visited a lot, so I'd say she was never lonely. Mrs Newman wouldn't ever be lonely, would she, John?'

Henry caught the tail-end of a glance that passed between them, and John didn't reply. All he said was that it had been a terrible shock to everyone when she had been killed like that.

Henry asked, diffidently, what had happened.

'Hit-and-run down on the front – that's what happened . . .' Ivy grew fierce. 'And the police ought to have done more to catch the driver, that's what I say . . .'

John Smith turned to Henry. 'You know how it is with maniacs who drive like that. The police hadn't a hope in hell of getting on to him. He'd be up the A13 and in London before the poor soul was cold. It was evening when it happened, and there was a bit of fog in from the sea.'

'Mrs Newman wasn't the kind to take chances; she'd have bin out in fog many a time . . .' Ivy gave a snort, and turned to Henry. 'She took that little dog of hers out for his walk every evening about the same time, between seven and eight. She always crossed at the same spot between the flowerbeds. She was a careful person; she'd never step out in front of the traffic like some say she did.'

'What a tragedy . . .' Henry's sad face was not put on; his earlier excitement at hearing the name had given way to a dull ache at the back of his mind that, later, he would have to come to terms with. Now all he wanted was to draw out the talk and, for his part, to listen. 'Was she found immediately?' he asked.

John Smith shook his head. 'Not at once . . . It was getting dark, you see, but then the dog started running up and down yelping its poor little head off. A couple took some notice of it and went looking for the owner. That's when she was found.'

Ivy nodded vigorously. 'They got a doctor from across the road, and he was on the spot straight away. But she was dead. He said it was instant. Isn't that what he said, John?'

'That's right. He said death was instantaneous. She didn't suffer.'

But those who are left will . . . Henry didn't know why the words came into his head.

He stayed with the Smiths until he had wrung every morsel of information from them; he didn't enjoy doing it any longer, but it was his job. Most of what they knew had been gleaned from the account of the accident in the local paper, and from comments by neighbours. This particular enclave of houses formed a small estate, and it seemed that most people knew each other. It was a permanent population not a transient one, and consisted mainly of retired couples, some widows, and, more recently, business executives whose companies were in the area – Southend a prosperous town and, in the opinion of the Smiths, could get along pretty well without being called the Las Vegas of Essex.

'I am rather surprised that Eastleigh should come on the

138

market at all,' Henry had said, hesitantly, 'if, as you say, Mrs Newman had family . . .'

'Oh, but they weren't young people,' Ivy said quickly; 'she told me she'd no children of her own. No, these would be more like older brothers, or maybe uncles . . .' Her voice trailed off, and again she gave that sidelong look at her husband. 'Wouldn't you have said they would be older, John?'

John had gone red, and began fiddling with the magazines on the counter. 'Well, they weren't youngsters, Ivy . . . And it wasn't for us to pry. Mrs Newman was a good customer. If she had her private life, then that was her privilege.'

'She didn't do bed and breakfast, then?' Henry enquired, innocently.

Both the Smiths almost held up their hands in horror at the very suggestion. No, Mrs Newman obviously had money of her own; there would be no need . . . Certainly not bed and breakfast. The people who stayed from time to time were all gentlemen – well, they took *The Times* or the *Telegraph*, didn't they? And they would call in at the corner shop for cigarettes, and sometimes chocolates – always the most exclusive brands.

John Smith's embarrassment at this turn in the conversation was palpable – not made easier by his wife's obvious enjoyment of it. Henry was reminded of George and Shirley Farley. John Smith was quite a good-looking man in his fifties, his beaky little wife perhaps somewhat older. When Henry had managed to slip in a query as to the late Mrs Newman's age, John had said she would be in her late forties, and Ivy had retorted: 'Make that her late fifties, but well preserved, I'll grant you that.'

Again there had been a small discrepancy about her name. 'She's down in my books as Linda Newman,' said Ivy stoutly, as if it had been an old argument. 'The other was foreign, somehow . . .' She blinked her black eyes across the counter at her husband.

'It was Linde,' he said, not particularly abashed; 'it was short for something German, but she hated anyone to suggest that she wasn't one hundred per cent British. After all, she supported the local Conservative party . . .'

139

'Enough of that, John.' His wife turned to Henry. 'We don't hold with politics, not in our business we don't.' Henry agreed with her that it was well to keep politics and business separated.

Shortly afterwards he left, having bought his paper, his local map and some Cox's orange pippins.

He told the shopkeepers that he hoped to renew their acquaintance at a later date, and thanked them for the information on Eastleigh.

At the estate agent's the very name of the property was sufficiently powerful to transfer him instantly from the languid blonde in the front office to the senior partner, Mr Wycroft. 'This gentleman,' she announced, breathlessly, 'is interested in the Newman property.'

My Wycroft rose, smooth as a dolphin from his afternoon resting place. 'Take a seat, Mr . . . er.'

'Henry Pocket,' said he, producing a plain card. 'I had several of your brochures yesterday and I have been having a look around.'

'Good. Good.' Edward Wycroft was having some difficulty in adapting to selling mode after a large lunch. 'And you are thinking of Eastleigh?'

'Well,' said Henry, cautiously, 'it's larger than my wife and I want, but there are grandchildren to be considered, and I am very attracted to the area. Is it an executors' sale?'

Wycroft looked sharper. 'Yes. The owner has unfortunately died, and it is the solicitors acting for the executors who are selling.'

'So, they might consider an offer below the asking price?' Henry could be sharp too.

The estate agent pursed his lips. 'That would depend . . . May I ask if you have yourself put a property on the market?'

Henry stretched back in the chair. 'Sold it for a fair price a month ago. So, there's no chain, if that's your problem. I have recently retired after nearly forty years with a solicitors' firm in Epping. No' – he held up a deprecating hand – 'not as a solicitor. I have been a legal executive with them, specializing in conveyancing.'

140

That made Wycroft sit up. This could well be a serious buyer, not one to fritter your time away and then be seen no more. 'Ah,' he said, 'so you know the ropes.'

'Some of them,' said Henry, modestly. 'But of course it's different when it's for yourself. I like the look of Eastleigh but would like to know just a little more of its history.'

Edward Wycroft spoke swiftly into his intercom. 'Bring me the file on Eastleigh, if you please, Corinne, and we would like some coffee, if you will be so good . . .'

She swung her tight-clad hips around the desk, and deposited a thick folder before departing to the coffee machine, which Henry had glimpsed and shuddered at on his way in.

He watched as Wycroft fingered through the documents: A land certificate, not a charge certificate, so there hadn't been a mortgage on the house. 'How old is the property?' he enquired.

'Let me see. Ah, yes. Built in 1970 as part of the Eastwood Estate. Very exclusive, Mr Pocket; there were only about ten houses built on that piece of land – a highly desirable site it was too.'

'Might I ask who the builders were, Mr Wycroft? The houses all look in good fettle despite their thirty years.'

'Not a local builder but a long-established Essex firm – been going since the First World War – M. W. Prentiss & Company. They'd several parcels of land in the area, but the Eastwood Estate was the best of them.'

'And the proprietorship register, Mr Wycroft?'

Wycroft studied the page in the document. 'Prentiss & Company retained the property called Eastleigh, although I believe they sold all the other houses. Then they let it until it was sold to Mrs Newman about ten years ago. And she of course was sole proprietor till her unfortunate death last autumn.'

Henry showed no interest in the death of the previous owner. He had already called at the offices of the local *Gazette* and taken extensive notes of the items on their files. They had not added much to what he had learned from the Smiths but, as press cuttings, they were a trifle more reliable than hearsay or gossip. However, so far as Henry's relationship with Mr

141

Wycroft was concerned, only the property called Eastleigh was of importance. To stress this, he agreed to a meeting at the property in two days' time, when his wife would have arrived to view their future prospective home. On leaving, however, he asked tentatively for the name of the solicitors acting for the sellers: 'I may have come across them in the line of business,' he explained.

'A firm in Chelmsford: Settle & Partners. Do you know them?'

'Indeed, I do. How very fortunate . . . Well, my wife and I will see you on Friday.'

Back at his bed-and-breakfast home at Rosebarn, Henry wasted no time. Up in his room he gathered together his wits, his notes, his pieces of paper, news cuttings, and carefully peeled and sliced apples by the telephone, and dialled Gillorns.

It was nearly closing time. Lennox Kemp had signed the mail, and was once again reading Bernie's snappy communication, short on grammar but long on terse, pithy comment – like a half-hour spent in a downtown police precinct on film. He stopped when he was told who was on the phone from Southend-on-Sea, and then he listened.

Several times he nodded. 'Settle & Partners – they've always been the Prentiss Builders' solicitors. Mervyn only came to Roberts because he thought old Cedric could do him favours with Newtown Council.'

Henry was asking a favour. 'Yes, what do you want?'

'Some kind of entry to Southend police. Just a name would do.'

'I'll have a word with John Upshire; he's bound to know somebody down there. I'll ring you back. You're not in trouble, are you, Henry?'

'I'm not, but someone is going to be.' Henry sounded grim.

It didn't take Kemp long to get what his operative wanted. John Upshire was on the point of retiring from his post as Chief Superintendent of the Newtown force, and he and Kemp had been exchanging favours for more years than they cared to remember. 'Tell your chap to ask for Inspector Thackery –

he's the man in Southend – and he can mention my name if he likes.'

Having phoned Henry Pocket and given him what he wanted, Kemp asked no more questions. Henry would file his report when he was good and ready.

In the meantime Kemp had a problem of his own: whether to tell young Franklyn the contents of Bernie's e-mail now, or wait until the morning. Either way there was going to be heartbreak enough. Dinah's friend would not easily be put to rest . . .

Eighteen

Dinah had felt an abyss yawn at her feet when Franklyn had talked about checking the airlines, and getting Kemp's private eye in New York on the case. Suddenly, what had been only a nebulous cloud of unknowing became reality, and the implications too awful to contemplate. She wondered if, in fact, she was being influenced by the book she was reading, scenting a mystery and following it up; but that was a mystery two hundred and fifty years old, and a fictional one at that. The man's disappearance and his son's search for him in the confusions and conspiracies of a divided land – it was the author's hand that had laid the trail and that would bring it to an end. The events of 11th September were real and terrible; the echoes from them would never die. Annabel's death was no longer a finite thing, the closing of a chapter; it had become a gaping question: to know or not to know?

The bland, Scottish voice of Sandy Duncan on the phone one evening in February came as a pleasant surprise. He'd been down in London for a conference; could he give her lunch tomorrow, and if Franklyn was available also . . . ? Franklyn shook his head; his time off from the office at the moment was limited. 'You go, Dinah; it's for you he'll turn on his Highland charm.'

And that quality was indeed to the fore as she sat with Sandy in the cocktail bar of his hotel. It was an effortless charm, a habit he might well have grown up with rather than being assumed as a prerequisite of the media image. She was reminded of characters in that book, the new Scotsmen, the smooth types who could sweet-talk the English soldiers but aye keep a dirk in their socks . . . She found herself slipping into the idiom, and told Sandy about it.

'It was a favourite of Annabel's mother. The lawyer asked if I wanted a memento, and it was all I could think of taking. Did Annabel ever talk to you about her?'

'Not a lot. It was her dad she'd quarrelled with, but when Mrs Angus buried herself in that wee croft on the island, Annabel said she'd not the heart to visit her. And that programme about the "Last Resort" – Well, that finished it . . . She said she'd be ambushed by the natives as if Bute was Hispaniola and she that general of Cromwell's who got chopped up when he landed. Always the one for clever remarks, our Annabel; they were meant to make us think . . .'

'So you didn't know she was going to Bute that last weekend?' Over the rim of her glass Dinah watched to see if the colour changed in his fair pinkish cheeks, but unfortunately a waiter approached at that moment to tell them their table was ready.

He had heard her, though, for he himself brought up the question while they were on their first course. 'When I saw you in Glasgow, Dinah, I didn't want to spoil your memories of your friend, so I glossed over what happened in our office that Saturday morning. I was pretty pissed off – if you'll forgive the expression – as you can imagine. When Mrs Bristow phoned me at some unearthly early hour and told me I wouldn't be going, she "had another project for me" was the way she put it . . . Aye the wily one, our Addy. Well, I considered not even turning up at the studio. All that blah she gave me about helping young Annabel, I thought, stuff that . . . But then' – Sandy leaned over and poured Dinah more wine – 'the word would go round that I'd got the hump; and maybe Mrs Bristow did have another project for me. You mind now, in the media business you have to look under the bushes, as it were, listen for the meaning under what folks say. After all, language is our business.'

'Do you speak Gaelic, Sandy?' Dinah was thinking of her book, and the people who thought in that other tongue the English were determined to tear out by the root.

'Tut tut,' Sandy admonished her, 'you should ask if I've the Gaelic. I have it, but in a small way. It got me started on Western Isles broadcasts, and it serves me well with

Adelaide, who likes anything the Scots have and the English haven't. Why she should think the English would want that mouth-twisting Hielan' nonsense is beyond me, but it's the great tongue for swearing in.'

'And you were all for swearing that Saturday morning?'

'I was that. I got in about ten. Annabel was already there, up early like the eager little bird, perky as peanuts; so I gave her all the stuff for her American trip, and told her to get on with it. My exit was swift, but dignified.'

Eating succulent slices of pheasant in a rather gooey sauce, Dinah felt she had not progressed very far; Sandy was simply repeating what they had already been told by Peter Mallen.

'And she said nothing about going to Bute?'

'Where on earth did you get that idea? She never went down to her mother's in all the time I'd known her. Besides, although I'd prepared our presentation for Laycock and Peabody carefully, and it was all in the folder, it had my personal slant on it – she'd have had to go through the whole thing again to get the right feel to it. It would have taken her the whole of that weekend; she'd have had to come back in on the Sunday, get cracking with a computer . . . There'd be no time for visiting her mother.'

'She was seen on Bute on the Saturday afternoon.' Dinah decided that directness was the only answer to Sandy's evasions. He was taking a second helping of sautéed potatoes, turning each one over cautiously as if looking for snails.

'Somebody was mistaken.' Sandy's attention seemed to be firmly fixed on his plate. 'Have you been talking to Peter Mallen?'

'He has been to see us, yes.'

'Now I understand. The man has it that his neb's been put out of joint over those last days of hers that he didn't figure in . . . Peter Mallen aye resented her career, that she kept him well out of it. Oh, I know he's had a dreadful loss . . .' Sandy Duncan waved a fork in dismissal, 'but he's got to realize he was never going to function in her life anyway.'

'That's what Mrs Bristow said.'

'And she was right. She was grooming Annabel as a presenter. Annabel saw herself as that and more – an aggressive interviewer, one to challenge the lads . . .' He stopped, and grinned, acknowledging that he himself might very well have been one of them. 'Peter . . . if he's coming up with some nonsense about that last weekend of hers, it's only because he's jealous.'

'Of you, Sandy?'

'For God's sake, no. Of her work, I meant.' Sandy seemed a bit rattled; he concentrated on chasing fragments of food around his plate before he said: 'Is it he who's putting Annabel on the Island of Bute that Saturday? If it is, he's dafter than I thought.'

Dinah put down her knife and fork. 'He's not,' she said, leaving him to fit in the answer to his query. 'That was delicious, Sandy,' she went on; 'thank you for having me.' She would have liked to say 'having me on', but thought it sounded too impudent. Instead, she simply smiled sweetly and showed him her dimples.

He responded by swiftly filling her glass again, and ordering another bottle.

He wants me tipsy, she thought, this bonny Highlander who gives nothing away. Is he worth sleeping with just to find out what goes on beneath his fair skin, and practised suavity? He's attractive, all right, but I'll bet even this girlfriend of his will never know the depths of him. He and Annabel, I wonder . . .

She must try again, secure in the knowledge that her Irish ancestors could outdrink any of his Gaelic forefathers, and he not having the knowledge of it!

Round about the sweet time, which was frothy anyway, she did a bit of giggling, flirting and flattery and, when it came to coffee in the overstuffed lounge afterwards, she said yes to brandy. He had helped her at the doorway, where she appeared to sway slightly, and perhaps it was that that gave him the idea she needed further sustenance.

Despite all attempts of his to wriggle away, Dinah kept up her obsession with her friend Annabel's last days. She herself felt that obsession was the right word, and if this had been a film, she would long ago have told the heroine to shut up. Sandy showed patience with this loopy creature, but it was thin as tinplate.

'That dinner party she went to – the one at Mrs Bristow's house . . . It was the last time Annabel was amongst, like, other people. I do wish I knew who was there.'

'Well I wasn't, for sure. Though I've been out there since, of course.'

'Oh, you're on the favourite pet list now, are you? Do you get good dinners?'

'I don't go for the dinners, but I've had to see more of Adelaide lately because of the new project.'

'I remember . . . You mentioned it. Wasn't Annabel going to do it at one time, or did I get it wrong? I don't understand you media people, anyway. We see you on the screen, then it's away to your other lives. Not that I've seen you, Sandy, though I'd love to.' She ogled him over the rim of her coffee cup and put it down a little off its saucer. 'Is it all very secret, this project?'

'Not any more. It's going to be seen next month. Of course, you won't get it down South till later, and there won't be the same interest. And you're right, it was going to be Annabel who was to do the interview of Adelaide Bristow.'

'And now it's going to be you, Sandy?'

'Yes. All the prepping has been done, and I'm just a tiny bit pleased with the way the programme's shaping. Quite a feather in my own cap, if I say so myself.'

'Cock of the North, eh?'

Sandy looked at her rather oddly and Dinah thought she'd better rein in her comments, which did sound rather too drunken . . . Back to business – she pulled herself together.

'Annabel went home in a taxi that night. She shared it with somebody called Bill. But he was a lord. Would he be a Scottish lord, Sandy?'

Sandy Duncan was trying to catch the eye of their waiter. As he turned away to order two more brandies, Dinah emptied her glass into the coffee pot for the second time. Her companion hadn't noticed, but the waiter did and gave her a knowing wink.

'Dinah, my dear, I've got another meeting tonight, but that's not till seven. How'd you like to keep a lone Scot company till then? We could go for a walk in the park, but it's raining and I get enough of that at home. My room's quite decent and there's a drinks cabinet. What do you say?'

The approach direct – Sandy could give that when it suited him. Dinah felt that it was now or never.

'You never answered my question.' She tried to pout, nicely.

'And what was that?'

'About the man in the taxi, the one Annabel went home with?'

Sandy laughed so loud the small table danced. 'Don't be daft, Dinah. You're talking about Sir William Erskine, and you make it sound as if there were shenanigans between them. Bill Erskine's one of Adelaide's oldest friends – and I mean oldest; he's near ninety. You really do take your extravagant ideas to great lengths . . .' It wasn't said in an admiring way. 'Seriously, I think it's time you gave up this obsession with the last days of Annabel.'

Dinah turned large, moist eyes upon him. 'Oh, Sandy, if you only knew how much I want to talk about her . . . I can't get those last days of hers out of my mind. Do you think she might have mentioned to this Lord Erskine that she was going to Bute the next day? I've no idea, of course, how long they would be together . . .'

Sandy swirled brandy in his glass, and looked at it gloomily. 'It's quite a run from Bearsden into the centre of Glasgow, if that's what you mean. I doubt they talked much. And anyway, it's a lot of nonsense, this tale of her being on Bute; there would never have been the time – not if she was going to be properly prepared for the American meeting. And that's made me think, Dinah, that if you go on with this trail, people will see you as one of these awful scavengers who can't leave Ground Zero alone.'

Dinah felt herself flushing; it wasn't simply that Sandy had shown her his nasty side, but she must admit he had a point.

Perhaps he saw that she was hurt. He added, hurriedly: 'If you have to pursue it, why don't you talk to Sir William Erskine himself? He's down in London a lot of the time – has a flat in Westminster . . . Now, forget all this, dear Dinah, and let's enjoy ourselves. What do you say?'

How long could she stretch this out? How long was a piece of string? Sandy Duncan had the overlay of politeness that went with being in the public eye, but at some point it was going to crack.

'This Lord Erskine, or Sir William, or whatever . . . I'm no good with the titled kind; I never know which from what. In the West of Ireland they could be little squireens, only one up from the gombeen-men, or they might be the real thing all the way back to Brian Boru . . .' The more nonsense she talked, the more exasperated was Sandy, his glowing inner eye already fixed on the room upstairs, the drinks cupboard and the silken coverlet getting pulled about . . .

'If you really want to talk to him, you can use my name. I interviewed him a few weeks ago as he's one of Adelaide's closest friends. And now, Dinah darling, let's get out of this stuffy place. My bedroom's airy and there's a view over the park . . .'

For a moment she thought he said 'eyrie', and saw herself in the talons of a great blond eagle being swept up to its mountain home. She'd think of something – she could always have a seizure, or fake a visit to the dentist. Why, oh why hadn't she brought her mobile phone that could trigger an SOS? She was struggling to her feet as Sandy leapt to his, over-tipped the waiter and made for the door.

The trilling signal was from his pocket, not hers. Testily he pulled out his own mobile. 'Yes?' he said brusquely. 'What, now?'

Dinah slipped into her coat and the shoe she had shuffled off under the table. The waiter was looking into the coffee pot as he cleared the crockery, and again she got a wink. I hope it's a good omen, she thought desperately. Sandy was sounding increasingly bad-tempered, yelping at the little phone as if it was to blame. He jammed it back into his pocket, and looked at Dinah like a child deprived of anticipated sweets.

'They've bloody well brought forward that meeting . . . three-thirty this afternoon.'

'And it's three o'clock now,' said Dinah, helpfully. 'What a terrible shame. Well, next time you're down, Sandy, give me a ring. I have enjoyed our talk. Cheerio . . .'

Still lamenting his loss of those enticing afternoon hours, Sandy Duncan showed her into a taxi, ordered one for himself and was soon whisked away in the opposite direction.

Saved by the bell, she thought, as she said 'Liverpool Street', and in the train going home she vowed never to touch alcohol at midday for at least a month. Then she slept all the way to Newtown.

'I've made your supper,' said Franklyn, 'though you don't deserve it. What if his phone hadn't rung?'

'Oh, I'd have got out of it somehow . . .' Dinah had rather enjoyed relating the story of her lunchtime exploit. 'Besides, Sandy Duncan's an attractive man – even though he's more aware of it than he should be. What I did get out of the encounter was that introduction to Sir William Erskine. If I use Sandy's name, at least it gives me a way in; then I can give him my spiel about wanting to talk to anybody who saw Annabel in those days before . . .' Her voice trailed off, and Franklyn realized that, under all the flip talk, Dinah was still unsatisfied, still longing for some voice – any voice – that might bring back to her the friend she had known.

He was himself more than interested, but for a harder reason. The facts he had found out on their visit North had not fitted; there had been too many loose ends. Now steps had been taken to tie these up, but he feared an inconclusive result.

'Mr Kemp says he will be hearing very soon from his investigator in New York. Bernie Shulman is giving it priority, apparently, because of their friendship.'

'What if . . . ?' Dinah had begun, but he stopped her.

'No surmises until we get facts. You do your bit this end – go and see your Scottish lord if he's in town, but I doubt he'll be able to tell you much.'

'I know it's a forlorn hope, but . . . Anyway, I'm going to write to him, send a polite note telling him my connection with Annabel, that I understand she was a guest at that dinner party, and that I'm trying to meet anybody she saw in those last days . . . Oh dear, I do seem to be repeating myself.'

'So you are. But that's the way with obsessions, and now we've come this far we must go on. Sounds a bit like the Macbeths,' he added, but with a grin to lighten the words.

'I think by then they were steeped in blood, weren't they? You do know how to comfort a person.' But she smiled, too.

Nineteen

Kemp was re-reading Bernie Shulman's e-mail – not an arduous task, since Bernie's style was pithy anyway, and the shortened forms of words, the acronyms and abbreviations fancied by users of the electronic miracle suited him down to the ground.

Got zilch from the airlines, as expected. Around 9.11 the records sink under scrutiny from anxious relatives, the FBI and NYPD. No hope of checking there.

Taft Hotel had a booking for a rep from Scottish firm, ClydeSight for two nights, Mon. & Tue. A/c pd but no one turned up. Certain of that. No, they didn't inform ClydeSight – no skin off their nose.

Tracked down the Greensmiths, habitat Greenwich Village – which suits them, both artists, vegetarian ex-hippies. Devastated by loss of good friend Annabel. They got a phone call Sat. 11.8 from AA saying she'd be in NY Monday to Wednesday 9.10 to 9.12. She wld contact them on arrival. She never did, nor did she show up at their home.

Delicate mission at Laycock & Peabody, they lost some of their best execs at that meeting on 81st floor, like Marty Laycock who'd two kids & his pal Joe Schwartz who had three . . . So, go easy, I think to myself . . . I get the facts: meeting scheduled for 8.30, all present EXCEPT the ClydeSight rep. This info came from a stenographer who was brought in from WTC typing pool to take notes. Name of Rachel Cronin. She escaped but deeply traumatized. Still on the payroll. I gets a peek at it – and her address.

153

Nice Jewish family caring for daughter Rachel. Don't want the media getting story, don't like the ghouls around . . . Me, I'm strictly kosher so I'm in. Besides I got a nice nature and don't mind showing it, so I gets talking with Rachel. Gee but that doll had a narrow escape. Seems L. & P's people got impatient waiting for the Scottish rep to turn up. Mebbe she's lost in the building, says one, or she's down in the washroom. You go look, they tells Rachel, so she trots off to find the lost rep. She's halfway down the stairway when it happens . . . She don't want to talk about it much. I go along with that but I ask just the same. What did she do? Sensible girl, she just kept on running down the stairs, down the stairs, down the stairs . . . She repeats it over and over so I stop her. She's getting better, her momma says, and they give me a meal. I don't ask any more questions, Mr Kemp.

That's all I got for you. Hope it helps. You want my opinion? Well I reckon this Annabel Angus she were never on a plane, she was never in New York, and she was never at the WTC on 9.11. I guess that in times of great confusion there's folk get lost. Ain't that so? Enc. A/c. Bernie.

This time the phrase did not irritate Kemp, but it made him think. Then he asked for Mr Davey, and when Franklyn was sitting opposite, he handed him the e-mail, with no comment.

Franklyn read it through twice before putting it down on the desk between them.

'What do you think?' he asked.

'That there's a problem, and it's not going to end cleanly. Dinah is not going to get what people now call "closure" on the death of her friend – if in fact Miss Angus is dead. I'm afraid my gut feeling is that she is. Too many months have passed for it to be a kidnap – which would have been highly unlikely in the first place anyway – and as for a deliberate disappearance . . .' Kemp shook his head. 'From what you've told me about her, I don't see her lying low all this time either.'

'Even before your chap in New York checked, I'd been

thinking along those lines. There seemed no reason for her simply to disappear. But it's true that nothing fits: the facts we've been told up in Scotland, the time scale – there's too many loose ends. I've not told Dinah the way my thoughts have been running, but yes, this report from New York simply confirmed my suspicions: Annabel never got on that plane on the Sunday night.'

'Then you are prepared to face the alternative?'

'*I* am,' said Franklyn, rather grimly, 'but I don't know if Dinah can.'

He told Lennox Kemp about Dinah's latest proposed foray into the world of Adelaide Bristow – that she was hoping to see Sir William Erskine because Annabel had shared a taxi with him.

'At any other time I would have dismissed that as a non-starter,' said Kemp, 'but in the light of this' – he indicated Bernie's e-mail – 'I'd want to meet anyone who had any connection with Annabel Angus during those last few days in September. Just run through them again for me to refresh my memory.'

Franklyn had gone through them so many times in his own head that the events, the conversations, the dates and hours, as retailed to either himself or Dinah by the people concerned, were clear as a map – but a map with essential features missing.

Kemp listened, then took a little while before he spoke.

'Hm . . . It sounds to me as if the sudden change of plans for Annabel happened either just before, during, or after that Friday night dinner party. Would you agree?'

'I hadn't actually thought of that, but it's obviously been on Dinah's mind. That's why she's anxious to meet this Scottish laird.'

Dinah had already suffered a disappointment, however. A note had arrived from Sir William Erskine to say that he would have been pleased to have met her but he was returning today – Friday – to his Glasgow flat. He commiserated with Dinah on the loss of her friend, and remembered kindly the girl who had shared his taxi after Mrs Bristow's dinner party. If, by any chance, Miss Prescott should come North again, perhaps she would let him know and he would see her. He gave particulars of his Glasgow address and telephone number.

It was a friendly letter, but it did nothing to raise Dinah's spirits. She could settle to nothing – neither study nor housework – and found herself mooning around the flat, restless and depressed. For once she found herself resenting that Friday evening get-together of Gillorns at the pub. It meant Franklyn would be late home and she would normally have cooked his supper; now she did nothing except wait for him. Like any moaning housewife, she told herself, stuck in the house all day while husband is at work . . . Shake yourself out of it, Dinah, she told herself; put on the brave face.

When he did arrive, and not late enough to be grumbled at, his news acted as a stimulus to her mind – shocking, of course, but somehow expected. Since their Scottish visit there had always been that doubt, that cloud of unknowing, a confusion of emotion and a desperate need for clarification.

'It's not something I've known,' she tried to explain, 'just that feeling of incompletion. At first I thought it was the manner of Annabel's death, but then I faced that squarely and realized it was the same for everyone who had had a friend or relative there. Time would perhaps not entirely heal, but each in their own way would come to terms. But this – the fact that she possibly wasn't there at all . . .' She looked at Franklyn with wide eyes. 'This is different, and it has to be dealt with.'

'That's what Mr Kemp advised – that it be dealt with, that we try to find out all we can, now that the whole matter is not just our suspicions.'

Without saying too much about the case of Annabel Angus, at the meeting that evening Lennox Kemp had addressed his staff on the question of professional ethics. What, he had asked, should a lawyer do if he found out scandalous or disreputable facts about a client while acting for him on another matter that had no relation to those facts?

The answers Kemp got ran, roughly, along the spectrum of the kind of work being done by each particular person in the office. Mike Cantley, for instance, who dealt with wills and probate, was all for lying low and saying nowt.

Perry Belchamber, who specialized in family law and divorce, took a different view. 'You have to be a bit of a psychologist,' he said, 'to understand people when they're involved in the legal process, just as doctors have to probe the whole body when a patient is ill. I don't say you have to take action when you find your client is not the loving father he's trying to convince you he is; but it certainly alters your judgement and your handling of the case if you find out he's a liar and a wife-beater. No, it's not something you can keep under wraps.'

Sally Stacey, specialist in company law and tax matters, tended to side with Mike: 'If it doesn't come under the assignment you are given by the client, then it's not really your business if you hear rumours he's defrauded the tax people in the past. Even if he's said to be a paedophile, if it's your job to do his tax return, you should do it, without prejudice.'

Most of the company present agreed that perhaps Sally was putting it a bit strongly, but they were forced to admit that knowledge of a client's true character should not be a hindrance to their chosen lawyer giving them full value. There were times when one's own feelings should be kept in the background; a solicitor acting for a particular client was neither judge nor jury.

'And do you pursue a case when the client is satisfied it has ended, even though you know it has not?' Kemp left them with that while he went to the bar for refills. That one certainly got them arguing, but in the end Sally, Mike and Will Summers, the cashier, came down hard on sending in a final account and closing the file. 'If the client is satisfied with closure of the case,' said Will, 'and pays the bill, then that should be an end to it.'

Franklyn had glanced at Kemp. From what he knew of the senior partner, this easy way out would not do; Kemp's insatiable curiosity was well known, and in the past he had carried on with certain murder cases even when the local police had given up. Franklyn wondered if, in this instance, Kemp was thinking of Annabel Angus, where there would be no client to meet the final bill, and where no one had

157

employed the firm of Gillorns to find out anything. He felt a rush of gratitude towards his employer, who could easily have shown no interest in Dinah's friend.

When he told Dinah, she acknowledged that, without Kemp's help, they would have been left floundering. In fact, they might well have tried to forget, put out of their minds any doubts about the death, gone on with their lives regardless – except that Dinah knew she would be haunted for ever by two images: the flaming towers and the bleak, cold cottage above the Firth of Clyde. She would not rest until she could blot both from her mind.

Franklyn knew his Dinah; it was one of the reasons why their relationship would be a lasting one. He looked across at her now, and made up his mind.

'It's Friday night,' he said; 'there are such things as trains, and one doesn't always need to book . . .'

'I don't know how you do it, Franklyn Davey . . . You were years tucked away in those dusty Chancery corridors, chewing vellum and living in dead documents, and yet you know exactly what I want at the exact moment I want it.' She threw herself at him. 'You're a fraud, you know; you should have been an adventurer, a pirate, a swashbuckling hero . . .' When she had finished smothering him with kisses, she got up.

'Eat first,' she said, 'then Euston, and the North-West Passage.'

In fact, their journey was pleasanter than they had expected, and they arrived in Glasgow to mild air and a pale sun. No March lion pawed the ground as the month came in gentle as a lamb.

They booked into the same hotel as on their previous visit, and at a reasonable hour Dinah phoned the residence of Sir William Erskine. The auguries continued in her favour, as he said he would be happy to see her and her friend on Sunday afternoon. Unfortunately, parliamentary business would keep him in Edinburgh till then.

Dinah came off the phone, delighted by her success. 'He sounds a nice old dear,' she said, 'with the softest of accents, like a grandee. He's not one of Labour's newest lords, then?'

'Far from it,' said Franklyn, who had been at *Who's Who*;

'it's an ancient title and Sir William would be more at home in that book of yours than in any modern House of Commons. Have you finished it yet, by the way?'

'Yes,' replied Dinah, sombrely; 'they've found the saddle from his horse, and the dirk that was used to kill him. They know where the body lies.'

Twenty

Inspector Thackery of the Southend police force happened to have a morning free of serious crime, and agreed to see Henry Pocket when he mentioned the name of Superintendent Upshire to the desk sergeant.

After a comment on John Upshire's possible retirement, and the fact that Tom Thackery had once served under him when he was in the Met, the inspector asked, pleasantly enough, what he could do for Mr Pocket.

'Well,' said Henry, diffidently and in the manner of one not wishing to cause trouble, 'you had a hit-and-run case here in Southend in October, I believe. A Mrs Linda Newman?'

'What of it? We never caught the blighter. You got something that might help in that direction?'

'No, sorry. It's just that I may have known the woman herself. I'm a private investigator, at present working on a case for Mr Kemp of Gillorns, Solicitors, in Newtown.'

'Oh, aye. I've heard of Lennox Kemp from John Upshire. Bit of an investigator himself. You want a look at the file?'

'If it's not too much trouble. I'm afraid it's not going to help your search for the driver of the car.'

'It was a van,' the inspector interrupted. 'Not that that makes it any easier to find. And there's no mystery about the identity of the victim. Mrs Linda Newman was well known in the town.'

Tom Thackery had a broad, bland face and cool, blue eyes. Henry thought he glimpsed a flicker of amusement in them as he scrutinized Henry carefully. Henry knew exactly what he looked like: working man on the verge of sixty, thin, nondescript – might as well have been wearing a grey mackintosh.

A file had been brought in and the inspector opened it. 'Would a photograph help?' Without waiting for a reply he took one from the file and handed it over.

Henry tried to keep all expression from his face, but he felt excitement nevertheless; this was the first time he had seen Sieglinde Prentiss in her middle years. The only photograph her husband had been able to give Kemp at the start of the enquiry had been one of her as no more than a girl in her early twenties, round-faced with slightly frizzy hair of an indeterminate colour between ginger and corn. Henry knew that Mervyn's man had used it in his pathetic attempt to trace her; Henry himself had ignored it on the ground the woman was now at least fifty and there would be little resemblance left. Now he stared at the studio portrait of a good-looking woman who had looked confidently at the camera from steady blue-grey eyes as if she knew her worth.

Her hair was dark blonde, expertly cut and styled like a smooth helmet high on her forehead. More Brunhild than Sieglinde, thought Henry, but with compassion. He handed the photograph back. 'Could be the lady I was looking into, but difficult to tell – mine goes back years.'

Thackery shook his head. 'Not likely to be Mrs Newman,' he said. 'She was well accounted for. Been in Southend more than ten years; nice woman, popular.' Again that odd glint in the eye. 'Were you yourself acquainted with the subject of your enquiries?'

Henry had to admit that he'd never actually met her. He changed tack and asked for more details of the accident on the promenade. The inspector obliged by giving him a quick run-down of the facts, which were more detailed but didn't differ from those given in the newspaper accounts.

'It was the nature of the injuries that led forensics to go for a van rather than a car – a lightish van, probably white. But aren't they all, these days, whether they're florists or builders? There was a brush of paint on the victim's clothes but nothing else to go on. She was struck on the side of her head – fracture of the skull; death was almost immediate – something to be thankful for, I suppose.' He paused. 'No difficulty in identification: her handbag was tossed on to the roadway and found intact. She'd

161

no relatives, but one of our local solicitors had been a close friend, and he identified the body. That would be Mr Edward Settle Senior. I believe his firm are the executors, but of course our only interest in the case has been to try to catch the culprit – and given the time that's passed, we've come to a dead end.' The inspector didn't altogether like the phrase he'd used, so he hurried on: 'As a matter of fact, we're in the process of wrapping it up, and closing the file. Like all hit-and-runs, it's hopeless trying to pin someone down, particularly in a town like this. All we could do was make sure as far as possible that it wasn't a local van. We did that, and now it would be a waste of our limited resources to go on.'

Henry could see the folder, and the photograph would soon be mouldering in the dead-letter office, so he made a tentative plea. 'Doesn't sound like my lady,' he said, 'but do you think I could have a copy of the picture?'

'Sure, why not?' Thackery rang through to the outer desk and the same young, fresh-faced constable who had brought the file returned.

'Could you make a photocopy of the photograph for this gentleman, please?' The constable went off with Sieglinde–Brunhild's calm smiling face, and Henry found the inspector's eyes were once again upon him with that oddly searching look.

Henry began to feel uncomfortable under the steady, slightly amused stare, so he asked if the police were sure it hadn't been a local van.

'We may not be the Met, but we're thorough, and we know our Southend firms and their drivers' records. But this is a town on the edge of the sea: vans and lorries come down from London with deliveries and they're on the fast route back within the hour. And, of course, we didn't know we were looking for a van until after the post-mortem.' He glared at Henry as if criticism had been made of his force, an impression that Henry hastened to correct.

'I didn't mean . . . I'm sure your men did all they could, particularly as the victim was a resident and popular.'

'You should have seen the turn-out at her funeral. Yes, Mrs Newman was a familiar figure to many of her neighbours, and well liked by them. People came from all over . . . Ah, thank you, Carey.' The young man had returned and handed a copy of the photograph to Henry. Tom Thackery stuffed the original back into the file and handed it to the constable.

Henry decided it was time he left, and rose to his feet. As he was being shown to the door, the inspector said: 'I'm sorry we weren't more help in your own case, Mr Pocket. I hope you find your lady alive and well.'

As Henry was going down the steps from the police station, he turned up his coat collar; the air had turned chilly. Before he reached the street he felt someone immediately behind him and, turning, found it was the young constable struggling into a duffel coat. 'Hold on a mo' . . .'

Henry stopped and waited.

'Fancy a pint?' The young man was buttoning up his coat against the wind. 'I'm off duty . . .'

'Don't mind if I do,' said Henry; 'a nice pub lunch would suit me fine. Anything to get out of your sea breeze.'

'Yeah, right freezer, innit? The Fiddlers on the corner's good and warm.'

Neither spoke on the way, since the newly risen harsh wind straight off the estuary would have blown their words away.

Once inside, Henry said: 'Allow me . . .' and bought the first round while he ordered haddock and chips for himself. The constable had shaken his head: 'Nah . . . the missus cooks an evening meal.'

It was only just twelve o'clock and the place was only half-full, so they were able to get a table against the wall in the darkest corner – a choice, in Henry's view, deliberately made by PC Carey. As Henry stood at the bar he took a good look at the young policeman – ruddy-faced, brash in his speech, he gave the impression of someone on tiptoe, anxious to go places.

Henry came over with their drinks, set them down and spread his hands, palms down, on the table top. 'So,' he said, 'what's all this about?'

Carey seemed to appreciate the direct approach. He grinned and took a long drink, then smacked his lips in satisfaction.

'That file the guvnor asked for – the late Mrs Newman – what's your interest?'

Henry confessed he didn't really have one; he'd been looking for someone but thought he'd probably got it wrong. 'Did you work on the hit-and-run?' he asked.

'More 'n most of them back there. Right lazy sods they've been over that one, and now they're wrapping it up . . .'

'And you think they shouldn't?'

The constable took a good fill of his beer before he spoke. 'Look here, Mr Pocket – I heard your name at the desk – was there something fishy about the woman you were looking for?'

'There might have been . . .' Henry allowed.

'Well then, don't be too sure you got it wrong. There was something more than fishy about the late Mrs Newman.'

'In what way?'

'The same way everybody clammed up, didn't want it investigated further, scared something might turn up . . .'

'Such as?'

'I'd seen her about – good-looking dame if a bit over the hill.' He stopped, possibly having realized the same might be said of his companion. 'And she was discreet about what she did. The neighbours might have suspected, but nothing was said. That's the way, ain't it, when there's bigwigs in the clientele.'

Henry affected innocence, pursed his lips and looked prim. Fortunately the arrival of his fish and chips enabled him to keep up this pose while PC Carey elucidated further.

'The ones from up London – they'd stay overnight; the locals'd visit in the afternoons. And by local I don't mean riff-raff, Mr Pocket. Rotarians, some of 'em, straight from their weekly do at the Castle Hotel.'

Mr Pocket unrolled his knife and fork from his paper napkin. 'Are you telling me Mrs Newman kept a disorderly house?'

Carey hooted with laughter. 'You're just like my old man; you talk like it was still Queen Victoria.' Then he sobered and said, with some spite: 'Don't bother me what she did; it's when the nobs start covering things up – that's what gets me.'

'You should get out,' said Henry, enjoying the crispness of

the batter and thinking it would be some time before he found the fish.

'I'm doing just that – getting a transfer to London. The missus – she's bored to tears in this hole, and after the way I've been treated over the Newman thing, I can't wait to get away.'

Henry showed a proper interest in the young man's career. 'You worked hard on the case and the higher-ups don't appreciate it?'

The constable nodded. 'You won't see all the stuff I found out in that file, Mr Pocket, 'cos it never got past the guvnor – and he's in cahoots with the Chief Constable, who's scared to get shit on his boots.'

'And who might well have been on Mrs Newman's list, eh?'

'You're quick on the uptake. Yeah, I wouldn't put it past any of 'em . . .' He laughed, unpleasantly, and gave Henry a wink. 'Come to think of it, it's funny the police at the top go in for a bit of discipline – they're always gabbling on about it to the lower ranks.'

Henry raised his eyebrows. 'That was Mrs Newman's speciality, was it?'

Carey nodded. 'Maybe they liked the bit of German in her. That's where she come from – least, that's what I heard . . . Domination – that'd be what it was about. I read it up in a psychology book. Middle-aged, respectable men, who're past it . . .' He looked at Henry, who bore the scrutiny with goodwill. 'Sorry, mate; I think old Thackery took you for one of them – your story of looking for some old acquaintance. But I think he got it wrong, and not for the first time. I think you're straight.'

Henry was glad of the implied compliment, and bought another round of drinks. When he came back to the table, he asked: 'Tell me some of the things that weren't in that file.'

'Tyre marks, for one.' The young policeman was eager to oblige. 'There was a slight smear of wet on the road, and I took the trouble to walk back along the line of a possible vehicle. I reckon it stopped a few yards from the scene, and someone

165

in heavy boots got out and walked back to where the woman was lying.'

'To make sure she was dead?'

'Right. But when I put in my report and asked for prints to be made at the scene, I was fobbed off – they said it was too late, too many other vehicles had gone along the prom by then. They should have cordoned the area off properly. I put that in my report, too, and they didn't like it.'

'I gather there was no family for identification?'

Carey gave a short laugh. 'None of the top brass would've needed that; they all knew who she was – even old Settle, who's in his dotage anyway.'

'What about efforts to catch the driver of the van?' Henry asked.

'All wind and piss,' said Carey, succinctly, 'made to look a lot on paper; but Thackery never really tried. Orders from above, I reckon: don't make waves. Like I said, a cover-up. Sure there was the post-mortem, and some white paint was found on her coat . . . How many white vans are there in the whole of London and south-east Essex? Don't make me laugh . . .'

'Did they put out a notice for witnesses?'

'Sure, they followed the book, but not so's you'd notice. I went round the neighbours – that's where I got the information about her so-called visitors; but nuff said, they only hinted . . . One thing was certain, though: the time she went out every night with that little dog, like clockwork, six-thirty to seven; out for half an hour, then back, same routine, same place of crossing the prom. Maybe that, too, was German. Anyone who knew her habits could have driven that van . . .'

'Hm . . .' Henry felt he wasn't going to get much more from the young man. 'You might just have done me a favour, Mr Carey. I'll of course have to report back to my principal to see if this helps our own case. If anything comes of it, I'll personally see to it that your work here gets merit points.'

The constable looked suitably gratified. He'd heard the name Superintendent Upshire mentioned; perhaps this old fogey Pocket meant what he said; there could be kudos in it for Carey . . .

'One thing more,' he said, as they left the pub; 'I'm no do-gooder, but the way that poor woman was bundled into her grave, no questions asked, just get her out of the way – well, it don't seem right . . .'

With which sentiment Henry Pocket was in full agreement, and in his heart of hearts (buried deep, like that haddock in batter) he felt a certain admiration for his own quarry, Sieglinde, who seemed to have taken life as she found it and made the best of it in the only way she knew.

'Those local white vans,' he said, when they were in the street, 'did you do the questioning?'

'Some. Weren't anything in it: two grocery vans, a painter and decorator, a video shop, small removal firm, and a builders' merchant. Got nothing outta any of them.'

'Remember any names?' Carey thought for a moment; he was proud of his memory. He reeled off: 'Webb's Grocer, Oakroyd's decorators, V.R. Videos, Pete's Removals, and Sam Mason, Builders' Merchant – I remember him all right, a right cocky bastard . . .'

Henry felt a surge of exultation. Gotcha! – that useless fellow Mervyn Prentiss had sent out on the first round of the search for a mislaid wife. And in the building trade too!

'Do you think you could do a bit of off-the-record questioning of that last name, Sam Mason?'

'I'd be glad to have another go at him. But it'll have to be on the quiet.'

Henry gave him one of his cards – not a plain one this time; in the corner it said: 'Gillorns, Solicitors, Newtown.' 'If you get anything, Mr Carey, contact either myself or Mr Lennox Kemp at Gillorns.'

Twenty-One

W hen Sir William Erskine entered his large, airy sitting room above Blytheswood Square where she and Franklyn were waiting, Dinah's first thought was the word 'hidalgo' though she was but vaguely aware of its meaning. Franklyn's equally instant reaction was 'King Charles I' – a triptych of portraits seen somewhere, though he couldn't remember where.

As they both struggled with their initial impressions of the man they had come to see, he had shaken their hands and gestured as to where they should sit. He looked particularly searchingly into Dinah's blue eyes with his velvet brown ones, and held her hand a little longer . . .

'Your friend . . . I have thought much about her. I am sorry she has been lost to you, but I am glad you have come. You will take tea?'

Indeed they would, for it meant their visit to this fascinating man (in their minds both had agreed as to that) need not be a short one.

Half an hour later, tea having been served by someone who could be nothing other than a parlourmaid, they were still under the spell of Sir William's old-world charm, his precise manner of speech – a lilt of West Highland accent lending piquancy to views that were surprisingly sharp and worldly.

He spoke with warmth of his long friendship with Mrs Adelaide Bristow – since she was just a girl, he said, for he had known her family – in particular the formidable aunts who believed in Scottish Nationalism when it had been as credible as the Flat Earth Society . . .

'And now,' he went on, 'they're out on a limb again . . . beyond the Fringe in the Scottish Parliament – is it not so?'

On Franklyn's admission that he knew very little of politics north of the Border, the old man gracefully changed the subject. 'That dinner party, now, where I had the pleasure of meeting your friend, Annabel – it was something of an occasion, I gather, though I was only made aware of that later. For me, it meant nothing at the time. I dine often with Adelaide when I'm in the North; I make a good, extra elderly man for her table.' The look Sir William gave Dinah could only be described as roguish. She smiled back; with his little Van Dyke beard and his head cocked on one side, he had a bird-like vivacity quite at odds with his age – which he had told them was ninety-one.

'Could I ask you something about that dinner party, sir?' Franklyn was trying to keep things in focus.

'Of course, Mr Davey. My memory has not yet failed me, even on matters that might seem trivial.'

'Was anything said about Annabel being sent to New York?'

The old man considered. 'Not immediately, no. Let me reconstruct the scene – as much for myself in the remembering of it. There would be a dozen of us – Adelaide's usual number – and a mixed bunch. Some Bearsden neighbours, a couple of minor politicians from Edinburgh, an executive from one of Adelaide's companies, a young artist of whom nobody had ever heard and, of course, your friend, the youngest of us – and by far the sparkiest.' The dark eyes turned inward, the melancholic Stuart features lengthened, and the voice faltered. In the pause Dinah was conscious of hanging on to his every word as though at a West End play with some famous actor onstage. She saw that Franklyn, too, was holding his breath.

When Sir William resumed, they were both startled, as if he had some way into their thoughts. 'Have you heard tell of a play called *Dangerous Corner*?' He addressed the question to Franklyn, whose brain was galvanized into action. 'Yes,' he said instantly; 'it's by J. B. Priestley.'

'In the thirties we were all of us intrigued by J. W. Dunne and his new concepts of Time . . .' The old man's voice slipped into reminiscent mode. '. . . and Priestley gave us more food for thought. A conversation, a moment in time, lives that can go either way – that was what was in it for me that night . . .'

Dinah was lost, but Franklyn was following. 'There was a turn in the conversation at the dinner?' he asked.

'We would have reached the pudding,' said Sir William. 'Adelaide aye had the sweet tooth, so the desserts from her kitchen were miracles of the pastrycook's art . . . There had been a pause while the main dishes were cleared. You must mind that I was up the other end of the table from your friend, who was nearer to our hostess. I only caught the end to their conversation. The refurbishment of cities was their subject, and the old argument: Edina, the Athens of the North and Glasgow, the old Second City of the Empire . . .' He smiled, as at some ancient, ineffable dream.

'And then . . .' Franklyn was now on the trail and anxious to keep nose to the ground.

'Something about a building in Bothwell Street – used to be a warehouse, now smartened up enough to be headquarters of a merchant bank.'

'Bothwell Street? But that's near the Central Station.' Dinah didn't know much about Glasgow, but she'd seen the street name close by their hotel. 'Surely there wouldn't be warehouses there?'

The old man smiled at her; his lips were still remarkably red and full. 'Not warehouses in your London sense,' he said, gently, 'but warehouses like there used to be in Glasgow. Fine stone buildings for the wholesale trade, whether it be furniture, fashions or, in this case, I believe for hairdressers' sundries – everything they could need for everywhere from a wee shop in a Highland village to the latest coiffeuse newly set up in Princes Street. I recall the name above the door back in the thirties – Gerard's, I think it was called . . .'

'And the conversation?' Franklyn said softly, trying to keep on course.

'Ah, yes, it was then . . . Your friend, Miss Angus, was laughing . . . "A merchant bank," she said; "well, it has come up in the world. It used to be a warehouse. My mother worked there."'

'And?' Franklyn prompted.

'I have not got the second sight,' said Sir William; 'I don't believe in such so-called superstitions . . . but . . . there was

170

something then in the air . . .' He turned to Franklyn, and said earnestly, 'I do not drink – another Highland myth demolished – so at dinner parties such as this I am more sensitive to changes in atmosphere, to tensions that develop – the more so when the wine goes round . . .'

'And it was there then?'

'Yes, it was. And I could not understand why. Voices seemed to sharpen, faces were flushed. I am used to seeing that, but on this occasion there was – how can I put it? – almost a fever . . . When the sweet had been served, and everyone went ooh-ahh, it was then that Adelaide said something about this young lady going off to New York on Sunday evening. It was an announcement that seemed to take everyone by surprise – including the young lady herself . . .'

'You think it was the first Annabel knew of it?' said Dinah, eagerly.

'As I say, I was not at that end of the table, so I do not know whether Adelaide had had a word with her earlier, but yes, I think your friend was taken by surprise.'

'Did she mention the trip when she shared your taxi back to Glasgow?' Franklyn asked.

'She was excited about it, yes . . . But there was something else, something in her manner, as if she was thinking not of the trip but of something else. Getting the cab had been difficult. I tend to leave such parties early and had already arranged for a man to pick me up at ten. I had no wish to break up the after-dinner party, which I know Adelaide loves; so I simply slip away without saying anything. On this occasion, when she saw me leaving, Miss Angus insisted on coming with me – much against the wishes of our hostess, I may say. It was a little embarrassing, but of course I couldn't very well refuse such an insistent young lady . . .'

'That bit of conversation,' said Franklyn, following his own line of thought, 'when Annabel said about her mother working in that . . . er . . . warehouse – did everyone hear it?'

Sir William sat back in his chair as if suddenly weary. 'There was a lull, certainly, and a silence . . . I think Adelaide broke it by saying how strange it was, and asking your friend for her mother's name. That seemed to get over the awkwardness, and everyone started talking again – about other things . . .'

'Could it have been just snobbery?' asked Dinah. 'The awkwardness, I mean . . . Annabel saying her mother worked in a warehouse.'

'My dear young lady, you don't understand. It wouldn't have been a warehouse in your London sense. I believe Miss Angus did say her mother was a shorthand-typist – nowadays you'd say secretary. In the thirties, that would have been quite a well-paid job in Scotland. Besides, how can I put this? Snobbery of that kind was never the thing up here; we've not got your English conception of class . . .'

Franklyn remembered hearing that every Highlander was as good as his clan, from the laird to the beggar at the crossroads – but that would have been in the old days, he was thinking; maybe a vestige of it remained.

'That corner of conversation,' he said, deliberately throwing back the idea to Sir William, 'which made you think of the play – was that the moment?'

'Yes. I've thought it over since and think I have the truth of it. For Adelaide never said the thing that was in my mind then and is still there now . . . But I said it to Miss Angus back there in the cab.'

'And what was that?'

'Adelaide worked at Gerard's, too. It was a lean time for her family when she left the school, so she learned bookkeeping, and her first job was as a ledger clerk at Gerard's. She was only there a few months, I understand. Then she got into university, the war came along, and I lost touch with them all until it was over. By then she'd married Major Bristow . . .'

'So, perhaps they knew each other, she and Annabel's mother,' exclaimed Dinah excitedly. 'What was Adelaide's family name?'

'Kelly. And she wasn't Adelaide in those days. Much too Victorian. She called herself just plain Ada . . .'

'Ada Kelly . . .' Dinah's voice faltered. 'And you told Annabel?'

'I wondered why Adelaide had not said. There had been that hiatus after Gerard's had been mentioned – there had been a

space, yet nothing had filled it. It was on my mind, you see . . .
Are you feeling all right, Miss Prescott?'

'What on earth were you doing, Dinah?' Franklyn asked
when they were back in their hotel, for she had been quiet on
the short walk through the Glasgow streets. 'Kicking off your
shoes and then rummaging about on the floor for them?'

'If I hadn't bent down I'd have fainted,' said Dinah, simply.
'I nearly did. I kept thinking only Victorian ladies fainted, but I
could still feel the blood draining from my face and I knew I'd
topple over if I didn't get my head lower than my knees.'

'You recovered quickly enough to babble on like a ninny . . .'

'I didn't want that nice old gentleman to notice . . . Come
to think of it, perhaps I should have let myself swoon – he
probably had smelling salts about somewhere. But all I thought
at the time was to divert his attention, and the Neil Munro
book proved a blessing. He told me it was the Gaelic in the
author that made for the style of writing, and you coming in
with your bit of history got us all clean away from that earlier
dangerous point . . .' Dinah threw herself into a chair as if
exhausted – which she was. 'Get me a drink, darling, from
that little bar thing . . . I know it's more expensive than gold
but I need it.'

Franklyn watched her swallow half a gin and tonic, rapidly.
'Now, tell me,' he said, '. . . about Ada Kelly.'

'I'm trying to get it straight in my own head first. I'll take it
slowly – what Sir William called "the remembering of it" . . .
It was hearing the name Ada Kelly that did it, that gave me
the shock, and now I'll tell you why. That time Annabel and I
were on holiday at her mother's cottage we had an argument –
well, just a discussion really, but it got into argument as things
tended to do with Annabel. In the college we were both at there
had been a spate of pilfering – nothing unusual in that. Students
were losing bits and pieces – bags, scarves, sports gear, wallets,
and cash from pockets – anything carelessly left lying about
simply went. Well, everybody knows students are always hard
up, but this particular epidemic of downright thieving was
getting our backs up. Annabel and I were talking about it at
breakfast with Mrs Angus hovering over us the way she did,
handing out eggs, filling teacups, making more toast . . . She

was never really part of these chats we had, but on this one she suddenly brought out a tale of her own about a place where she worked before the War where there had been the same kind of petty pilfering going on. I remember the thing she hated about it was that someone was pinching from girls' overalls, or from handbags left in desk drawers, and those girls couldn't afford to lose cash. She said sometimes money was taken out of their pay envelopes.'

'It's a common enough happening,' said Franklyn, 'wherever you get a lot of people – offices, schools and colleges. Nasty, but true. Did Mrs Angus say whether they caught anyone?'

'She did. She came in early from lunch one day, went into the washroom and left her handbag on her desk. When she came back there was this person taking money from her purse. Must have made quite an impression on Effie Angus; she says the culprit was standing there with two half-crowns in her hand.'

'What happened?'

'She went straight in to the office of her immediate boss – I think she said he was the cashier – and told him. It wasn't someone from outside the office; it was one of the other girls who worked there. Well, at that Annabel jumped in with both feet. "You snitched on a colleague, Mother. What an awful thing to do, telling tales . . ." I could see all she wanted was to get at her mother; they'd reached that stage in their relationship when she would blow up at the least thing. Anyway, Mrs Angus just pursed her lips and said nothing. In the afternoon she and I took the dog out – Annabel said she'd what she called "prepping" to do for one of her projects. Her mother and I walked down the glen below the house, and I asked her what did happen to the girl caught stealing. She told me the firm – they were Quakers and very good people to work for – simply gave the person her cards and told her to leave immediately. For the sake of saying something I just asked if she'd been one of the typists, because I knew that was what Mrs Angus had been. She said, no, it was one of the ledger clerks, a girl called Ada Kelly, and she'd never seen or heard about her again. It was the summer of 1939, she explained, and everybody was on the move. She herself had got married that year, and she'd completely forgotten the whole incident until that very morning when our talk had brought it back . . .'

'And Ada Kelly, according to Sir William, is now Adelaide Bristow, the scourge of sleaze in high places, the bane of backsliding ministers . . .'

'It's not that I'm thinking of, Frank, but whether Annabel picked it up: the mention of that place where they'd both worked just before the War, Mrs Bristow asking what her mother's name was – and then, in the taxi, Sir William telling her that his old friend had been a ledger clerk in the same firm . . . Wait a minute: Annabel didn't know that part of it; she wasn't there when Mrs Angus told me the name of Ada Kelly . . .'

Franklyn was working it out. 'But at that dinner party she'd heard enough. So, what would she do? She would go straight down to Bute to see her mother and find out more . . .'

'So we know why she went to Bute.'

'And we know she got there because she was seen on that bus. But what she found there, we don't know.' Franklyn was grim. 'And did she ever leave?'

'I don't think I can handle this,' said Dinah. 'Should we go on?'

'I don't think we have any other option. Have you got that number of Sandy Duncan's?'

Dinah gave it to him, her thoughts miles away. I don't want to know any more, she told herself; I don't think I can bear it . . . That walk down the glen in summer years ago, a name mentioned, a name remembered . . . Oh, why did it have to be me?

Franklyn had got through to Sandy Duncan, but the voice he heard him use was one he hardly recognized. 'That you, Duncan? Franklyn Davey here. I'm coming right over. No, I don't give a damn what you're doing or who's with you; I want you face to face with me. Understand? I've not got all night, I've a train to catch. No, Dinah won't be with me; this has to be just you and me – and no more lies, Duncan, no more lies, or I'll see that it all gets into the press . . . Yes, that's what I said . . . I'll be with you within half an hour . . .'

He called room service, and ordered a taxi to be at the door as soon as possible. Only then did he turn to Dinah. This, to her, was a new aspect of Franklyn: coldly incisive, sure of his ground, and unmistakably angry. He shook his head. 'No, Dinah, this is strictly between Duncan and me; he's run rings round us long enough. I'll take my bag with me, as I've no idea how long this'll take. Settle up here, my love, and meet me at Central Station in time for our train.'

He closed her still-protesting lips with a kiss, then collected up his belongings, shouldered the bag and left.

Dinah sat down on the silk coverlet of the bed and tried to pull together her bewildered thoughts. After a while she felt better; she too had plans.

Twenty-Two

H enry was back at the corner shop, buying his morning paper and hoping for a gossip.

'Still interested in the Eastleigh property, then?' Mr Smith greeted him like an old friend. Henry explained that an appointment had been made with the estate agent to inspect the house as soon as his wife came down from London. He rather liked the idea of a wife – at present visiting a sick relative – and wondered about her name. Something pretty but dated: Maureen, perhaps, or Violet . . .

'Of course, all Mrs Newman's stuff will have been cleared out; she had some nice things, antiques, you know . . .'

Ivy Smith popped up from behind the counter. Henry wondered if she lived down there. 'All her stuff went to the saleroom. Got good prices at the auction, I'm told . . . Not clothes, of course; neighbours say they went to charity, but not in Southend. Well, it wouldn't be proper, would it? I wonder what happened to all her dog leads?'

'Why?' asked Henry, bemused. 'Did she have a lot of them?'

'Quite a collection, she had. Always buying them. D'you remember her showing us that last one, John?' Ivy turned back to Henry. 'Not long before the accident she'd got a new one. Very posh: blue suede with gold studs. She brought the dog in just to show me. Real good leather, it was; she said she'd had it made special.' Mrs Smith sniffed. 'That poodle of hers was spoiled, that's what I say . . . But ladies on their own, like she was – they get fond of their dogs, don't they? Talk to them when they get lonesome . . . Not that Mrs Newman was like that; much too brisk and businesslike, wasn't she, John?'

But John kept his head well down as he arranged the

daily papers along the shop shelves, and only muttered that Mrs Newman had been a good customer and was missed. Addressing the top of his head, Ivy Smith remarked that many gentlemen in the town would have said that, leaving Henry in two minds as to whether the words spoken were as innocent as they had sounded.

Henry took up his paper and said, 'Good-day.'

After morning coffee and a bracing walk along the promenade he walked into the police station and enquired if he might have a word with Constable Carey. Fortunately the young man was writing up reports in the back office and looked pleased at the break. He drew Henry along to the far corner of the front desk, just out of earshot of the duty sergeant.

'Sorry to bother you again,' said Henry, 'but I wonder if you know what happened to the dog lead after Mrs Newman's accident?'

'Funny you should ask. I forgot to tell you, but it was in my notes – the notes that got ignored. There weren't any sign of a lead. I persisted in looking because the neighbours that knew her said she changed dog leads to match her own clothes! Seems she had them specially made – well, she'd know where to get leather goods, the line she was in . . .' Nudge nudge, wink wink . . . Henry found PC Carey's smirk distasteful but managed to get into smile mode just to show that they were both men of the world.

'I understand the little dog was running loose when Mrs Newman was found. Could it have pulled its lead out of her hand?'

'No way. I think whoever got out of that van, he let the dog off the lead to stop it yelping and drawing attention. Then he scarpered.'

'Surely he'd have thrown the lead away – perhaps over the railings into the sea?'

Carey looked at him with pity. 'It's obvious you don't know the place, Mr Pocket. Tide's way out, see? There's only mud, though they try to bring in sand to make it look better. And those sands, they were well and truly searched that night – though what clues they hoped to find down there beats me.

Just to make the police look good, a line of men searching the foreshore – that got on the late news . . .'

'Any luck with that local chap with the white van?'

'Mason? Nah. Seems he's moved away, gone back to a previous employer, firm of builders up your way – Newtown, isn't it? I spoke to the wife; she said they're selling up – not enough work round here. It's more likely he made himself unpopular in the trade – got a reputation for shoddy work . . .'

Henry could well believe it, but the shoddy work that Mason had done for Mr Prentiss might well have been preordained. That was something to be thrashed out with Mr Kemp when Henry made his own unofficial report on what this nice town of Southend-on-Sea had thrown his way in the matter of Sieglinde Neumann. It was with real sadness that he turned at last from the spot on the promenade between the two flowerbeds where she had stepped into the road, and realized that, from the streets of Scarborough and the cemetery beside the Weser to the house here with its smiling windows open to the wintry sun, he had always had that hope in his heart that one day he would meet her. Now he was sure that could never be.

'How can you be certain it's the same lady, Henry?' He knew Lennox Kemp was paid to be sceptical, so he had to marshal the facts into proper order, and try to answer the question without recourse to mere speculation.

'I took the liberty, Mr Kemp, of writing to Mrs Farley in Scarborough to ask if there was a photograph of the house-keeper among her mother-in-law's possessions. I did not wish to cause dissension in that household by approaching George Farley – he had made his contribution by way of the postcard – in view of what I had discovered since of Sieglinde's later proclivities. Mrs Farley sent me a picture taken one summer in the garden of the elder Mrs Farley with her housekeeper. It's only a snapshot, but clear. Police Constable Carey was good enough to obtain for me a copy of the photograph from the file on Mrs Linda Newman.'

Henry removed the two pictures from his envelope, and

placed them on the desk facing Kemp, who picked them up and studied them.

'I agree with you, Henry. There's no doubt it's the same face – a few years older, but age seems to have been kind to Sieglinde Neumann . . .'

'And there is the postcard sent to George Farley to say she had settled down in Southend. A comparison of prices in the selling and buying of property shows that she received a high price for the Scarborough house because it had been a large family home, while her next seaside residence was acquired surprisingly cheaply from the original builders, who had been renting it out . . .'

'This, of course, is where it gets interesting,' said Kemp. 'I'm presuming you saw the price from the Land Registry copy entries and I'll not ask how you managed it . . .'

'I read documents upside down,' said Henry, who was proud of the accomplishment. 'Mr Wycroft had the Land Certificate on his desk.'

'Hm . . . And the builders were M. W. Prentiss & Co., the same firm as Mervyn says he was so busy trying to revive that he hardly noticed his wife had gone. I think we can take it for granted that he knew all about the site in Southend . . .'

'And when she wanted a house there, he handed one over – discreetly, of course.' Henry's eyes met Kemp's as they came to the same conclusion.

Kemp was the first to speak. 'He always knew where she was . . .'

'But he sent me on a fool's errand into Germany . . .'

'Where you were supposed to find that she had died there over ten years ago, for which happy conclusion he has paid my fee.'

Henry Pocket actually smiled. 'Well, I'm glad you got your money, Mr Kemp, because we've not finished with this case, have we?'

'We most certainly have not.' Kemp sighed. 'In this instance I did not particularly like my client, so I kept scrupulously to the rules. But in the light of what you and I know, Henry, that death in Southend seems to have been suspiciously timely . . .'

'In my work there are no rules,' said Henry, piously, 'and I have not met your client. But I do not like what I have found about the death of his wife. You say it was timely. Did he have a reason to want widowhood thrust upon him?'

'It would have been tidier had she died in 1989 when the Wall fell, for then there would be no further enquiry because – what's the phrase: "it was a time of great confusion"? But yes, he does wish to be a widower.'

'His wish has been fulfilled twice,' said Henry, sarcastically. 'I just wonder if he had a hand in bringing it about . . .'

'Time we got down to business, Henry,' said Kemp, briskly. 'Perhaps it's fortunate that his man Mason has returned to Newtown. I'll see if I can get the local force to have a look at that van . . .'

'Which will have been all cleaned up and repainted by now.' Henry was disposed towards pessimism.

'Not if it was already inspected by the Southend people, and they found nothing. You say they weren't trying very hard, but Mason may think now that he's got away with it. In any case, I'm after bigger fish than Mason.'

'Someone set him up in that builders' yard down in Southend – a lot of money, those in the trade said, for someone who wasn't much good at the job . . . Someone's been using people, Mr Kemp, just like I was used.' The old disgruntlement showed in Henry's voice. 'I was being led by the nose right from the start. Didn't I say so? Go here, go there, follow the yellow brick road . . . Only when I showed some initiative, Mr Kemp, did I get on the proper trail, and it was never intended I should.'

'You're quite right, Henry. But you weren't alone. I was also misled.' Kemp was notoriously slow to anger, but the more he thought about the various ploys of Mervyn Prentiss, the angrier he became. He must shoo Henry out of the office before his feelings became apparent.

'You must let me have your final account, Henry, and leave nothing out. In the meantime I shall make my own enquiries and you must lie low for a while. Take a little holiday; you deserve it.'

Henry took the complete folder simply marked with the initials 'SN' – he still liked to think of her as Sieglinde

Neumann – from his case, leaving it empty save for the inevitable Granny Smith and packet of sandwiches. He handed the folder over to Kemp, and forbore saying: 'This is Your Life'. Henry thought up jokes sometimes but rarely spoke of them.

'A holiday?' he said. 'I don't think I'll take it in a seaside resort.' But there was always Maureen Miles up in Yorkshire . . .

Twenty-Three

The morning after Henry Pocket's last visit – and he was going to miss the little grey man – Lennox Kemp was greeted by another piece of unfinished business: young Davey wondered if he could spare some time.

'It'll have to be the lunch hour,' Kemp told him; 'I'm up to my eyes in real paying customers till then.' He was only joking, but realized from Franklyn's indrawn breath that the point had been taken. Kemp softened his tone. 'Get some sandwiches for us, Frank, and we'll use my office. I gather you've some serious news?'

'Yes, sir . . .' It was rare for any of his staff to show that kind of respect; young Franklyn was very much on his high horse this morning.

But it had been difficult for him to remain so when burdened by a tray of coffee, sandwiches and the inevitable folder, which he had spent his time on the train carefully composing.

With most of the story told, and half the meal eaten, he sat back exhausted. Because of the work he'd had to do before arriving at Euston he'd not slept. Kemp looked at the dark circles below Franklyn's eyes and the lines that were new to the youthful features, and thought, This young man has the concentrated energy when it's needed, and the intellectual power to fuel it; he'll go far in the profession . . .

All he said, through, was: 'How did you break Sandy Duncan down?'

'It wasn't difficult when I told him what we knew about Ada Kelly and Adelaide Bristow.'

'He had no idea?'

'None at all. But now he's joined the band of those in the know: Dinah, Mrs Bristow, myself and now you. Sir William

183

knew that Adelaide had worked at Gerrard's, but of course he knew nothing of the thieving. The firm itself made no record of events; presumably, if one looked them up, they would show a ledger clerk called Ada Kelly worked there, but that would be the end of it. She left. Dinah did ask Mrs Effie Angus about other members of staff, but she said she knew the cashier had died in the war. The two directors of the firm, who simply handed Ada Kelly her cards and asked her to leave at once, were Quakers, and elderly even then. They took their action more in sorrow than in anger. They spoke to Effie Angus quietly and said they would be obliged to her if she said nothing of the matter. She was so impressed by their obvious sincerity that she promised to say nothing, and she kept that promise – already, Dinah told me, she regretted even having talked of it at breakfast; she wished she'd kept her mouth shut . . .'

'Did Sandy Duncan realize how deeply he was implicated in something very nasty?'

'It dawned on him by degrees . . .' Franklyn remembered the slow horror that had taken over the normally imperturbable persona of the television presenter as Franklyn had beaten him down. At first he had naturally denied being anywhere otherwise than at his flat that weekend.

'And my girlfriend will vouch for me,' he'd blustered.

'Is she here tonight?'

'No, I sent her out for a Chinese – and not to bring it home . . .' He'd smirked at Franklyn's incomprehension. 'She's Chinese, you fool, and she'll say anything I tell her to.'

'I don't see Mrs Bristow accepting a false alibi from a Glaswegian lily-girl.'

It was the mention of Adelaide's name that had started the rot . . .

'What's all this about Mrs Bristow? You said on the phone—'

'That her secret was out. It came unstuck at her dinner party on the Friday night, and by Saturday she began to take drastic steps. Phoning you was only the first.'

Franklyn had played it cautiously with Sandy Duncan,

letting the truth come out in dribs and drabs so that it could be gauged how much Sandy knew, or didn't know.

'In the end,' he now confessed to Kemp, 'I had to tell him, and I'll swear he hadn't an inkling. Mrs Bristow had been clever; she could use the enormous power she had over Sandy to make him do whatever she wanted, and ask no questions. To get the promotion he wanted, the boost to his career he was desperate for, he fell in with her plan like the idiot he is. Under all the smart talk Sandy Duncan's shallow as a serving spoon.' It gave Franklyn great pleasure to come out with the phrase – made up for a trace of jealousy that still rankled after Dinah's afternoon frolic in the London hotel . . .

When Franklyn had spelled out the connection between Annabel's mother and the owner of ClydeSight, Sandy had collapsed. He had drunk two whiskies straight off, and fallen on to his sofa, white-faced. 'And this is true?' He'd muttered. 'This is what happened?'

'He wasn't putting on an act, Mr Kemp; all he was doing now was saving his own neck. So he came out with the whole story of that weekend, right from the early call he'd had to say he would not be going on the New York trip, asking him to be in the office to brief Annabel and see that she had the correct papers. That was straightforward enough, but what Mrs Bristow hadn't reckoned on was Sandy's anger, his resentment at being passed over – that was how he saw it.'

Sandy's fury had boiled over when Annabel had come into the office and treated his careful presentation of the New York project with casual indifference, as if her mind was elsewhere. That did it: he'd walked out on her, hoping that when she got to the States she'd make a fool of herself . . .

Then Mrs Bristow had phoned again in the afternoon when he was – as he'd already said – at home with his little Chinese friend. Now his employer was the one to be angry: Annabel wasn't in the office; why wasn't he with her? He had been told to keep close to her until she left for her plane on Sunday. Where was she? Of course, Sandy said he didn't have a clue, and felt like telling the old bat that he wasn't Annabel's keeper, as he'd put it to Franklyn. Then Mrs Bristow had calmed down, and told him the reason she was sending Annabel to New

York instead of him was that she had a special job lined up for him.

'She must have made it all very plausible and tempting,' Franklyn told Kemp, 'because he left immediately for a meeting with her in the deserted lounge of a Glasgow hotel, where she had often met members of her staff who were in line for promotion; and it was there she told him what he was to do.'

Mrs Bristow knew a lot about Sandy Duncan – that he was temporarily strapped for cash, that he'd taken delivery of a new sports car on the strength of the promotion he hoped would follow a successful American trip. He hadn't yet shown it off to anybody at ClydeSight and, now he wasn't up for the States meeting, he was glad he hadn't, as he might not be able to pay for it. There it sat outside his flat. Would he drive his boss to Wemyss Bay to catch the Rothesay ferry? Of course he would.

She had told him she had something personal for Annabel Angus to take to friends in New York and she had forgotten to give it to her on Friday. She had guessed that Annabel had gone to see her mother in Bute – Sandy had admitted to Franklyn he'd no idea why she should think that – in fact had argued with Addy on this very point. Well, in that case, Addy had said, I'll just leave them with Mrs Angus; it's a family matter . . . And that had been all she would say about her reason for going to Bute. But the manner of it – that had been the sticking place (her very words, according to Sandy).

In addition to telling him quite bluntly that she would not only be paying for their small journey to Bute but also the full cost of his new red sports car, she had called for complete secrecy. He was to tell nobody – not then, nor afterwards – where they were going, nor anything else about her reasons or the fact that she was looking for Annabel.

'That, I knew for sure,' Sandy had told Franklyn, 'was the whole reason for Addy's masquerade: She wanted to find out just where Annabel had gone since she'd left the office before midday on Saturday. But,' he finished, wearily, 'I wasn't to reason why; I wasn't even to think . . .'

'Now,' said Kemp, 'go slowly once again over what Sandy

Duncan and Mrs Bristow got up to that Saturday evening.' He began to take notes.

They had driven to Wemyss Bay and caught the seven o'clock ferry to Rothesay. When they had disembarked on the quay, Sandy had asked if they knew where they were going, and Mrs Bristow had told him she had never been to this cottage called Glenhead before but had had a description of it from Annabel; and, of course, she herself had visited Bute at the time of the showing of 'The Last Resort'. That, she said, was the reason for the present secrecy; the film documentary had been so unpopular on the island, she did not want to be recognized.

'In fact,' Franklyn said, 'Sandy said she was got up like a Scottish Widows advert, swathed in a black cape, her head and face covered in silk scarves. And she kept well down in the car while he drove out of the town.'

'Now we've got two women arriving incognito at Glenhead,' said Kemp, 'but will we ever find out what happened next?'

Sandy had been told to pull up at the top of the track where there was a mailbox in the hedge saying 'Glenhead Cottage' but he was not to wait. He was instructed to take the car for a drive, and return in an hour's time – that would make it between nine thirty and ten o'clock. Mrs Bristow indicated that her business would have been concluded by then. She assured him she was perfectly capable of walking what looked like a rough road down to the cottage, and he didn't doubt it. She had been a well-known hill-walker in her time.

Sandy had taken his fine car down to the sea and raced it along sands far from village or hamlet – just marram grass on the edge of wrack-strewn shore. He had let the hood down – his companion had insisted on keeping it up – and put the vehicle through its paces, to his entire satisfaction.

'To my way of thinking,' Franklyn observed at this point, 'Sandy was completely taken over by his car, the joy of it, the possession of it which – thanks to Mrs Bristow – he was now certain of.'

The long Scottish twilight had still lingered in the sky when he'd come back up the road and seen the figure of Adelaide waiting for him in the shadow of the hedge. He'd said she was pale and rather shaky on her feet, the effect of coming up the track in the half-dark, she'd said, and once in the car she'd been silent for a while. 'Back to the town?' he'd asked. 'It'll be too late for a ferry to the mainland . . .'

'I can't stay here,' she'd said; 'I'd only be recognized . . .'

'Hold on a minute . . .' Kemp interrupted Franklyn's story. 'What's your opinion about this hostility on the island? Was it really serious?'

Franklyn thought about it. 'Annabel made a drama out of it when talking to Dinah, but that was just in character. Sandy Duncan said it was all crap – taking the professional line that there's no such thing as bad publicity – because the ratings went up for ClydeSight after the newspapers slated the documentary – so much so, in fact, that there had to be a second showing . . . I tend to agree with him.'

'So, people were simply using it as a means of camouflage.'

'Right. Sandy says that Adelaide Bristow didn't mind showing up at the funeral of Mrs Angus in a blaze of publicity, so why should she have bothered to hide herself that weekend before?'

'Good question. Sounds like Sandy's only an idiot when it suits him. Anyway, did they manage to leave the island that night?'

'They did. It was a Saturday and there was a late ferry. He drove her back to Bearsden from Wemyss Bay with, according to him, hardly a word out of her. She was cold, she said, she was tired; she practically went to sleep on the journey back.'

'Did she say whether she'd found Annabel at the cottage?'

'She told him, no . . . Whatever it was, she'd left it with Mrs Angus. Sandy says by then he'd realized it was all cock and bull, but who was he to argue with the queen bee who was paying for it all?'

'What was the main bribe?' Kemp was seriously interested in what a young man would be looking for as a further step up the media ladder at that point in his career.

'The coming programme in the New Year – the profile of that important Scottish personality, Mrs Adelaide Bristow – would be entrusted to him as producer and presenter: the very project that, according to Peter Mallen, had been promised to Annabel Angus.'

'Hm . . . Worth lying your socks off for. And, of course, the price of a sports car. Money does make the world go round . . .'

'It's certainly the key that winds up the media. I almost feel sorry for the likes of Sandy. Without Mrs Bristow the whole project is dead in the water. In fact, if she goes down, so does the whole of ClydeSight.'

'What does Dinah think of all this?'

Franklyn looked uneasy. He hadn't told Kemp that Dinah had not come back with him; she had not been on the platform when he'd gone for that train at Glasgow Central; he'd had no option – he had to take it. Work awaited him at the office; he was not a freelance; he still owed a duty to his employer. And that employer was watching him with some sympathy.

'All right, Frank, so Dinah couldn't tear herself away?'

Franklyn nodded, grimly. 'I bet she's back on Bute,' he said.

'You think she'd go there on her own?'

'I'm sure of it.' Franklyn sighed. 'Once Dinah's got an idea in her head she'll not let it go . . .'

'Could be dangerous . . .'

'Surely no one would . . .'

'Your Dinah is now in possession of information that some-one may have already killed for. If they've killed once, they'll do it again. Have you tried getting her on her mobile?'

'It's switched off. Or the battery's run down. Do you really think . . . ?' By now Franklyn was becoming agitated. He regretted not having stayed in Scotland once he'd guessed where Dinah would make for. 'She would go to the cottage,' he said, miserably.

'Right. I'm going to ring George McCready. At least he's the man on the spot. We've no right to contact the police – they'd be next to uselesss. And we've no evidence to apprehend anyone. Nor do we know for certain that Dinah is in danger. All I can do, Frank, is tell George that Dinah might be on the island, might be at the cottage, and ask him to keep his eyes open.'

Unfortunately there was no reply from the McCreadys'

bungalow – only the answering machine to say they were both away for the day, and to please leave a message . . .

With that, Lennox Kemp would have to be content for the time being. As for Franklyn, his day's work was tormented by thoughts of Bute, so far away and suddenly so sinister.

Twenty-Four

Dinah would have loved to be on Bute by now – two o'clock in the afternoon – but the weather, about which Franklyn had been so philosophical, was against her. A front swept in from the Atlantic with the kind of winds that tore off chimmney pots, and the ferry company decided not to risk their squat little packets in seas that were screwing up the Clyde estuary as if it was tissue paper.

So she must wait, reading old magazines in the lounge of the bed-and-breakfast establishment where she'd booked in the night before, a mile or so up the road from the quay at Wemyss Bay. Only in the late afternoon, when the winds had subsided and the tide looked sullen but navigable, did the ferry put in an appearance, and Dinah went aboard alongside the other pedestrian passengers from the bus she'd picked up in Gourock. The experience reminded her of backpacking; but never in Nepal, Thailand, Indonesia or Australia had she met such a dismal, damp and dispirited lot as disembarked on Rothesay pier in a mist thick as porridge.

In sheer desperation she went to the nearest hotel, where the bar was closed, and the tea room was closed, and a surly porter gave her the key to a room on the first floor that was only marginally warmer than the street outside. Dinah thought herself intrepid, but the full weight and significance of the Scottish weather was stripping her pride to shreds. She boiled water and used a tea bag. The milk wasn't even fresh; it was that ultra-violeted stuff – what on earth were all those cows in the fields for?

Looking out of the window, beyond the grey veils of netting, she saw the gold letters of 'Robert McFie & Son' spread across the wide windows of the building opposite, and felt immensely cheered. At least she had a friend in this barren land . . . But she need not call on him yet. Her mission might involve him at some time in the future, but for the present she was on her own.

She asked, and was told that, aye, there'd be a bus from the square for where she wanted to go, but she'd just missed the last one and it'd be an hour before the next. Par for the course, thought Dinah; the Fates are against you.

She actually found a fish bar that was not closed for the day, shut down for redecoration, or suspended for bankruptcy proceedings, and was fed some rather good haddock and chips before taking her place in the short queue waiting in the bus shelter. By now it was getting seriously dark, sky and water over the bay merging into one black-and-white picture grainy enough to please the most ardent photographer. The bus lumbered up, and everyone got on and shook out raincoat, anorak, waterproof hat and tousled umbrella before settling down in small huddles of uncompromising silence.

Dinah had never travelled this shore road by bus before. On that idyllic holiday they had spun along merrily in Annabel's zippy little car, stopping only to photograph seals sunning on the black rocks – the resulting prints always a disappointment: glistening lumps of speckled blubber but no hint of the lamplike eyes or whiskered astonishment. Dinah had tried to get closer, but they were off, slipping from the stones with barely a ripple.

Now, of course, she could see nothing, the windows misted up with the breath of her fellow passengers, and anyway, it was dark. Difficult even to tell where they were or hazard a guess at the speed of the bus, which simply jolted along from stop to stop – fortunately there were few – sometimes gathering momentum downhill, slowing and grinding its gears up the small rises. As folks got off, there were muttered goodnights from those left on board as the descending passengers disappeared in the gloom, it might be to cosy hearth and home, it might be into Hell and everlasting night . . . Dinah realized that she was herself becoming a victim of the pathetic fallacy, her mood swung low by the depressing weather, the handfuls of vicious rain being thrown at the driver's windscreen till his wipers screeched in protest, the only other people within her reach being muffled up in silence, an alien tribe . . .

She recognized a darkening – if it was possible – outside as they passed between the two woods just up the road from the cottage, and she went forward. She had asked for Glenhead, and the driver had not forgotten. He even wished her a gruff goodnight as her feet found the solid road. No one else on the bus took the least bit of notice.

She stood for a moment within the shelter of the hedge and looked down towards the sea. The astonishing thing was that over the sands and the edge of the water there was a line of light, a break in the clouds above, a glimpse, no more, of the riding moon. On this, the south side of the island, the wind was less strong, coming in short guests as if tired of its journey, and the rain had stopped.

It was easier going down the drive than Dinah had expected; it was winter and the hedges were bare and let in the light from the sky so that she could see and avoid the ruts and the rough patches where the tufts of grass were taking over. It had been Mrs Angus's pride that the road to the cottage had originally been a metalled one – made to the orders of the most enlightened of the earlier lairds who owned the land – so that it could never become a mere mud track; and it was the ring of road metal under her heels that Dinah could hear now – that and nothing else. A whisper of wind, a rustle of twigs, the rest was silence . . .

The creaking of the field gate split that silence. Mrs Angus had averred she could tell when folks were coming by the sound of the opening gate, and tonight Dinah could well believe her. As she turned to push the stave back in place, she was conscious of an after-image: something had caught her eye even as she turned away. Now she stopped and stared across at the cottage, surprisingly white as the moonlight caught it, with its background of dark hedge and distant wood; but it hadn't been moonlight – not that pearly radiance, and not from outside. The light she had seen, but that had briefly and instantly gone, was inside the cottage, it had shown itself at the window . . .

A neighbour? Mrs Cluthie, perhaps? Prospective purchasers

already biting? Dinah told herself she could always count herself as one of these, if challenged. Having come this far, she must keep to the path she had chosen.

The night had sharpened her eyes. As she came nearer to the croft, she could swear there was still a light in the window, but now it appeared to flicker. She was suddenly reminded of the end of *The New Road* – Drimdorran, the murderer, desperately lighting candles as retribution stalked him. Certainty struck her – though in ordinary circumstances Dinah would have given it no more credence than she would the pathetic fallacy – that this was where Annabel had met her death . . .

She skirted the coal shed and knocked loudly on the back door before trying the sneb and finding it giving way to her hand. The outer room was dark, with only a pale square showing the window, but Dinah knew her way across to the kitchen door. She thrust it open and stood back, staring into lamplight. The oil lamp was on the dresser, but another was being held aloft by Adelaide Bristow. The face of a ghoul, thought Dinah, seeing the great black pits of eyes, the darkening hollow of the throat, the red gash of the mouth. But she knew it was only the exaggerating effect of lamplight.

'What? No electricity?' she asked. She heard Mrs Bristow give a sigh, which could have been of immense relief. The lamp was put down on the table by the window, and Mrs Bristow seated herself in the chair where she must have been when she'd heard the noise of the gate. 'Thank goodness, my dear, that you are not a burglar. I really had no fear of such, but it is late at night for visitors to be calling. May I ask why you are here? It's Dinah Something, isn't it? You were that friend of Annabel's who called at the office . . .'

'Yes, I am Annabel's friend.'

'Do sit down, my dear. At least we have warmth, although our canny Dougal McFie has turned off the power.' She gestured to burning logs in the fireplace, and indeed the kitchen did seem almost cosy.

Having sat down on the other chair by the fireside, Dinah was not surprised to be offered, a few minutes later, a cup of tea. Go with the tide, she told herself, but collect and marshal your thoughts, keep your mind in discipline, remember facts and cut out all random surmise. As she watched her elderly companion warm the teapot with water from the kettle already boiling on a swing above the fire, Dinah was thinking: What use was all that academic knowledge I learned in college about the way the mind works if I cannot, in this dire situation, make some use of it?

I'm not a policeman, she thought; I'm not even a lawyer. Far less am I an undercover agent with a pistol in my jeans. Yet somehow I have to outwit this woman, and do it without her being aware of it. To start with, I have the advantage of superior knowledge: I know all about Mrs Adelaide Bristow; she knows nothing of me. Keep it that way for as long as possible.

'Fortunately, I brought milk with me,' Adelaide was saying, 'when I came to the cottage today, and of course I had the keys. Dougal McFie was only too anxious for me to have them . . .' She paused to let the message sink in, as she brought two cups and saucers over to the table.

'Because you're buying the croft?'

'Yes. Funny, you should call it that; most people say "the cottage".'

You're buying it because it's here Annabel Angus is buried, and once the place is yours no one will suspect that her bones don't lie in that other graveyard, that other place of lamentation. Sudden anger made Dinah burst out: 'It was a terrible thing, to use that . . . that atrocity . . .' Fortunately the hissing of the kettle as the water from it streamed into the teapot must have covered her words.

'What was that? There, the tea's made . . .' Mrs Bristow came back to her chair. 'Let it rest a little. Now, did you say why you came here tonight, Dinah?'

'Much the same reason as you, Mrs Bristow.' Dinah gave a nervous laugh. 'I thought I might like to buy the croft, and a sudden impulse made me come and have another look at it.'

'So late at night, and in such weather, too . . .' Adelaide seemed to speak to herself. 'Ah, let me pour you a cup.'

'It was a romantic notion.' Dinah seemed to be floundering. 'Silly, really. I was reading this book – it belonged to Mrs Angus . . . I was quite carried away. The whole idea of

Scotland, the Highlands and the misty islands, the history of the clans, the glens and the desperate wars . . . It was called *The New Road* . . . Stupid of me, really, but I must admit it began to influence me. I thought of just buying a corner of it . . .'

'It was meant as a counter-blast to all those romantic notions of the likes of Walter Scott,' said Mrs Bristow severely, as she poured out the tea, 'and a history lesson to those who still thought Bonnie Prince Charlie had been good for the Highlands. I've no sugar, I'm afraid, but I have these . . .' She went over to the couch, where her capacious handbag was lying, and rummaged in it. Now is the moment she'll produce the small automatic, thought Dinah, turning in her chair to watch her; but it was only a green-topped tube.

'Yes,' said Dinah, 'I'll have a Sweetex.' It rolled into her hand straight from the pack, so it could hardly be poison or a sleeping pill.

The tea was good, strong and stimulating. 'I needed that,' she told her companion. 'The journey in the rain was terrible. Have you a car?'

'I gave up driving some years ago, Dinah. I took a taxi from the town, but of course I've made preparations to stay the night.' She looked across at Dinah, and her features in the firelight were now soft and gentle, the grey hair gathered into a bun low on her neck. 'You are very welcome to stay,' she said, without inflection, 'now that you are here.'

Dinah shook her head. 'I've booked into a hotel in Rothesay, so I don't need to trouble you, Mrs Bristow. If that phone is working, I could call a taxi.'

'Another of Dougal's wee economies, I'm afraid. The phone is not working.'

Dinah blessed the mobile lying in her shoulder bag and hoped the battery was keeping up. But before that . . .

Putting her cup down carefully on its saucer, she said: 'Sandy Duncan says that Annabel came here that Saturday . . .'

Mrs Bristow rose and drew the kettle back from the glowing logs. 'What Saturday was that, dear?'

'The eighth of September. The weekend before she died.'

'You know Mr Duncan?'

'Yes.'

Mrs Bristow leant forward and put a hand on Dinah's knee. Dinah tried not to flinch. 'Mr Duncan is a very resentful man,' Adelaide said quietly, as if he was in the room and she didn't want him to hear. 'Annabel's death has taken him in strange fashion. He is, I am afraid, somewhat unstable, so I shouldn't take much notice of anything he says.' More sharply, she went on: 'When did he tell you this tale?'

Dinah shrugged. 'Oh, just lately,' she said. 'And I don't believe Sandy Duncan's simply upset: I think he's frightened.'

Mrs Bristow was sipping her tea in affected, ladylike manner, but Dinah could feel her tenseness. Yet the voice was soothing, meant to be comforting. 'My dear child, you too have been upset by your friend's death. You too have been behaving irrationally. All these questions, all this speculation about Annabel's last few days – don't you see it has become an unhealthy obsession for you? I am older than you and more experienced, and I have seen cases like yours: friends who cannot let go, relatives who cannot mourn properly without trying to analyse their loved ones' last moments . . .'

Dinah kept seeing in her own mind the pages and pages of text she'd had to swot up before the psychology papers in exams. If she held fast to these, she could disregard, indeed laugh off, the pseudo psycho-babble being used on her, as the warmth of the fire and the solace of the tea combined to make her drift into happy slumber. Perhaps that had not been a simple Sweetex tablet after all. She shook herself, and concentrated on what she, Dinah, knew about the other woman, because that was her only weapon, and she must stay alert for the moment when she would reveal it.

'I'll have another cup, please,' she said, handing over her empty one, 'but no sweetener this time. Perhaps I am a bit obsessed, Mrs Bristow. It was reading that book that did it. The mystery of what really happened to the hero's father, Paul Macmaster . . . He was a fugitive after Glenshiel – did he drown in some loch on Lovat's land, or did he die in France? He was supposed to have gone abroad – just like Annabel – and perished there in those times of great confusion; but he didn't, did he? He never left Scotland; he was stabbed in the back and his body buried in the glen. It was that story got me thinking . . . What if Annabel never got on that plane, was never at the Trade Centre that dreadful morning? Six months since, and no word from her . . .'

Adelaide had been sitting motionless, listening to the farrago of nonsense that Dinah was making up as she went along – not entirely making up, because she was aware of an undercurrent carrying the words, an undercurrent of belief that had built itself from all the facts she'd gathered in these last weeks. Now Adelaide Bristow stirred. She put down her cup and saucer on the table and rose to her feet. 'I think,' she said slowly, 'that you are in delirium, Dinah. Perhaps you caught a chill out there in the rain, and you have a fever. You must not attempt to return to Rothesay tonight. I will make up a bed for you; there are hot-water bottles and plenty of quilts, and I think I can find some aspirin . . .'

'I am not in the least ill, Mrs Bristow. You see, I know that you were here in this house on Saturday the eighth of September last year. You came because Annabel was here, but you also came to see Mrs Angus.'

Mrs Bristow was handing Dinah another cup of tea, her eyes large and luminous, staring straight down on her. Everything seemed to be happening in slow motion. I've seen this on television, thought Dinah, she's been putting something in the tea. Dinah got up, took her cup out into the scullery and rinsed it under the tap. She filled the cup with water and drank it off, then did it again. When she returned to the inner room, Mrs Bristow was sitting relaxed on the sofa.

'Do you feel better, my child?' Dinah was getting sick of being addressed as either an infant or a fledgling chick. 'I'm all right,' she said, brusquely, 'but I shan't rest till I find out what happened to Annabel.'

'I don't know how I can help you, Dinah. Have you been sharing these fantasies of yours with other people?'

'Oh yes, several people, in fact, who can confirm they are not fantasies.'

'I suppose you can call them up on this.' Adelaide had a silk shawl round her shoulders; she moved it to reveal her hand holding Dinah's mobile. 'Well, I don't think you'll be needing it tonight.' The woman put the phone down on the carpet, took off her smart high-heeled boot and brought it smashing down on the instrument. 'There,' she said, 'that's sorted out.'

Dinah cursed herself for being a fool. When she had gone out to the scullery with the tea, she'd left her bag on the table. But at least she had succeeded in forcing the other to show her hand – and a strong, mailed fist it had turned out to be. Soft-spoken, doe-eyed, grey-haired and elderly Adelaide Bristow might be, but she was the enemy – and she had killed Annabel as easily as she had destroyed Dinah's phone.

Dinah sat down at the other end of the sofa. 'The battery was flat anyway,' she said. 'But my friends know where I am . . .'

'And what is a broken phone between friends? You simply dropped it, my dear.' Adelaide yawned. 'You have wearied me with your nonsense talk; I'm going to bed. You can have the sofa if you like.'

Did she really think she could get away with it? Dinah could either leave or sit the night out by the dying fire. Somehow she must again force the issue – the breaking of the mobile was merely a gesture and easily enough explained. As Mrs Bristow started to get up, Dinah took her arm, firmly but not roughly. 'Did Mrs Angus tell Annabel about knowing you when you both worked at Gerard's?'

'She didn't get the chance to.'

A perfectly straight question and a perfectly straight answer. Who needs psychology? Dinah pressed on.

'Because you took Annabel away? She'd been here hardly an hour, not even time to unpack . . . What did you tell her? Something urgent back at the office, and you had a car waiting at the road end?'

The one admission had been enough, however. Adelaide Bristow had slumped down on the sofa beside Dinah, clutching her handbag in her lap. It was one of those made of some thick material – tapestry or chenille velvet, or even carpet – meant to hold a lady's embroidery, knitting or crochet work, and looking to be in complete harmony with its owner. She was fiddling with it now as if searching for a scrap of lace to sob into. Dinah knew better and was quick to knock the bag away, but not quite quick enough, for the small automatic was out and pointing at her, even as the bag, unheeded, slid to the floor.

Dinah sighed. 'I guessed you'd have one of those. But shooting me is going to take a lot of explaining . . .'

The hand holding the gun was steady, as were the great dark eyes. The sorrow in the voice seemed genuine. 'It is a pity you came, Dinah, and a pity you know so much. But shooting you would be foolish. I rather think an accident . . . It is dark outside and the ground is rough; you could easily fall. Get up, please . . .' Even in this situation Adelaide didn't forget the courtesies. Dinah sat still.

'I can put a hole in your foot that might go unnoticed. Please get up.'

Dinah moved slightly, but as she did so, there were noises outside – the loud barking of a dog, the high screech of a woman. 'Come back, ye wee bugger, come back here . . .' Then there was a wild scratching at the door, and the barks got louder.

'Stay exactly where you are and don't move' – Adelaide rose but kept the gun pointed at Dinah – 'while I deal with this unfortunate interruption. If you start anything, Dinah, I'll shoot the woman and she'll be on your conscience.'

They could hear Mrs Cluthie at the back door, and even Adelaide must have realized that the neighbour possibly had a key. Her presence of mind did not desert her as she opened the inner door and called: 'It's all right; I'll catch your dog for you . . .' as the Scottie tore in, barking his little head off.

This is becoming a farce, thought Dinah, as she heard Mrs Cluthie's well-remembered voice raised in apology. 'Ah don't know whit gets intae him, really I don't. One moment he's wi' me and then he's off across the field an' Ah'm left with the lead in my hand. Oh, Ah'm that sorry – I didnae mean to disturb you . . .' Dinah could see the woman peering in, trying to see who was in the living room, but the doorway was blocked by Mrs Bristow, somehow grown larger as she stood swathed in her voluminous garments like the angel of death. Even Chummie was cowed, stopped barking and allowed himself to be caught and put back on the lead.

'I'll say goodnight to you, then,' said Adelaide Bristow in a tone that allowed for no dissent as she followed the dog and his new mistress to the back door. But nothing could stem the tide of Mrs Cluthie's talk, when she'd the mind to let it all out and the breath left in her body.

'It's the well he makes for every time. Ah canna keep him away from it. He's through the wee hedge and sitting on top of it till I have tae drag him off. Back there at the end of the year I thought there wis a smell. Ah wis for telling Mr Dougal McFie, but I didnae want to interfere . . .'

'Quite right. I am the new owner of Glenhead, and I would be obliged if you would restrain the animal and not disturb your neighbours again. Goodnight, Mrs Cluthie.'

So she did know her name, thought Dinah, listening to this short exchange. Remembering names is something politicians are good at as well as thinking on their feet . . . Now what?

But even as she heard the back door being slammed shut and the bolt shot home – the old-fashioned one Mrs Angus had never needed to use – Dinah felt some satisfaction: she knew where Annabel's body would be found.

The well. It had served the inhabitants of the croft for generations with sweet water until Mr and Mrs Angus had modernized the house and put in piped water like everybody else; but Mr Angus would not allow the workmen to fill in the old well. 'You never know,' he'd said, 'when the public supply might be cut off.' This tale was much repeated by his widow, because she was afraid of the well: someone might fall in, she'd said, meaning Chummie. Mr Angus had planted a thick hedge round it, and had it securely covered with a heavy board. This had never been enough for his wife, who would still call out to people: 'Make sure the lid's on the well . . .'

Naturally, that familiar cry had become a subject for mirth from Annabel, and also a reason for investigation. She and Dinah had pushed aside the wooden cover and gazed down into the interior. Alas for Mr Angus's hopes of using the sweet water in case of emergency – he'd forgotten that, in laying pipes, the workmen had killed the spring. If there was water left, it was far, far below, and the old well had been deep . . .

201

One half of Dinah's mind was occupied by these memories while the other, on a more practical level, was wondering why she hadn't sprung up from her seat and tried tackling this elderly woman when her back had been turned. Until Mrs Cluthie was safely outside the door, she hadn't dared to move; Adelaide was right, if the neighbour was hurt, it would be Dinah's fault. And now it was too late, as the gun was once more in evidence, pointing at Dinah's head.

'I have to think out what to do with you, my dear.' Mrs Bristow took the chair by the fireside, where the logs had by now crumbled to ash.

'You could always shove me in the well with Annabel,' said Dinah, crudely. 'I'm sure there's room for one more body.'

'I'm afraid you don't understand. It was necessary. She would have spoiled my work, my duty to keep my people out of sin . . . Annabel Angus would have ruined all that. I could no longer have spoken with the voice of virtue.'

She's mad, thought Dinah; she's toppled over the brink . . . and I'm just the one to help her. She continued speaking with relentless precision:

'Annabel knew there was something and like the good researcher she was, she'd have got to the truth in the end – that you, who were supposed to be the scourge of the dishonest, were yourself a thief and a liar. She'd have done a fine profile of you on television, Adelaide Bristow, once the true story was out. Your reputation would have been in shreds, and quite right, too, in my opinion.'

The hand holding the automatic was close to Dinah and she was glad to see the tremor that ran along the arm; but the woman was aware of it also, and tightened her grip on the gun.

'I could not take the risk,' she said quietly, as if talking of some everyday occurrence. 'Not when Annabel had a hint of it. She would have questioned her mother another time. There would always have been another time . . . My chance was then, only then.'

'Was it when you were out of the door, the two of you? Annabel with her travel bag and her coat on . . . What happened?'

'Will you see that the lid's on the well?' It was sheer mimicry – the sound Dinah remembered as the voice of Annabel's mother. It was as if a ghost were calling . . .

'So I said to her, why not do what your mother says, Annabel? And she laughed . . . It's only a little way round the hedge, she said, and I followed her. There was a pile of logs . . . There is an impulse that comes . . .' Adelaide Bristow was speaking to herself more than to Dinah. 'And the impulse is the strength, the strength for good, the strength that is mine. And then I moved the cover from the well.'

Shock had Dinah by the throat, yet she had to stammer: 'Was she dead when you . . . you tipped her in?'

'I am not a cruel person. I hit her a second time and heard her skull crack. Yes, she was dead before she disappeared.' Something in what she had just said halted Adelaide. 'Dead before she disappeared,' she repeated. 'How strange that sounds now . . .'

Dinah was reliving the scene as coldly as she could; later her emotions would flood in. 'And Mrs Angus heard nothing?'

'Of course not. We had already said goodbye to her in the living room, told her not to come to the door because the evening had grown chilly. I talked to Annabel all the way up the rough drive, Dinah, I tried to explain to her why I had to do it: to save the name of integrity . . .' She was nodding to herself as if it was a tale told many times but that still needed talling again.

'No one else knew – only Euphemia Kerr – and she'd never have spoken if it hadn't been her own daughter doing the asking. I've been explaining it to Annabel ever since . . .'

Dinah nodded, as if in agreement. 'It was her spirit that was with you all the way up the rough road, Adelaide. But it went back down the glen when you got into the red car with Sandy Duncan and he drove you home.'

'Yes, that's the way it was. How clever of you to find out. And next day I attended a luncheon party in Edinburgh and made a speech . . .'

Dinah gazed at the woman in sheer astonishment and even admiration. It was true: Peter Mallen had checked the newspapers. Mrs Bristow had attended a function at Holyroodhouse

203

and made a blistering attack on any backsliders in the Scottish Parliament, on Sunday, 9th September.

It reminded Dinah suddenly of something else. Ignoring the steadily pointed gun, she raised her voice in anger. 'And you attended a service in St Giles' commemorating the Scots who died in the World Trade Center attack! How could you use other people's misery for your own ends? It was monstrous . . .'

The woman took no notice of Dinah's flare-up. She shook her head slowly from side to side. 'She would have died hereafter . . .' she said; 'don't you see? Annabel would have died in New York on September the eleventh . . .'

The twisted logic was awe-inspiring and took Dinah's breath away. The woman wasn't totally mad; was there nothing one could say to throw her off her course?

'No one else knew that you had worked at Gerrard's and that you stole money – only Effie Angus . . . And then she died.'

'Ah, that . . . That was the Lord's will. I had no hand in it.'

'But you came back the day after the attack in New York. You said you couldn't make anyone hear, but you could have got in, because you had the keys – Annabel's keys, which you would have taken from her purse before you threw the body down the well.'

'I came to tell Effie Angus that her daughter had died in New York the previous day. I came on that errand of mercy so that she wouldn't hear of it in a cruel manner.'

Dinah shook her head fiercely. 'No, you came to threaten the old lady.'

'You are wrong, my dear; I came to help her in the dreadful tragedy of her daughter's death, and to offer her whatever compensation my company could afford.' The tone of deep sincerity with which the words were spoken would have convinced anyone that the speaker herself believed them. 'But Mrs Angus was dead when I entered the bedroom; she had had a heart attack. Out of respect for her, I withdrew and informed the police in Rothesay.'

'But not before you'd taken a good look round the cottage and eliminated all trace that you'd been there, that day or any other. That's why the dog didn't bark all the time: he'd food and water in the scullery where his basket is. Mrs Cluthie said there was a mess by the door, but Chummie had been none the worse for being shut in.'

'I am not a cruel person,' Adelaide said again. 'There was nothing I could do for Mrs Angus.' She gave a great, deep sigh. 'It was the Lord's will, and only He knows if she ever heard of the New York tragedy. I hope she was spared it . . .'

'But Annabel didn't die in New York!' Dinah burst out. 'She died here at the back of the cottage, beside the woodpile.' She remembered the smell of pine resin which rose from the logs when the afternoon sun used to reach them that summer when she and Annabel had sunbathed in the little garden. In a sudden frenzy she brought her knee up and kicked out savagely at the level gun. But Adelaide held on to it, and fired. Her aim was deflected and the first bullet hit the ceiling as Dinah slid off the sofa and dived for the woman's legs. Now Adelaide had a firmer grip on the automatic and she brought it up sharply under Dinah's chin.

'Don't try anything like that again, Miss Prescott, or I'll be forced to kill you before I can arrange a more benevolent accident.'

Twenty-Five

It had been a busy afternoon at Gillorns, but Lennox Kemp found time to ring the Bute number every hour, without success – still the dull thud of the answering machine. At six o'clock young Davey had drifted in, hoping for news, but Kemp shook his head.

'I tried to reach Dougal McFie,' said Franklyn, 'but his office is closed. It's something to do with a trades holiday in Rothesay. Apparently all businesses shut down for it.'

'And the McCreadys take off for Glasgow. Don't worry, their answering machine says they're only away for the day, and that has to be limited when you're on an island.'

'It's not the tourist season, so the last ferry would be about now from Wemyss Bay,' said Franklyn, remembering the timetable. 'So we should hear something from McCready soon. Unfortunately, I've got that meeting with the tax people.'

'I'm staying on here anyway, so I'll take the call when it comes. John Upshire's coming in to see me about another case. Off you go and dazzle the commissioners with your expertise.'

Franklyn gave a wan smile as he left. Kemp had some sympathy for him: Dinah was off on a frolic of her own, and if she was in danger, what could they do at this distance? Kemp wondered if he should indeed get in touch with the police in Rothesay – but just what, exactly, could he tell them?

His thoughts were interrupted by his favourite local police officer, John Upshire, retired this very week and anxious for a talk. Kemp brought out a bottle of Scotch – a rare occurrence in this office – in celebration.

'Well, this makes a change,' he said, filling their glasses. 'Water?'

'I'll take it straight, thanks. One of the best things about retirement is that I can sit and talk to folk wherever I like, and I can come into this office without someone later bringing it up in court!'

'I thought that when you rang and suggested we meet in the Cabbage White. Unfortunately, I have to stay in the office – I'm expecting a call. Now you're retired, John, neither of us is bound by protocol; we needn't be looking over our shoulders when we meet. But I gather you did have something to tell me?'

John Upshire grinned. He was happy in his retirement, but there were loose ends he wanted tied up, and this was his opportunity.

'Just a word in your ear,' he said, taking an appreciative drink. 'The roof of the Council Chamber is about to fall in.'

'So soon? I thought it would take much longer. What's happened?'

'An employee of Prentiss, the builders, name of Mason, has been arrested and taken to Southend police station, where he has been charged with the murder of one of their residents.'

'They got evidence?'

'His wife has a Yorkshire terrier; Sam Mason gave her a rather posh dog lead. Specially made, it seems – the only one of its kind.'

'The idiot. He kept it! I always say you should never send a boy to do a man's job, and never use a fool for a mission. And there's more?'

Upshire nodded. 'Now we come to the serious part. Mason has made a full confession; says he was paid – not half enough, according to his statement. As you've probably gathered I've had a long confab with Tom Thackery. But it'll all be out in the open by tomorrow. They've pulled in Mervyn Prentiss for questioning. The talk is conspiracy to murder.'

Kemp was silent: the denouement had come more quickly than he had suspected. Ironically, it was Mervyn's meanness that had been his downfall; he had used cheap labour, just as he'd done in the building trade. Henry Pocket had been right about Mason: he was a bad workman and so proved the weakest link in the elaborate edifice erected by his boss.

John Upshire accepted another drink. 'A young police constable called Carey made a careful note about that dog lead, spoke to neighbours who described it – blue suede with gold studs. Then Thackery found who the makers were. I understand someone you sent had known the victim?'

'Not entirely. And I'm not the one who's retired, John.'

'Meaning you can't speak yet?'

It was an uncomfortable moment for Kemp; he was glad when the phone rang.

'George? Yes, I've been trying to get hold of you. Dinah's in Bute; she may try to get into the cottage. This may be a false alarm, but . . .'

George McCready muttered only a few words, and Kemp put the phone down.

'Trouble?' asked John Upshire.

'Too far away. You remember George McCready?'

'From the old days. He used to be in the Met before he took up with that detective agency. Well, if he's on the spot, you've nothing to worry about.'

When John Upshire had left, slightly miffed that the solicitor was not yet ready to share the part he had played in the Prentiss matter, Lennox Kemp paced the floor of his office – a tiresome habit and unproductive. He knew he must stay till there was further word from McCready, but the enforced inactivity didn't improve his temper. He could not get rid of the thought that he should have taken more seriously young Franklyn's anxiety for his girlfriend . . .

As an antidote, something to get his brain working on while he waited, at last he sat down at his desk, took out the papers from the Prentiss folder and began making a note of his version of the Sieglinde Neumann story.

When she had first left Mervyn, she had managed on the few thousand he'd given her, and she'd kept in touch by postcards; but the Scarborough venture had been her own: she had found a home and wages and become independent. For the first time, she showed up as a good person, competent and kindly to her aged employer, and she received a proper reward: the gift of a house and the respect of the Farleys. She had also discovered independence, and a certain talent in herself.

Mervyn Prentiss had not known of the Scarborough episode in his wife's life, but Kemp had no doubt that she had got in touch with him when she wished to settle in Southend – it was Essex, after all; she was back on his ground. And it seemed that he was pleased enough to see her; in fact he had encouraged her to buy one of his best houses in the town. Was it because she had let him in on the secret of her successful business? Kemp rather thought so. When Sieglinde had turned up some ten years ago, a handsome woman, confident in her ability to provide a service for gentlemen, he must have been tickled pink. She'd had no wish to resume her original marital status; she had found her own place in society, and she liked it.

Whether Mervyn had availed himself of his wife's services could only be guessed at, but some cosy arrangement would have been made, and the provision of wealthy clients might well have been part of it. How did that song go? 'There is a house in New Orleans . . .' Only in this case it would have been Leigh-on-Sea; and of course nobody in the circles where Mervyn moved would know the real identity of this little woman, who was both discreet and obliging – and who cooked the most delicious suppers.

All must have gone merrily until Mervyn had met Alicia Simon and been spurred to thoughts of marriage by the twin lures of money and prestige. He would have seen a quiet divorce as the answer – rather like the Simpson one in some out-of-the-way corner of England where nobody would notice. But what of Sieglinde? She liked the life they were leading; she liked having him around if she wanted him, and she certainly didn't want him marrying anyone else. Sometimes the simplest people could be the most obdurate. Sieglinde must have dug in her little heels. He could have tried to divorce her on the grounds of their separation for years; but what would a judge have made of the peculiar arrangement the husband and wife had enjoyed in the house at Southend?

Mervyn Prentiss had not dared antagonize Sieglinde, for she might well have made trouble for him; she might even have had persons on her books to counsel and advise her on aspects of matrimonial law. A quick divorce was not on the cards, so Mervyn must think up another way to rid himself of a now-unwanted spouse, and a right mish-mash his devious mind had contrived. To satisfy his new bride's papa, his former wife must have died respectably, preferably before the advent of gentlemen's relish to Southend, and at a period when dates and certificates need not be a prerequisite.

Well, there was always that 'time of great confusion' when the Wall came down and East and West Berlin were united in one joyous free-for-all, and when no questions need be asked if one long-exiled heart should have burst under the strain. The tale of the return of the native contained just sufficient romance to assuage any doubts about the nuts and bolts holding it together.

Kemp had no doubt that the Rinteln address found so fortuitously in that writing desk had been known to Mervyn for some time, and all that had remained for him to do was throw enough money at the Dieters, father and son, so that they came up with a suitable grave at the right time. It was doubtful if they need face any charges; they would know nothing of the cold-blooded murder on the Southend promenade.

For that killing carried out by a hired hand, Mervyn Prentiss would pay the price . . .

The telephone at his elbow jarred on his thoughts. But it was only Franklyn Davey, his meeting over and anxious for news from Scotland. Kemp had to tell him: nothing so far . . .

'If you don't feel like going home,' he told him, 'you might as well share my vigil here in the office. Bring some food. We may be here for some time.'

Twenty-Six

It was black dark in the tiny bathroom that had been contrived out of the original dairy at Glenhead. Dinah looked up at the tiny square of light that was the window, but it was far up on the wall, and anyway much too small even to get a hand out. Adelaide Bristow had pushed her through the door, closed it and firmly locked the other side. With the gun pressed into her back Dinah had had no choice but to do as she was told. 'Get in there, and stay till I work something out. I need time to think . . .'

In the last ten minutes, as they sat together in the living room like two friends finishing hot drinks before retiring for the night, Dinah had felt the other woman's sanity was draining away, as if the brain, so full of addled thoughts, could hold no more. She herself had said little – simply listened to the muttered words: 'I must have time; I must make time. Like I did with Annabel that weekend – sent her off to New York to give myself time to think . . . Give myself time to go and see Effie Kerr – she's Effie Angus now, mustn't forget that. She'll see reason – no need for her to say anything. There'll be money for her. But Annabel won't let go; she's young, she's hard, she won't be bought. I had to do it, you see, there was no other way. It is my destiny to speak for my people, and Annabel will realize that . . .'

It was a monologue, spoken in a tired tone, as if the words had been said many times before, and always into empty space; but despite the meandering voice, the silences and the broken phrases, the hand that held the gun was steadfast. It had fired once, and Dinah was in no doubt that Adelaide was capable of firing again, and again.

'I must make a plan,' the weary voice began once more, 'for

211

an accident. You were putting out the lamp, Dinah, weren't you? But you've never handled oil lamps, have you? so you didn't know how to do it. Or I might have asked you to fill it in case either of us needed it in the night. Yes, that would be better. You would be pouring in the fluid, and then . . . What could have happened? A spark from a log in the fireplace, and you dropped the can. Yes, that might be it, but I need both hands to fetch the oil can. I think it would be better if you were in the little room at the back, Dinah, so that I can work out the unfortunate accident that's going to happen. Up, up, my dear, on your feet, and walk into the bathroom. You can always use the toilet, for you must be very afraid by now, and being afraid weakens the bladder.'

'I'm not afraid of you, Adelaide Bristow,' said Dinah stoutly and in a voice steadier than her heartbeat, but she let herself be pushed to the door, out into the hall, and finally into the bathroom. Heroines may do great deeds in the books, she thought, but I'm waiting for the Fifth Cavalry to come riding to the rescue. So far, they had given no sign.

George McCready had been called a slow-moving policeman in his day and, depending on who made the accusation, he might have agreed that he had never been prone to action without previous planning; but he would have added that convictions on his evidence tended to stick, even up to and through the machinations of the appeal courts. In short, George had always gone by the book, even back in his time with the Met.

On hearing the urgent messages on his answerphone, and talking to Lennox Kemp, George still had no idea what he was looking for out at Glenhead Cottage, so he took all necessary precautions.

'What was the name of that neighbour?' he asked Grace, because he knew she would have the answer.

'A Mrs Cluthie, and here's her number.'

George explained tersely to the voluble neighbour that there might be something amiss at Mrs Angus's croft. After that it was difficult for him to get a word in.

'That woman's there. I never liked her, and what's she doing in the house?' Mrs Cluthie dropped her dialect when on the telephone, but not the steadily flowing current of her speech. 'Says she's bought the place, but that canna be. There's not been the time, Mr McCready, *that* I know; but she's there the now, and keeping other folks out. And with a rude tongue that I'd niver thought to hear. Something's going on – you're right there. That Bristow woman – I niver liked her though she might have the gift of the gab. She's trying to hide someone. There was someone in there with her, but she'd not let me in to see.'

'You still have a set of keys, Mrs Cluthie?' asked George, patiently.

'Indeed I have. It's no use you trying to get in the back; I heard her shut the bolt when she got me out. You'd best get in the front.'

'Could you meet us at the road end in about half an hour, Mrs Cluthie? And I shall be bringing the police with me.'

'Indeed I will. I'm right glad there'll be the police, Mr McCready. My house is close to the road, and I've never been feart; but Glenhead's different: I'd niver go down there again whilst that woman's there. It's the keys she's wheedled out of Dougal McFie; he'd niver staun up to the likes of her.'

'I'm taking the Land Rover,' George told his wife, 'and I'll pick up Sergeant Crawford on the way. Can't be too careful, so we'll play it by the book.'

He knew the police station in Rothesay would be closed, but Crawford was a golfer and he'd often picked him up from his home.

'You've a rumour of a break-in?' he enquired of George. 'So I'd best be in uniform. Can you no tell me more?'

George shook his head. 'Could be just youngsters mucking about, the place being empty and everyone knowing about it. Yes, the sight of a uniform could do the trick if that's all it is.' Archie Crawford was a man in his forties, built large, but quick on his feet, as many a Rothesay teenager had found out to his cost. There was never much crime on the island; no one had ever scrutinized the figures, but local legend would have said that Archie Crawford looming round corners in the town, or suddenly rising from the back of a hedge out in the fields, scared the pants off local wrongdoers and terrified errant tourists before they could even think break-in or burglary. And, of course, it wasn't easy to leave Bute without some kind of notice, unless you swam the Kyles – and few crimes would be worth that enterprise. Both men in the Land Rover were silent. The wind had dropped entirely, and instead of rain there was a fine mist through which the pale moon shone fitfully. When they reached the turn-off in the road, Mrs Cluthie stepped out from the shelter of the hedge.

'Oh, I'm that glad to see you. It's yoursel', Sergeant Crawford, the very man.' She handed him a bunch of keys. 'That's the one for the front, the wee silver Yale. Ye'll no be wanting me?' Mrs Cluthie at any other time would have liked to be in on the act, but tonight her encounter with Mrs Bristow had robbed her of any confidence, and she would be glad to be sitting safe in her own home. 'But ye'll let me know if things are all right, Mr McCready?' She looked up at him on the high seat of the Rover.

'You just get yourself home, Mrs Cluthie,' said the sergeant, 'and I'm sure Mr McCready will come himself and tell you all's well. And he'll return the keys to you. Would you like me to see you home?'

'No, thank you; I'll be fine. Get yourselves down to yon place; I'm thinking there's something funny going on.'

'Maybe that rumour you heard was genuine,' said Archie Crawford as George swung the vehicle on to the rough track. 'Mrs Cluthie wasn't surprised to be asked for the keys?'

'She's got the dog that belonged to Mrs Angus. I think there's some trouble when it keeps running back to the croft and disturbs folk.'

Archie frowned. 'There shouldn't rightly be anyone there. Mr McFie asked me to keep an eye on the croft, but it's a long way down the glen and there didn't seem the need.'

The big car took the road easily enough, and turned in at the field gate of the cottage. The sergeant got out and opened it with its usual screech of hinges. He grinned at George, and shrugged.

'We're not going to be a surprise party,' he said, 'so you might as well drive up to the door. I'll be at your back on foot, and do a bit of a recce round the place to make sure there's nobody out there. There's lights in yon wee windows; that'll be the kitchen and living room. Looks like an oil lamp.'

George braked the Land Rover just short of the little lawn with a few flowerbeds that Mrs Angus had tended so carefully in her time. He jumped out, made for the front door, and knocked sharply on it even as he found the lock and fitted the key.

Both women had heard the noise of the field gate, and the sound of the Rover crossing the paddock. Dinah was the first to hear the key in the lock. She gathered breath into her lungs, pulled herself up beside the door and bellowed: 'Watch out, she's got a gun! She's got a gun!'

George heard her as he pushed open the front door, and he stopped. Archie Crawford heard her as he padded round the back of the cottage and looked up at the bathroom window where the shouts were coming from. He nipped to the front and followed George into the hall with the living-room door on their left. He gestured to George to keep back as he himself took up his position, flat against the wall by the jamb of the doorway. Stooping low, he leant forward and flicked up the old-fashioned latch. The door creaked open wide.

There was little light left from the fire, but there was an oil lamp on the table shedding its pool of radiance on two objects; a key and an automatic pistol. Before either man could reach it, Adelaide Bristow came out of the shadows carrying a large oil container, which she threw into the path of Sergeant Crawford. Even as he side-stepped it, she grabbed the gun and whirled around as he tried to come up behind her. She pressed the trigger and kept her finger down. The noise of the explosions was deafening, but the bullets went wide of their mark.

'Holy shit!' Archie was more surprised than afraid. He threw the woman to the floor in a rugby tackle and prised the gun from her fingers. 'Who the hell is she?'

George McCready was more concerned with the key. He took it up and opened the bathroom door. For the first time that evening Dinah had been really scared in these last few minutes. The sound of gunfire, the knowledge that Adelaide was quite, quite mad and capable of any mayhem, Dinah's own ignorance as to who her rescuers might be, and whether they had been shot in the attempt . . . Her legs wobbled, her throat was dry, she was on the point of collapse. 'George,' she said, 'have you come on a white horse?'

He brought her in and sat her down on the sofa. Sergeant Crawford was on the floor, sitting on the rump of Adelaide Bristow and breathing hard as he fastened the cuffs on her wrists. 'I hate to do this, lady, but assaulting a police officer is a crime, and taking shots at him with yon wee gun is attempted homicide. I'm afraid I have to restrain you.'

He pulled her to her feet firmly but surprisingly gently, and put her in the chair by the fire. He turned to George and Dinah. 'I suppose I shall be told at some time what this is all about. It is with real sorrow that I now recognize Mrs Adelaide Bristow, but in view of her actions tonight I have no option but to keep her fast: she might well be a danger to herself as well as to others. Do you think you could find her coat so that I can take her to the car?' He had addressed Dinah.

'Not before we look into the old well,' she said; 'there's a body . . .'

Sergeant Crawford sighed, as if this night could hold no more horrors for him.

'And I think you should bring Mrs Bristow along too.' Dinah could almost feel sorry for the woman, who was sitting upright, muttering to herself, the amber eyes now dark and demented; but Dinah was thinking of Annabel Angus and of another night back there in September when she had still been alive . . . And there was that ghost of a second voice: 'Will you see that the lid's on the well?'

George McCready undid the bolt on the back door, and the four of them trooped out and into the garden. The hedge masked the place, but George pushed the thorny branches aside, and finally they stood looking down at the neat wooden collar fitted so expertly over the old stones. Sergeant Crawford held the old lady, so it was George and Dinah who stooped and pushed the lid aside.

Even on the summer day when Dinah had last looked into the depths of the well it had seemed sinister, but now, as a faint wind rustled the hedge and the moonlight caught the slimy moss growing round the brim, then died into the darkness below, she knew it had become a place of death. George McCready shone his torch down, down. Dinah caught her breath. There was not only the smell of stagnant water, but the unmistakable stench of rotten flesh. She steeled herself to look, then drew back and let George take over.

'Yes,' she said to him, 'it's the camel coat . . .' And the tears came. She stumbled back to the house without a glance at the madwoman standing meekly now in the care of Sergeant Crawford.

Lennox Kemp and Franklyn Davey had been drinking, on and off, for the last three hours, and both were feeling the effects. 'I've never so much as had two whiskies in a row before this,' groaned Franklyn, conscious that tonight he had broken a record. He hadn't been able to resist his employer's invitation to share the late-night vigil in the office; he had brought takeaways and been fuelled by fiery liquid.

Greasy cartons lay about on the desk; they refilled their glasses countless times, and they talked, but afterwards neither could say what they had talked about. Nothing mattered in the long waiting time but what was happening away in the North, across a stretch of water, in a fold of the hills above the Clyde – something they could not manipulate or manage, something totally out of their control.

It was after midnight when the call came. Kemp grabbed at the phone.

'Yes . . . George? Is everything . . . ?'

He listened as Franklyn staggered round the desk and almost wrenched the phone from his hand. 'George,' said Kemp, 'speak up; there's two of us here want to listen.' He put the receiver down on the desk between them, and Franklyn laid his head beside it.

'. . . I was saying . . . Dinah's safe in her bed. Grace has just given her a cup of Ovaltine. It was a terrible scene out there at Glenhead, Lennox. The Bristow woman is mad; she tried to shoot a policeman. No, he's all right. And, I'm afraid the body was in the well. Yes, the Angus girl . . .'

'And you, George?'

217

'I'm OK – and the girl did splendidly, tell that young man of hers. Adelaide Bristow's off her trolley. She's admitted she killed Annabel Angus – my friend the local bobby took it all down, played it by the book . . . Tell you about it later; I'm tired now. It's been a time of great confusion . . .'

Kemp put the phone down, images swimming in his head: the broken Wall, the falling Towers. Franklyn had gone back to his own chair. Kemp wagged a finger at him.

'That's all you need, Franklyn my boy, when someone has to disappear. That's what you choose as your vanishing point: a time of great confusion – and then you make sure people are looking in the wrong direction . . .'

But Franklyn Davey was neither listening nor caring. In the visitor's chair he was fast asleep, a soft and silly expression spread all over his face.

Kemp called for a cab to take them both home.